Letters

By Buz Sawyers

Aignos Publishing
Honolulu, Hawaii
2014

Published in the USA by Aignos Publishing, Inc.
1910 Ala Moana Blvd, #20A
Honolulu, HI 96815
www.aignospublishing.com

Printed in the USA

Edited by Jennie Oliver
Cover art provided by Buz Sawyers
Art Design by Liang Han Yu / Zachary M. Oliver

13-digit ISBN: 978-0-9895191-8-2
10-digit ISBN: 098951918X

Aignos Publishing

Honolulu, Hawaii
2014

Dedication

This book is for Aunt Madge, who always told me, "Be patient; you'll know when the right subject comes along for that first book you're going to write."

This book is also dedicated to Clem Countess, who completed Aunt Madge's prophesy when he gave me copies of the James Durrett letters at Aunt Madge's memorial service.

Aunt Madge was right. Thank you, Clem, for finishing what she started.

Foreword

The American Civil War is recorded as one of the most devastating wars in history. Over 500,000 Americans lost their lives; families were divided in their loyalties to the Union or the Confederacy, sometimes pitting brother against brother---father against son. This novel follows the battles, triumphs, and tragedies of the 18th Alabama Volunteers of the Confederate Army as seen through the eyes of a young soldier.

The characters and events are based on actual letters written by my great-great uncle, James Durrett, a teenager who fought for three years in some of the bloodiest battles of the war. In addition to James's letters, written eyewitness accounts from other soldiers who served in the 18th were invaluable as resource material for factual events describing the battles and trials of the regiment.

I have included James's unedited letters in the text of the story to lend not only authenticity, but also to give the reader an opportunity to make his or her own judgments about his character.

Chapter One

"PRIVATE THOUGHTS"
James & Harry

APRIL 2, 1865
SPANISH FORT, ALABAMA

The snipers' proficiency had become more deadly with practice. The slightest move, the slightest exposure could cost a man his life. Simultaneously, cannons bombarded the Confederate positions twenty-four hours a day, giving no moments of solitude, peace, or safety for the weary warriors of the South. James could hear the echo of cannons and the vibrations of the gunboats firing from across Mobile Bay. He wondered if he knew the names of those dying at moments of impact. The sun would set soon, at least then the snipers would stop their target practice for the evening.

Letters

James Durrett, at age nineteen, had seen enough death and terror in the past three years to last him a lifetime. He was at the end of his tour as a Confederate soldier, as were all his friends, but he was no longer the same idealistic youth ready to experience adventure and act out heroic fantasies of courage as he charged into battle. Too soon, he realized that war was not an adventure or a fantasy. War was brutal with no discrimination of age or color. War was random when it concerned fate.

He sat on the damp ground next to the small campfire. His knees pulled up beneath his chin, arms wrapped around his legs. He stared straight ahead, looking at nothing in particular, pondering the circumstances as they were. He knew this was the end. Not just of his tour, but the war. The word around camp was that there was a constant, never-ending build-up of over 55,000 Yankee troops being brought in to wipe out the besieged city of Mobile and to bring this God-forsaken war to an end. James wanted the war to end alright, but not at the price he and his comrades were about to pay. The Yanks were thirsty for blood, and there would be no mercy at the end. No quarter given.

Mobile, Alabama was the last stand for the South, and there was nowhere to run. Approximately 4500 Confederate troops were left to withstand the final Yankee assault. And now, here at the end, all that was left of the Confederate Army was a ragtag, starving, battle-fatigued bunch of veterans. As a last-ditch, desperate effort, the generals in their misgiven wisdom, had even recruited squads of boys from Mobile, barely thirteen- years-old, to help reinforce the dwindling numbers of able-bodied soldiers on the picket lines. The "Boy Brigade," as it was dubbed by the vets, was enthusiastic and eager for Yankee blood; they harbored the same fantasies James did three years earlier. However, their inexperience and unwillingness to listen to advice caused heavy casualties in their ranks. The snipers easily picked them off and cannon fire blew them apart as they ran in terror for cover. Mercifully, they were finally pulled back to re-enforce Fort Blakely, ten miles behind the lines. James could see no point in sending children to an assured and senseless death---for any cause---right or wrong.

James's own family had felt the brutal effects of the war. His oldest brother, Tom, was hopefully still alive somewhere up north in a Yankee prison, since being captured at Mission Ridge. His father was back home, a battered man, old beyond his years now, with the spirit sucked from his soul from a Yankee Minie ball that ripped away a piece of his throat. Leaving him less the man he was than when the war started. Henry, his cousin, had been by his side the past three years helping him to keep his hope and will to stay alive. Hopefully, one of them would make it back home. James knew his fate would end here, in the swamps of Mobile Bay and the picket lines of Spanish Fort.

Then, there was his mother. He could only think of her as she was before the war, trying not to consider her own pain. Her letters were brief and social, not daring to express her true thoughts and pain with her sons in constant danger. She did her best to keep everything upbeat and give only good news from the home front. But James knew...he knew she feared for him and Tom and their safety, regardless of her effort to glaze over the uncertainty of their future. Tom's future as a POW was as precarious as his own. He'd heard the rumors just like everybody else. Conditions in prison camps were brutal and consumed with disease. Thousands were dying daily.

Every soldier at his side, trapped in the slushy marshes and swamps of Spanish Fort knew the war was over. They'd be overrun in a matter of days and there was no retreat with Mobile Bay to their backs and Yankee forces on the other side waiting for them. If the South were winning, that would be one thing, then maybe there could be some justification to all the loss of life and shattered bodies. But the South was done, never to be the same again.

James felt moisture escape from his eye and the slow, wet progress as it trailed down his cheek. Without realizing he was even speaking, he muttered, "What is the point in dying now?"

On the opposite side of the Confederate picket line, the Union camps were a bevy of activity with fresh troops arriving every day. There was no way Harry would have ever guessed he'd be celebrating his eighteenth birthday on the shores of Mobile Bay, instead back home in Ohio. He'd been with the 96th Ohio Regiment almost two years now; even the veterans in his unit said that if Harry had joined the war when it began, he'd probably have more kills than California Joe, the most renowned sniper in the Union Army.

Harry Morgan had a reputation for his ability and uncanny

prowess as a sniper, but he was not a popular figure among his fellow soldiers, regardless of how many kills he had under his belt. He loved what he did too much, and it bothered even the most battle-hardened vets.

"Ever' body here wants this damn war to end exceptin' Harry," a beardless youth grumbled, who just wanted to go home alive and in one piece.

Harry heard what the soldier said and turned to face him with cold, lifeless eyes, "Not to worry fellas, there's always somebody that needs killin' somewhere, even when this war is done." Harry reached down and picked up his Sharps rifle. "Well boys, time to go," he said with a sly grin, "them Johnny Rebs need somebody to help 'em keep their heads down. See you at suppertime."

With that, Harry retrieved the rest of his gear, preparing to return to the sniper's nest he'd staked out for himself. He wanted to get there before sunup.

"Just like shootin' ducks in a pond, boys---ducks in a pond," he called out as he retreated to his perch.

Chapter Two

"THE BEGINNING"
Harry Morgan

APRIL 29, 1862
CAMP DELAWARE, OHIO

Harry Morgan and his father, Horatio, watched the organized mayhem take shape at Camp Delaware, Ohio. Hundreds of men from local counties were in lines and gathered in groups getting orders from their company commanders. Civilians everywhere slapped the backs of friends and relatives, congratulating them for their bravery. Mothers and sisters cried, fathers were proud, and younger brothers were envious.

The 96th Ohio Volunteers were mustering and preparing to train for battle. Colonel Joseph W. Vance, Commander of the 96th, purposefully rode his mount through the ranks of soldiers. He cut a distinguished figure in his tailored uniform, tall riding boots, and a wide-brimmed hat cocked to the side. While he observed and made judgments, his spurs and saber seemed to rattle and jingle in unison as his steed high-stepped through the camp. Colonel Vance was a popular and respected leader among his men, and they were willing to fight through hell for him. Little did they know---they were about to do just that.

Harry and his father observed the enthusiasm of the soldiers and the gawking civilians as young boys and men prepared for war.

"It's a shame to see so many people excited about dying," Horatio said sadly.

"Come on, Pa. This is excitin'. We're gonna whip them Johnny Rebs, and these guys are gonna come back home heroes," Harry said with pride and envy.

Horatio glanced down at Harry and realized, sadly, that his son was totally enthralled with the grand illusions of war. "Son, these boys are joining a fool's brigade. They think they're running straight to glory and guns a' blazing. But I'll tell you now---when they see their best friend with his head blown half off, or hears one of those Minie balls whistling by their ears, they'll discover that those pretty blue uniforms they have on aren't worth the wool they're made from."

Horatio Morgan was the wealthiest man in his hometown of Bellefontaine, Ohio. He owned the Morgan Bank and Morgan's Mercantile Exchange. Mr. M., as he was known, loaned money to people so they could spend it for supplies and trade at his store. He was known to be fair to those who were willing to work, but had no use for those who didn't. However, the one thing most of the townspeople didn't agree with was Horatio's savage, unpatriotic distaste against the Union's participation in the war. Horatio wasn't against the cause of the war. He wasn't in favor of the South leaving the Union, and he abhorred slavery. He was just against war, period. He was thankful that Harry was only fifteen and too young to be involved in this destructive enthusiasm.

Harry, on the other hand, would not be dissuaded from his desires to join the army. His father's point of view had nothing to do with him, and while he knew it had something to do with freeing the Negros he wasn't even sure why it had become war. He didn't know, didn't care. "Pa, they should let me join that outfit. You know darn well I'm as good or better a shooter than any of them boys are. Look, there's 'ol Gregory Paul," he said, pointing at a tall, slender young man. "Ever'body knows he can't hit the side of a barn if he were standin' six foot from it. Why should that idiot get to go and not me?"

Horatio snapped back, "Because he's eighteen-years-old and his pa's an idiot too!"

Harry recognized that he'd gone too far with his old man and knew it was time to curb his enthusiasm.

Horatio knew his son was right about the shooting part, at least. There wasn't a man in town he couldn't outshoot, and everybody knew it. Harry had an uncanny eye when it came to handling a rifle. He hunted every day in the woods and fields around the county, learning to read tracks and trails like an expert. And while he wished to run full bore into a Union uniform, in his patience tracking game, Harry was unmatched. He could lay in ambush in the trees or under the brush for hours, waiting for unsuspecting prey to appear. Horatio was also aware that his son had some kind of extra sense when it came to tracking, stalking, and waiting, but he wasn't sure of his motives.

He enjoyed the kill too much. Even in these hard times when food and supplies were scarce, he never brought home his kill.

Right or wrong, Horatio indulged Harry when it came to rifles, though. His son was big for his age and easily handled the long, cumbersome rifles of the day. His favorite was a Sharps Model 1859, .54 caliber, breech-loading rifle; the one preferred by the legendary California Joe. It wasn't as long and weighed less than the Enfield rifles used by most of the infantry on both sides of the war. A true marksman could shoot accurately up to five- yards with a Sharps rifle. Harry was a true marksman.

"If this war ain't over before I'm sixteen, I'm gonna join Berden's Sharpshooters," Harry bragged. "Ever'body knows that's the best group of shooters and snipers in the whole dang Yankee army. I'd love to be linin' up them Southern devils in my sights alongside ol' California Joe."

Horatio stared down at his son with hard eyes. "Harry, there's no glory in killing a man. It's not like shooting a bunch of dumb animals. These devils, as you call them, were shooting the eyes out of rabbits before they wore long pants. They're going to be shooting back. They see blue---they're going to shoot you."

Harry shrugged and mumbled, "Not if they can't see me."

Horatio had seen and heard enough. Hearing his son talk about killing a man like it was some varmint in his sights was disturbing. Unsettling.

"Come on, Harry. Let's go home," Horatio said, grabbing his son by the sleeve. "I've seen enough." There was no need worrying, Horatio thought to himself. This war would be over and done with long before Harry ever reached his sixteenth birthday. At least he prayed it would be so.

Harry looked over his shoulder for one last look at the huge gathering of soldiers. He smiled.

Chapter Three

"REMEMBERING THE BEGINNING"
James Durrett

June, 1863

James Durrett was seventeen-years-old and he'd been a soldier the better part of a year now and had already killed more men in battle than he wanted to think about. Unfortunately, firefights were not the only enemy that soldiers of war had to encounter. The demanding life of living in a mobile city, constantly on the move, among thousands of soldiers kept a man on edge just as much as life on the front lines. Measles and dysentery wreaked havoc on the troops, killing hundreds and leaving too many unable to perform their duties. Monotony and boredom combined with homemade liquor and bad tempers made for jeopardous situations. Boredom was a soldier's worst enemy in camp; it gave a man too much time to reflect on things he'd rather not think about. James realized, in hindsight, that nothing prepares a person for the lasting effect that lingers in his soul after his first fight. You can drill, march, practice, and brag about all the Yankees you're going to kill, but you're never prepared for that first Minie ball that whizzes by your head and kills the man behind you. It was only by God's grace that the three of them had made it this far unharmed.

James, his brother Tom, and cousin Henry were among the first to join the 18th Alabama Volunteers back in September of '62; he was only sixteen, Tom twenty-one, and Henry was eighteen. Convincing his mother and father to let him join had not been an easy task, but with Tom's help they'd finally relented. Tom swore that he'd watch over and protect him. Pa smirked, "Yeah, but that's like letting the fox guard the chicken coop. Who's going to keep *you* out of trouble?"

More against his mother's objections then his father's, both parents finally relented and allowed him to enlist as long as he was in the same unit as Tom and Henry.

It only took a couple of weeks of getting organized and outfitted with weapons and uniforms, that the Eighteenth moved out to Mobile, Alabama, where they joined in force with other Alabama regiments. James was surprised to see that some companies still hadn't received any muskets or ammunition; for some, what they did have was defective. "Hell of a way to fight a war," Tom said.

Six months of intense training followed, preparing the boys for the next three years of their enlistment. Eventually, under the command of General J. K. Jackson, all regiments prepared to disembark for Corinth, Mississippi. Their time had finally come to perform.

James had been ready to do something besides learn to march and drill, chop timber, and march and drill some more. In all these months, he hadn't seen one blue Yankee uniform, but upon arrival in Corinth, he had a feeling that things were going to be different. Troops arrived from everywhere, noise and confusion was abundant. Officers scampered everywhere atop their mounts; troopers marching through their drill routines, and artillery rolling in columns awed the new recruits. Most of these men had never fired a gun in anger, much less to kill. The smell of blood had not yet filled their nostrils, but their time was coming soon.

The rumor mill had it that Generals Price and Van Dorn were soon to arrive with veterans who'd already fought in Missouri and Arkansas. When the battle weary units finally arrived, the green recruits all stopped at their duties and stood in respect as the generals and their troops marched in smooth rhythm into camp. One could see they were proud and felt like conquering heroes, come to show us how it was done. However, James could also see that beneath their bravado, lay a deep-rooted weariness.

"How do you think we'll look a year from now, Tom?" James had asked.

"Alive I hope," Tom replied grimly.

Time dragged by until the first week of April. Training became more intense, restrictions and curfews were enforced, and there was less idle time for mischief. Finally, around mid-April, the Eighteenth received orders to cook three days rations and prepare for a long and difficult march. The time had come for them to put to use all of the torturous and mundane hours of drills and target practice the men had endured for the past months. The weather had turned nasty and rain pounded them unmercifully on the first night; muddy roads hampered the mobility and movement of the heavy artillery and the wagons that carried supplies for the thousands of men marching to battle. Many times soldiers took on the same duties as the mules, pushing and pulling, straining to keep the mobile army in motion.

The Eighteenth's first sight of a real battle's aftermath was upon their arrival at Pea Ridge. The grotesque picture of wounded soldiers and contorted, lifeless corpses jolted the Eighteenth from any previous visions of a clean, heroic war. It had officially started. Some were scared to death, some anxious to begin, some ready to run. Little did the boys know that before a second night would fall---thousands would lie dead on a field of courage and blood.

At sunup, Sunday morning, firing began among the pickets as skirmishers pressed forward to bring on the engagement. The Eighteenth was brigaded with the Nineteenth, Second, Seventeenth Alabama, and the Second Texas Infantries. Initially James's unit was in the reserve line, but was soon relegated to the front column. The enemy seemed to be taken completely by surprise by the Confederate presence, and as the Rebels passed through the enemy camps, they found that they'd been engaged in cooking and eating breakfast. In many instances, the breakfast was half-cooked or eaten, preparations set for a leisurely meal. The enemy was obviously surprised by the attack. For three days, the Yanks retreated; on the third day, the enemy made their last stand. They'd been engaged in desperate and intense fighting for perhaps thirty minutes when they heard the command, "Cease Firing!" shouted up and down the lines.

James saw a white flag, or rather a white handkerchief tied to a long stick being held up. Firing ceased and Colonel Wheeler rode to General Prentiss, the Union commander, and offered to take his sword; but Prentiss declined to give it to him on the grounds that Wheeler was an inferior officer of lesser rank. Prentiss proved to be a most surly, crusty prisoner, cursing everything in sight, even to the soil of the country, snarling and snapping at everything. The Eighteenth Regiment was ordered to carry Prentiss's Brigade of prisoners to Corinth, and did not participate in the final engagements on the following day.

James remembered the noise and first time warriors cowering in fetal positions behind trees or any other kind of cover they could find. Cannonballs exploded, blowing men and beasts apart. Splinters from shattered trees pierced soldier's bodies like arrows, men cried for their mothers, screaming, and praying to die. But, he had done his part; he didn't run. He didn't soil his pants the way some did. He remembered being frightened, only a fool wouldn't be, but not cowardly. He was mechanical in his firing and loading. He was accurate. He walked away from the battle physically and emotionally drained trying not to think about the men he'd killed on the battlefield that day.

Unfortunately, the Confederate taste of victory was all too brief. Union forces reorganized and responded with a brutal counter-attack that sent the snake-bit Rebel army running. James's first taste of victory was bittersweet; a taste he would encounter many times before Mobile Bay in 1865.

The Confederate troops retreated back to Corinth to lick their wounds and reorganize. James's unit had a lot of "wound lickin" to do as 125 out of 450 of his comrades from the Eighteenth lost their lives on the battlefield. Much shifting around of companies and officers took place because of losses absorbed by various units. In the shakeup, Captain Inge of Company E was promoted to Lt. Colonel and Captain Hunly of Company I, to Major. These were moves that the Durretts were glad to see, since they knew both men. It had been a costly initiation and a brutal reality, especially for the new recruits. In total, 25,000 brave men from the Union and Confederate armies lost their lives on the battlefield.

In spite of their losses, James and the boys were riding high on their first excursion into combat; they'd survived the worst. There was hope in knowing the Yanks could be whipped and the Johnny Rebs would make short order of anyone who got in their way next time. With hardly any rest or time to savor the down time, the Eighteenth got their marching orders again. Their ultimate destination was Wartrace, Tennessee. They had two more encounters with the Yanks on their way. With each battle, James became more confident, more determined to live, and more deadly. Yet, his common decency as a person never wavered. It seemed to James that he was two people--- one in battle, and one out. At Blackland and Murfreesboro, he demonstrated uncanny prowess with his rifle and was gaining a reputation among his peers as a deadly marksman; however, no one considered him a cold-blooded killer. He was a soldier fighting for his cause. The Eighteenth finally arrived in Wartrace, Tennessee on New Year's Eve, December 31, 1862, where they settled in for the winter and spring of '63.

On a mid-June morning, James sat in the shelter that Tom, Henry and he had built so they could stay dry during the rainy weather. They were in pretty good shape compared to some of the other boys. They had good shoes, warm clothes, and food from home to get them through. Those that had to rely on the meager hard tack rations dispersed by the Quartermaster were in a bad way. It was hardly enough to keep a man alive.

He decided to write home, but before he pulled his writing supplies from his bag, Luther Megs sloshed by, kicking up mud with every step. He stood in front of James, looking down on him with a smirk. Luther was tall, over six feet, and probably didn't weigh 150 pounds soaking wet.

"What're you doin', Jamie – writin' to your momma?" Luther

said, slurring his words. James could tell he'd been drinking again.

"Yeah Luther, just writing home---you know, keeping in touch with the family," James answered calmly.

Luther was from Tuscaloosa, same as the Durretts, but they didn't travel in the same circles. He was a drunk and a thief that did odd jobs around town just to make enough money to buy his next bottle. Ira, James's father, would never hire him, even banned him from ever stepping on their farm again. Luther never let an opportunity pass without reminding the Durretts of their lack of human kindness to the downtrodden.

"You damn Durretts is a bunch of mamma boys," he ranted. "And your brother Tom, he ain't as tough as he thinks he is, you know. He thinks he's some kinda top soldier 'round here." Luther straightened up his shoulders and looked around the camp to see if anyone else was around. "Yeah---I could whip him on my worst day. Yep, just might do that today if 'n he gets in my way." He took a swig from the bottle grasped tight in his hand. "An' one more thing," he added, pointing his finger at James and stumbling back a step, "think I'll write a letter to your momma – so's she can get a letter from a real man. Know what I mean? She'd probably like that, don't you think? Right, Jamie boy?"

James stood up calmly, unfettered by Luther's words. "Well, that's mighty fine, Luther. Didn't know you could write. If you can't, you can tell me what to say and I'll put it down on paper for you."

Luther's face turned beet red as he took a threatening step forward, this time jabbing his finger at James's face. "Ah, hell on you boy," he growled. "You Durretts are an uppity bunch. You got money, an' land, 'an you don't know what it's like to be church-mouse poor and have nuthin'. Ya'll strut 'round here in your good boots 'an warm jackets, whilst the rest of us is stealin' boots an' food off dead Yanks. It just ain't right to have more than the rest of us."

Luther stepped up closer, nose to nose with James. His breath reeked of homemade hooch and tobacco. "You Durretts better watch your backs, Jamie boy. Hate for sumthin' to happin' in the heat of battle." He winked and gave a crooked grin, "Know what I mean, Jamie boy?"

Without another word, he slowly turned and stumped his way down the path through the trees. After a few steps he stopped, turned, and raised his arm level and pointed his finger at James like a pistol. That crooked grin appeared again and he whispered, "Bang", just loud enough for James to hear him. Then he turned and stumbled off through the muddy trail.

"That boy won't see the end of the next battle, know what I mean, Jamie boy?" said Tom, mocking Luther as he stepped from behind the shelter. He walked around and smiled at his little brother. Tom was also over six foot tall, but he weighed closer to 200 pounds. He and James had always been close and watched each other's back, during peacetime and war. Tom knew that James could take care of himself---in a battle or one on one. But he couldn't help being protective.

"I wasn't worried, Tom," James laughed. "I heard you behind the shelter, stifling your giggles when I told old Luther I didn't know he could write."

"So---you writin' your momma, baby brother?" Tom said, mocking Luther again.

"Yeah, I wish momma and the girls would write more regular from home," James sighed. "Want me to tell 'em anything? Put in a word for you?"

"Nah---I'm gonna 'em write too---you know how us momma's boys are. I'll see you later, I'm gonna check in with the sentries, just to keep myself busy."

James settled in to write his letter home.

June 14, 1863
Wartrace, Tennessee

Dear Mother,
We are all well this morning but have not heard from home this week. Tom got a letter from Jane yesterday but it was dated May 31st. She stated that she would go home on the 17th on this month. We have moved since I wrote to you. We are about 3 miles from Wartrace in a very pleasantly situated place. But we do not have good water. The water is rotten limestone water and not very plentiful at that, though we do not expect to stay here long. We are in Tennessee now and it is a place in which a soldier does not get much rest though I suppose it is as good as any. It keeps us from becoming attached to any particular place, which would not in any way be military. Which last word I have learned heartily to despise. Dear mother you need not trouble yourself about sending me anything in the way of clothing, not knowing when you would have a chance to send anything. I have drawn clothes, 1 pair of shoes, 1 pair pants and 1 pair of drawers, which was all that I needed. I was nearly barefooted when I got the shoes. I have got a splendid pair of shoes with very thick heavy bottoms, which will withstand the rocks and hills of Tennessee finely. Tom did not draw anything. He speaks of taking a pair of shoes the next chance he gets which will probably be in a few days if we stay in one place long enough for the Quartermaster store to get up with us. The weather is very cool up here for the time of the year. There was a heavy rain here last night and we did not have our tent staked properly and the rain blew in leaked in under the tent and come in on

us generally every way.

There is a great deal of interest and suspense among the soldiers at this place about Vicksburg as I suppose there is all over the Confederacy, as there ought to be. I am afraid there is too great confidence put in the agency of great Generals and armies and not enough in the one that gives the victory and causes the defeat. If this war is brought on us as an affliction I am awfully afraid that as a nation we are becoming more hardened and wicked instead of being more humble as we ought to be. I do not think it will be a disadvantage to me to be in the army if I live to get out of it. For I am learning lessons every day that will be of use to me as long as I live. Painful lessons though they be of human nature. Still it will all be of service to me in life. I learn a great many of the weaknesses of men that it is a humiliation to me to know of. I simply find out more than I like to know about some men. I know now why you never would let us associate with everyone. The less one person knows of another to a certain extent, they like them better. Friendship is like the glow of foxfire, it shines beautifully till it is brought to light and it proves to be nothing but dull rotting wood and it will not do for one person to depend too much on another for friendship. If a man goes at that he is depending on a broken stick for support. Enough of that. When you write to me I want to know if the bees are all dead or if Papa saved any swarms this year. I hope I will be at home this time next year to attend to them. How is my dog getting along in this troublesome world? Give my love to Papa, Jane, Becky and John B. and Dear Momma receive the love of your affectionate son.

- *J. A. Durrett*

Chapter Four

"DRUMMED OUT"

JUNE 1863
WARTRACE, TENNESSEE

James always felt better after writing home. It was the one straw he had left that reminded him that a normal world still existed. He wasn't sure he could endure this war any further without the companionship of Tom and Henry. Those connections to home were important. People imagine that soldiering is marching to bands in victory and sitting around the campfire bragging about how brave they are and all the exciting exploits that occurred in battle. However, James discovered that being a soldier was hard labor, never having enough to eat, fighting disease, and protecting oneself from one's own comrades.

The Eighteenth was brigaded with the Nineteenth of Alabama. Each unit had to clear the timber from a number of acres for marching drills and commissary supply disbursement. Digging up pine tree roots was not James's way of thinking to become a better soldier. His once soft hands were now calloused from swinging an axe. On the other hand, boredom and monotonous repetition of daily duties had its dangers also. If you were assigned nighttime sentry duty, it could be especially difficult to stay awake and efficiently man the post. Many times, those on duty would sleep, leaving their comrades in danger of a surprise attack. Slackers, thieves, no-counts, complainers, and cowards were dealt with severely in the army. Deserters were shot by a firing squad without trial. However, if they punished everyone that complained in the army, there wouldn't be anyone left.

The Durretts stayed together most of the time and tried to stay away from the slackers and troublemakers. "Guilt by association," as momma used to say. Those who didn't pull their weight or tried to get out of work ended up doing twice as much as everyone else, but there was no toleration at all for thieves. James, Tom, and Henry were about to witness the severe results of stealing from your own people.

Matt Rupert came running up to the shelter where the boys were cooking biscuits in a Dutch oven and a large pot of potato soup beside it. He was out of breath and holding his side when he arrived. "You boys need to come on!' Ol' Luther Megs got caught stealin' some food from Captain Moxley's tent last night, an' he's 'bout to be drummed out!"

Tom grinned. "I knew that boy was too stupid for his own good," he said, pulling the soup from the fire and standing up. "Well gents, shall we go enjoy the show?"

Besides desertion, stealing was one of the worst crimes a soldier could commit against his fellow comrades, and only a fool would steal from an officer. The penalty was severe. The culprit first had his head shaved and then he was "drummed out" of the service. As badly as the South needed men, there was still no room for a thief. Once the thief's head was shaved, a band would march ahead of him on the parade grounds playing "The Thief's March." He, then, had to follow the band throughout the camp, displayed in shame for all to see. All the while, a guard detail followed close behind to prevent any attempt of escape. When the tune was over, the band and guards would turn and leave---casting the thief from camp with no supplies or weapons, leaving him to fend for himself.

James and the boys could see the band, for what it was, getting into formation and preparing for the march. They saw a circle of men who were hooting and hollering at some spectacle in the center of the bulls-eye.

"What's a drumming out, Tom?" asked James, never having experienced one before.

"It's when a thief gets what he deserves. He gets a new haircut and a butt kickin' before he's sent home. Times are tough enough without stealing from your own." Tom obviously had no sympathy for Luther; he'd made his own bed, now he could lie in it.

Luther was down on his knees in the middle of the circle, his hands tied behind his back. As one soldier held him still by his shoulders, another proceeded to shorn his long, shaggy hair with a pair of dull shears. The cutter roughly grabbed fistfuls of hair, snipping and gouging clumps next to the scalp, sometimes slicing skin and all. James could see small trickles of blood dripping down Luther's butchered scalp.

"You bastards!" Luther yelled. "Ya' yella' bellied bastards! I'll kill you if'n I get the chance! I'll be back---you'll see!"

"If'n you come back, you thievin' bastard, I'll kill you ma'self," the cutter yelled back and then spat in Luther's face. "You're lucky we don't kill you now, you thievin' coward!"

James winced as he watched Luther's humiliation. He got no pleasure from it, even though he didn't like him. This was the worst of human degradation; he didn't see the point in humiliating a man to this degree.

"Damn, Tom," said Henry. "Ol' Luther's so mad he's foaming at the mouth like some ol' rabid dog."

"Can't say I hate to see him go," answered Tom, "but we haven't seen the end of that rascal. I'm 'fraid that boy holds a grudge something bad."

Once Luther's head had been sheared like a sheep from its wool with uneven patches of stringy hair hanging limp, he was brought to his feet. The band formed in order, blew a few warm-up notes, and began their parade, playing an off-tune rendition of "The

Thief's March." Soldiers quickly formed two lines, creating a gauntlet so Luther could be paraded for a final time before his peers. Luther followed behind the band, his head held high, yelling curses and threats to everyone he saw. Three armed guards marched behind--- prodding him viciously with their rifles whenever he attempted to slow the pace. Luther spotted the Durretts standing in line together.

"Hey, Durretts---getting run outta this chicken outfit is the best thing to happen for me. I'll tell your momma hello when I see her!"

Tom bolted from the line, his face blood red and fist clenched. He charged straight at Luther, head and shoulders down, crashing his shoulder directly into the thief's stomach, knocking him hard to the ground. He straddled Luther, pinning his shoulders down with his knees. Their faces were nose to nose and Tom smelled his foul breath. He whispered straight into Luther's horrified face, "Luther, I ain't gonna dirty my hands with you right now 'cause I've got family to take care of whilst this war's going on. But if you ever cross my path again–I promise---I'll strip the skin off your back one-inch at a time. Never mention my mother's name again. Know what I mean, Luther?"

At that moment, Luther knew he was lucky to be alive, his lips quivered as he took in all of Tom's threat. Then, Tom wrapped his big hand around Luther's throat and pushed himself up --- putting his full weight on his victim's scrawny neck. Luther's eyes bulged, thinking his neck was about to snap. Tom stood, straightened himself up, brushed off his clothes, and faced the band.

"Play it up boys," Tom said between gritted teeth, "and get this trash outta here before I lose my temper," he instructed.

The band started up without further encouragement, and the guards grabbed Luther underneath his arms and jerked him to his feet. He didn't shout any more curses or threats; he stared in a catatonic daze at his feet and stumbled his way to exile. The band finally stopped the music when they reached the tree line; the procession of soldiers ceased, and the guards cut the ropes from Luther's hands, pushing him into the woods.

"Why don't you head for that Yankee camp, Luther? One look at that pretty head of yours 'an they'll skedaddle on back to New York as soon as they set eyes on you!" A guard taunted as the thief groped a tree to steady himself.

Luther slowly turned to face his tormentors, "I know you Al

Clayton, and I'm not done here yet! Nobody makes a fool of Luther

Megs! You just remember what I'm saying! All of you!" He yelled,

sweeping his hand back and forth across the crowd. And with that

said, Luther turned and disappeared into the brush.

Chapter Five

"OFFICER MATERIAL"
TOM

JUNE 1863

When the orders from Command came down to bug-out, James and the boys were glad to finally get out of Wartrace. The water was rotten with limestone and an epidemic of measles had killed almost 200 men among the five regiments brigaded there.

"Let's get out of this hellhole," grumbled Tom. "I'm tired of watching people die from things that don't come out from the end of a rifle barrel."

"Now Tom," said Henry, "is that any way to talk 'bout our fine army? We've got all the comforts of home here. Rain five days a week, dysentery, measles, and bad tempers. You really want to give this all up?"

James couldn't help getting in his two-bits, "Yeah Tom, I think you should get some of those gold bars on your shoulders. You'll get a horse and won't have to march anymore, and you'll get a shiny new sword to boot! You always said you could do it better than most these fellas running this army now."

Tom aimed a finger in James's direction, "Now little brother, you know how I feel 'bout officers. They're good ones and bad ones. Only trouble is---the good ones get killed and the bad ones get promoted. I'll just take their orders---and then change 'em up a bit."

Just then, they heard the clattering hooves of an approaching horse and rider. "Speaking of officers, look who's comin' our way," Henry said, pointing up the trail. "Maybe he wants to promote you to a general, Tom."

"Yeah, right," Tom mumbled, "never happen. That'd require making a decision."

It was Colonel Inge, one of the good ones. Actually, the

Durretts knew Colonel Inge from home. His family had a farm in Tuscaloosa County, same as them. They were good neighbors and could always be depended on if needed. Richard was older than the Durret boys, but they'd still been close in the past.

"Afternoon gentlemen," Inge said, reining in his horse and noticing the lack of salutes, "stay at ease."

James snapped to a mock attention. "Sorry Colonel, we didn't realize it was an officer. Normally when we see one galloping around on a horse, he's usually waving his saber in the air yelling, "Charge to the front men and take no prisoners!"

Inge smiled. "Well, you don't know how close you are to being related to an officer in your own family." Inge shifted his gaze to Tom and nodded. "Tom, go to the Quartermaster and get three stripes for your tunic. You're the new first sergeant for your platoon. Otis Yarborough died from the measles last night. Muster your men together and get them ready to move at dawn," Inge instructed with a stiff salute. There was no humor in his voice; it was all business. "Congratulations Sergeant Durrett."

Tom stood dumbfounded, "But Richard – uh – Colonel, sir!

Letters

You can't do this!"

The Colonel snapped back, "I not only can, but I just did. We've got a tough road ahead of us, Tom. I need a body I can trust and whom the men'll follow orders from. You're the man." 'Tween disease and desertion---there's not many left that can get these boy's attention like you can. You'll do just fine, Tom. I'm counting on you. I'm running out of good leaders, and I need somebody to snap these boys back into shape, somebody to watch my back. Should have done this a long time ago."

Tom rubbed a meaty hand through his hair, shook his head and mumbled, "I'll be damned."

Colonel Inge winked at James and Henry and then threw his head back and laughed. He pulled his saber from its scabbard, waving it overhead, turned his horse in a tight circle, and yelled, "Charge to the front men and take no prisoners!" He galloped away.

Tom twisted around and glared at his little brother and cousin. They immediately snapped to attention and saluted.

"Sir! Permission to speak, Sir!" Henry called out in a sharp, crisp voice.

"Permission to go to hell, soldier," Tom barked. "I've got some stripes to pick up. You boys better have this pigsty cleaned up by the time I get back or there'll be KP duty for both of you for the whole damn march!"

Tom turned tromped down the hill in a huff, while the boys continued to mock his plight behind his back. After a brief distance from the camp, he stopped and turned back to look at James and Henry. It'd been a long time since he'd seen them laugh out of just pure joy. Laughing can cleanse the soul, Tom thought. There hadn't been much of that since they joined the army. Deep down inside, he was glad to take a position of authority. Things had gotten too loose around camp. No one paid much attention to orders anymore, especially from the officers they had no respect for. He knew they'd take his orders or they'd pay hell.

As Tom made his way down the trail, an uneasy feeling came over him. He was glad to break camp finally, but there was a bad feeling in his gut about the upcoming march. Mother Rumor, the heartbeat of every camp, had reared its ugly head the past few days, passing from campfire to campfire about a big push coming up. Talk of an upcoming fight always stirred mixed emotions of dread and excitement. Grown men who would kill the enemy at the drop of a hat, suddenly turned sentimental, yearning for home and family, and started writing letters home filled with love and affection. Tying up loose ends. The boys needed a morale booster. The South had been getting beat up pretty bad ever since Shiloh; Gettysburg and Vicksburg were now in the hands of the Yanks and they controlled the Mississippi River. Losing the Mississippi cut off the main source of supplies for the Confederates and rations were getting thin. When stomachs rumbled and growled, so did the soldiers.

Tom straightened his shoulders and put some snap into each step as he approached the Quartermaster's supply depot. "Hey! Mr. Quartermaster! Lt. Cohill! You've got a payin' customer out here!" He yelled smartly.

"It's time to polish the toe of my boot on somebody's back side," he whispered to himself.

Chapter Six

"FIRST KILL"
HARRY

JUNE 1863
BELLEFONTAINE, OHIO

It had been almost two years since Harry and his father

watched the inauguration of the green recruits of the 96th Ohio,

preparing for war. News of ongoing victories and defeats were

plentiful in the newspapers and letters from loved ones. It was

unfathomable to the locals the number of casualties inflicted upon the

nation. A body count of fifteen to twenty thousand casualties in any

one battle was not unusual; in the Battle of Gettysburg alone, over

50,000 men had been killed.

None of this deterred Harry in his enthusiasm to fight,

however. If nothing else, then it inspired him even more. His prowess and marksmanship was so fine-tuned that killing animals had become a bore. There was no challenge, no incentive---no thrill. It was time to move on to bigger and more challenging game.

He left the house with his usual rations and supplies packed in his knapsack, a full canteen, and his Sharps rifle. School had been out about a week now and he was never so glad for something to end. He hated school, but not because of the learning. He learned because he knew being educated was the best way to beat somebody else's ignorance. Harry always intended to be a step ahead of everybody else.

The war, of course, was his obsession. There wasn't a day that went by he didn't read the local paper and any other outside material he could get his hands on about the war. Whenever a local from town returned from fighting, he questioned them until they ran him off. Most didn't seem to want to talk about it. If any strangers came through town, h'd know it and pestered them in the same manner until they'd shoo him away like a fly.

Harry heard that Gregory Paul, who joined in '61, had returned home, and he went by to see him. Gregory's left arm had been amputated above the elbow. He looked even more gaunt and thin than when he'd left. He told Harry he didn't want to talk about the war. The whole experience was just too unnerving to reminisce.

"Don't go Harry, there's nuthin' glamorous about it," he stated. The youth had turned and walked away in disgust.

The thing about school that ate at Harry like a blister on his toe was the cowards and momma's boys. He could handle the little kids, they didn't bother him none, as a matter of fact, he was their protector from the older boys. They knew if they got picked on, all they had to do was go to Harry and he'd take care of the bully, in a severe manner. They also admired him because he talked about going to war and killing as many Johnny Rebs as he could. It was the mama's boys his age that got on his nerves. They'd rather play war than be in it. Hardly any of them had their own rifle, and those that did couldn't hit anything unless what they were shooting at was herded into a barn for them. The older boys stayed clear of Harry. He was a bully to them and they feared for their lives when they were around him. He liked it that way, too. Many a parent had visited with Horatio about his behavior and made threats about talking to the law. "Something's wrong with that boy, Horatio," one parent told him. "He needs to be either locked up or put in the army."

That's exactly what Harry wanted---to get in the army. He'd already turned sixteen a few months back, and with his size he looked closer to seventeen or eighteen. He was old enough to join now, but there was one holdup---Horatio. The recruiter told him he'd need Horatio's permission and signature, even if he were sixteen. *My time's comin'---sooner than you think Ho-ra-she-o. Sooner than you think.*

Harry was in rare form today. He was excited. He couldn't wait to get to the woods and set up. He had a plan and he hoped it'd come together for him.

"Creatures of habit. That's what people are. Watch. Study. Predict. Execute," he whispered to himself.

It was a five-mile hike to the sniper's stand he'd prepared. Once he entered the forest, he became one with the landscape. His instincts instantly kicked in. He became aware of every sound, every movement. Quietly, he weaved his way through the woods with barely a sound.

Harry was finally only a quarter mile from his destination, and he automatically slowed his pace and moved with most care. He had practiced this maneuver constantly since making his decision about today. When he was about fifty yards from his destination, he lay flat on his belly and began to crawl, keeping his Sharps cradled in the crook of his arms as he crept forward. Finally, he came to the small clearing. He went straight to the spot he'd prepared a month earlier. He was protected from the heat of the sun and roaming eyes. The bushes along the edge of the clearing were tall and thick. He'd scooped a shallow bed where he could lay flat and comfortable under their protection in the shade, while waiting for his target.

Another hundred yards into the clearing was a small log cabin. The shuttered windows were opened and occasionally he saw the inhabitants pass by. He watched as smoke lazily rose from the chimney, and he smelled the faint aroma of cooking food. All of Harry's senses were on fire. Everything was in tune. Off to the side and behind the cabin was a small barn with a circular fence in front of it. There was a mule in the corral, other than that no other livestock was in sight. This struck him as unusual when he first discovered the cabin, but not anymore.

Everything would come together today. He had the means, now, to finally fulfill his destiny. Horatio would have no choice but to help him, and if he didn't---the consequences would destroy everything he'd worked for all his life. A "no lose" situation. He couldn't help but giggle about his good fortune.

Harry had come upon the cabin purely by accident several months earlier. He knew these woods backwards and forwards, but never knew anything about this place. It had to have been built within the past year. There didn't seem to be much farming or activity going on by the owner, except at night. The cabin's mysterious, sudden appearance and lack of work made Harry suspicious, so he stayed low and out of sight. He was intent on watching and finding out what was going on. He knew there were people inside because there was smoke coming from the chimney and a mule in the corral; however, no one came out of the cabin until about an hour before dusk. The first person he saw was a tall Negro man who stepped out on the porch, walked to the front edge, and stood as still as a statue---just staring out over the open ground. He seemed to survey every foot of the pasture and the edge of the woods before making a move. Harry's position was high on the branch of a tall oak tree that night, about thirty feet from the edge of the pasture. He lay on his stomach on a nice fat branch, his Sharps rifle ready if needed. He watched every move of the man.

The Negro reached over and took what appeared to be a walking stick that leaned against a porch post. He stepped from the porch and turned to go to the barn. When he reached the barn door, he twisted around and surveyed the open field one more time. Then, Harry saw him do something unusual. He knocked on the barn door, waited a few seconds, and went inside.

Harry wondered, "Now who the hell knocks on a barn door before he enters? He afraid to wake up the cows?"

The man stayed in the barn about thirty minutes and then came out. He struck out across the open field and headed straight towards Harry's direction, swinging the walking stick in rhythm with every other step. Harry didn't panic, but his heart raced. Not from fear--- but excitement. Confrontation.

As the Negro approached, Harry could get a better look at the man. He was big, maybe 6 foot, 4 or 5 inches tall, weighing over 250 pounds. He was a very imposing figure as he purposely marched towards the edge of the pasture. His overalls looked worn, but clean. Not tattered like most black men he'd seen in town. He definitely didn't have the look of a farmer. The most noticeable feature about him was his eyes, not only the intensity, but also the color. Instead of the normal dark brown color he was accustomed to, they were a light brown, almost hazel. He was constantly alert and his hazel eyes and head never stopped looking back and forth, searching. The Walkin' Man, as Harry came to call him, stopped at the edge of the clearing and peered into the dense woods. He didn't step into the foliage though; he turned and started walking the entire perimeter of the field. Once he'd made a complete circle, which took about thirty minutes, he returned to the barn, knocked, and went inside again.

"Damn peculiar," whispered Harry.

The Walkin' Man was in the barn only a few minutes when Harry saw lights glimmer through the cracks of the barn door. Suddenly both doors swung open and at least fifteen to twenty Negroes began to stream from inside. They strolled towards the front of the cabin, stretching and appeared to be taking in the fresh air after breathing the manure and stale hay from the barn. But, it was the appearance of the last man, calmly strolling through the barn doors with a look of satisfaction that quickly sucked the air from Harry's lungs. It was Horatio!

"I'll be damned! Ol' Ho-ra-she-o is runnin' coloreds from the South! The ol' coot is part of that damn Underground Railroad!"

The Underground Railroad was a secret network of people, colored and white alike, who smuggled black slaves from the plantations of the South to Northern states where they could be resettled. Even though the organization's intentions were good, the large influx of former slaves northward brewed resentment among some of its citizens.

As Harry watched, a plan began to formulate in his mind. Now he had the goods to blackmail Horatio. He would get what he wanted on his time schedule, not his old man's.

This will be like shootin' ducks in a pond, he thought.

Time had passed, preparations made, and now it was the moment of truth. Harry had been in his position almost two hours. He had trained himself to ignore the discomforts of staying in one position for extended periods of time. The shade from the heavy foliage of the bushes and the coolness of the ground kept him comfortable. As before, he was in tune to every sound and movement around him. The sniper's life is one of loneliness and patience. Waiting for that one shot; that one opportunity to make the kill. Harry was not one for socializing, so the part fit him perfectly.

It was about an hour before dusk. He knew the Walkin' Man would be making his appearance soon. Sure enough, within minutes, he emerged on the porch, surveyed the pasture, and then strolled to the barn. "Creatures of habit," Harry smiled.

After the Walkin' Man left the barn, he began his survey of the perimeter of the woods. He passed within fifteen feet of Harry, never breaking his stride, never suspected. Harry knew if a person gets lazy and falls into a routine, it becomes a habit, and habits breed carelessness. The Walkin' Man was getting careless.

Once the perimeter had been surveyed, he returned to the barn, knocked, and opened the doors. Harry watched as ten newly liberated slaves emerged into the fresh air. He brought his Sharps to his shoulder and aimed. His target was talking to another man, his back towards Harry's position. He continued to talk with the other man. His gestures were quite animated, as though the men were in a heated discussion. The target turned towards Harry, throwing his arms up in what seemed exasperation.

Harry squeezed the trigger smoothly without hesitation. The report from the Sharps was loud and kicked forcefully against his shoulder. The target clutched his chest as if in confusion and then collapsed to the ground. The Walkin' Man was dead.

As Harry reloaded, the realization of what happened struck the other slaves, and they immediately began to scatter. They ran hunched over, heads low, and scrambling for cover. A woman and a small child of about ten-years-old, burst from the door of the cabin, running at full gallop to the body of the Walkin' Man. Harry aimed, fired, and killed another slave loping hunched over towards the barn for his own cover; he fell dead before reaching the doors. Even Harry drew the line with women and children.

Confusion consumed the survivors as they scattered into the woods behind the barn. Harry quietly backed out from his position, taking care to stay flat on the ground. After crawling at least one-hundred feet on his belly, he stood, brushed the leaves and dirt from his clothes, and calmly began his walk home.

"Like shootin' ducks in a pond."

Chapter Seven

"FINAL CONFRONTATION"
HARRY

JUNE 1863

That night, Horatio sat in his big over-stuffed chair reading a book. He heard Harry's heavy boots clump onto the porch. Confrontations between the two were beginning to be more common, and Harry grew bolder and more defiant with every argument. Very subtle changes had begun to come over Harry. He spent more time away from home, he was moody, and often made snide comments as though he knew something Horatio didn't. His forays to the woods had been more frequent, and his insistence about joining the army was more determined.

Letters

Harry stepped through the door, dropped his gear on the floor, and then carefully propped his rifle in the corner. His appearance seemed more disheveled than usual; his clothes and face were smeared with dirt.

"What in the world happened to you?" asked Horatio, incredulously.

"Been huntin'. Where'd you think I'd been?"

"It's just that you've been out after dark almost every night, and I worry about you."

"What in the world can happen to a soul 'round this damn place? There's nothing going on, for Pete's sake. Besides, some of the best hunting is at dusk. All kinds of varmints start stirring around. You know---getting ready for the night's activity," Harry smiled.

Horatio sensed a sudden change in his son's demeanor, he was relaxed, almost jubilant, "Sit down, Harry. We need to talk."

"I know", interrupted Harry, "but 'fore you start preaching again, I've got something to say. So save your breath." He paused for effect. "I'm leavin' Horatio, and you're gonna help me get what I want. I ain't the only one been going to the woods at night. Am I---fa-ather?"

Horatio's jaw dropped, his face blushed with astonishment. "What---what do mean?" He stammered.

"Let's not play games, Horatio. You know exactly what I mean. That little cabin in the woods. Coloreds in the barn. That big buck that runs the place for you."

Horatio knew he was caught. Horrible scenarios flashed through his mind. Everything ruined. His future, the railroad's future, the lives of the escaped slaves all in the hands of his demented son. "What do you want, Harry? What have you done?" He asked with resignation.

"I want to join up with the 96th. They're down in Vicksburg in one of the biggest battles of the war, and that's where I want to be."

Horatio stood, his book dropping to the floor. "Now Harry, we're not going to---"

Harry stomped his foot on the floor with such force that it rattled the furniture and pictures on the wall. "You ain't exactly in a position to tell me what I can and can't do, old man! I got the goods on you. And I'll use 'em to get what I want! I don't give a hoot 'bout you and them damn coloreds. You do what you want, but I'm outta here, and you're gonna help me! Hell! Even the coloreds are fightin'! Coloreds that you been bringing up from the South. If they can fight, it's only right that I should too!"

Horatio's face was blood red, his fists clenched tight by his sides. Harry had him backed into a corner, but he was damned if he'd let him berate him like a child. "You don't tell me what I'm going to do, young man! You may think I'm some soft old man who's never raised a hand in anger and have no concept of what war and killing is all about! You know nothing about my past or me. You think you're the only one in this family that has a passion for adventure. The difference between you and me, Harry, is our motivations. Any time I ever raised a hand against another man was when there was a just cause. Not just to have the pleasure of killing a man. Now if you want something from me---you ask and talk to me like a man. I'll help you to get what you want under my terms, not yours. Do you understand me?"

Harry just stared back at Horatio with a crooked grin and a knowing glint in his eyes. It momentarily unnerved Horatio, so he continued talking, buying time to settle himself and get back the high ground. "Yes---I'm running slaves out of the South, and I also know the risks involved. But I'll tell you this---you will do nothing to interfere with it or you will be the one backed in a corner. If, and I emphasize if, I help you---as I said before, it will be on my terms." When he was done, Horatio's tone was firm, leaving no doubt that he meant every word.

Harry's controlled façade broke and the surprise from his father's tirade showed on his face. He'd never seen Horatio explode like this. What was he talking about? Had he killed before? Was there more to this man than met the eye? Horatio almost scared him for a minute.

Harry shoved his hands into his front pockets. "What do you mean? Are you tellin' me that you've killed a man before?" Harry asked with a hint of admiration and curiosity in the question.

"I'm telling you not to underestimate me, Harry. Now there's something I want to ask you and I want a straight answer." Horatio hesitated. His mouth grew dry. "Why are you so anxious to kill another man?"

Letters

Harry relaxed, he thought a minute, and looked Horatio straight in the eye. "I'm not sure if that's it or not, Horatio. At least I'm not as anxious as I used to be," he quipped, the crooked smile returning. "I can tell you that. I'm not built to be a banker or store clerk. I don't care 'bout money. It's the thrill of the hunt. Being on the edge. I can't really explain it. But I do know this---if'n I stay here any longer, I can't be responsible for my actions. Fighting in this war is just something I have to do. I can't explain it. It eats me up every day. It's time for me to go---and you know it."

"Don't you see these boys coming home every week in a box or with half their bodies blown apart?" Horatio asked desperately.

Harry shrugged. "Those idiots stand in a line facin' other idiots in a line, and they take turns shooting at each other. How stupid is that? I'm a sniper! Nobody sees me. They won't even know where the shot that kills 'em comes from! Right now, the 96th is down in Vicksburg beating on Rebels like they're a bunch of mangy dogs, and I wanna get in on it 'fore this war's over!"

Horatio's shoulders slumped, eyes staring at his feet. He'd fought this battle long enough and it was time to break the standoff.

He didn't want Harry in his house anymore. "We'll go to Camp Delaware tomorrow and get you signed up." Horatio said flatly, slumping back into his chair, exhausted from the verbal warfare with Harry. He was afraid of the damage his crazy son might do to his link with the Underground if he stayed around any longer. Changes would have to be made and soon.

Harry decided not to say anything about the Walking Man. He'd let Horatio find out about that on his own. He got what he wanted.

Chapter Eight

"VICKSBURG"
HARRY

JULY 1863

The Union Army victory at Vicksburg, Mississippi was one of the most brilliant military campaigns of the war. For General Ulysses S. Grant, it was the battle that brought him recognition for his brilliant military strategy and eventually catapulted him to the rank of General-in-Chief of the Union Army.

Since October of '62, Grant had made several failed attempts to crush the Confederate forces that were under the command of Lt. Colonel John Pemberton. Finally, towards the end of March of '63, Grant made a final push, but the Southern forces were able to withstand two brutal assaults. Pemberton was determined to hold the city of Vicksburg at all costs. A defeat would cut the Confederate states in half and greatly disrupt the shipment of supplies to soldiers in need. Grant was finally convinced that a long and protracted siege was the only sure way of defeat for the Confederates.

The siege of Vicksburg began with the repulse of Grant's final attack on May 22, 1863, and lasted until July 1st. As the siege progressed, disease and starvation reduced Pemberton's 20, 000 man garrison. The city's residents were forced to seek the refuge and protection of caves and bombproofs in the surrounding hills. Hunger and daily bombardments by Grant's forces finally compelled Pemberton to ask for surrender terms on July 3, 1863. Grant finally agreed to terms and even paroled the bulk of the Confederate force. Ironically, many of these same men would later oppose Grant's forces at the Battle of Chattanooga, Tennessee, one of the bloodiest battles of the war. All told, almost 20, 000 men died at the Battle of Vicksburg, with casualties being about equal to both sides. With the Confederate loss of Vicksburg, Pemberton's worst nightmare came true. The South was cut in half.

Letters

The 96th Ohio, still led by Colonel Vance, worked with Grant's army and was an important part of the siege. After the surrender, they were ordered to Jackson, Mississippi to prepare for a major campaign in Louisiana. Harry finally joined his home unit while they were garrisoned in Jackson. It had not been an easy task to get Harry hooked up with the 96th. There were many units, which were easier to get to, but Harry wanted his home unit; it's where he wanted to be. One thing about Horatio that Harry admired---he didn't mind stepping on toes and going over subordinate's heads to get what he wanted. For once, he agreed with Harry. He needed to be with the 96th.

"If you're going in, it's going to be with John Vance. There's no better officer and gentleman in the army. Plus, you'll have some friends and people you know that will be able to help you and show you the ropes."

Harry grimaced, "I'll proudly serve with Colonel Vance, he's a military genius and he's always at the front of the lines with his men. He's not one of those damn campfire generals. But, as for those other fellas---I don't need 'em or their advice. Why would I take advice from somebody who's stupid enough to stand in a line in front of the enemy and let 'em use them for target practice?"

"I know," conceded Horatio, "you told me already."

When Harry was finally in camp with the 96th, he was taken to Colonel Vance's tent, per his letter of introduction. "You must be somebody special, boy. I didn't know ever'body got a personal "howdy-do" from the Colonel when they come in camp," said the smirking corporal as he escorted Harry.

"My name's Harry Morgan---not boy."

"Really? Well your name is mud around here, 'til you prove yourself. You're barely off your momma's milk, boy. They's men 'round here that'll stomp you in the ground as a warm-up before breakfast, if'n you're not careful."

Harry quickly turned and pointed the barrel of his Sharps at the corporal's crotch. "And I know just what I'll serve 'em for breakfast, too."

The corporal never flinched a muscle or gave any indication of fear. "You've got grit boy, you'll do just fine. But if you ever point that Sharps at me again, you better pull the trigger."

"I will," said Harry.

The corporal gave a quick little grin from the corner of his mouth, "Good. Now let's go see the Colonel."

Harry waited outside the Vance's tent about twenty minutes before a lieutenant finally opened the flap back and said, "Come in Private Morgan."

The Colonel was already standing, bent over a large table with maps strewn all over the top. Harry snapped to attention and gave a crisp, correct salute, "Sir! Private Harry Morgan reporting for duty, Sir!"

Vance looked up from his maps at Harry, amused. He was a changed man from that first day when he was prancing around his troops on his beautiful stallion at Camp Delaware in '61. The clean, tailored uniform seemed to hang on him, and his eyes looked weary and sad. His appearance didn't concern Harry, in fact he liked it. The look of war.

Vance smiled, snapped to attention and returned Harry's salute. He grinned at his aide as his salute dropped. "At ease Private Morgan. We have a tendency to relax formality around here after the seriousness of the war sets in. Did you have a good trip?"

"It was okay, Sir. I'm just glad to be here."

"Well, we'll see about that, but we're glad to have all the fire power we can muster. I understand you're a crack shot, Mr. Morgan. Do you think you're up to snuff to be a part of our sniper unit? Those boys are a different breed all together from the rest of the troops. It takes great discipline, not just being a good shot."

"I'm fully aware of that, Sir. I believe it's the place I'm supposed to be and best serve you and the army, Sir."

"One thing about those Rebels, son. They can shoot the eyes out of a turkey at five-hundred yards if it suits them. Their snipers are the best I've seen. Those country boys were shooting squirrels out of trees when ours were chasing skirts in the city. If you're as good as I've been told, then we can sure enough use you."

"Thank you, Sir," answered Harry.

"The lieutenant here will take you to your unit and get you in order. He'll make sure you have everything you need."

"Just plenty of ammunition, Sir---that's all I need."

The Colonel gave a small smile, "I'm sure we can handle that then, Private Morgan. We're going back to Vicksburg in a few days and prepare for a big push to New Orleans at the end of August. That's no military secret, your unit has already been told. I hope you've made the right decision Harry---it's going to get a lot worse before it gets better."

Vance motioned to his aide. "Lieutenant, help Private Morgan find his unit. Good luck to you, soldier."

"Thank you, Sir."

Harry turned and walked out of the tent. Except for seeing Colonel Vance from a distance in camp, or watching him charge to the front of his troops in the heat of battle, he never got to talk to his commander again. That suited him just fine. It was also the last time he said "sir" to anybody.

It didn't take Harry long to settle in. He didn't fraternize much with the soldiers in his unit, except when they were on the move from campaign to campaign. He had more enemies than friends, but that didn't bother him either. He preferred it as a matter-of-fact. His comrades may not have cared for Harry's cockiness and sour attitude, but they did admire his marksmanship. His reputation grew and continued to follow him as the 96th move ever southward.

Nine months after Harry joined the unit, in April of '64; the gallant Colonel John Vance was killed at the Battle of Sabine Cross Roads, in Louisiana. Harry stayed out days at a time without returning to camp, so he was unaware of the Colonel's death until days later.

"I'm sorry to hear that," Harry said. "He was a good man." Then he turned and walked away from the group of soldiers.

"That's the nicest thing I've heard that son-of a-bitch say since he's been here," a soldier smirked.

News from the war continued to flow back to Horatio in Ohio. He never received any letters from Harry, but he was fully aware of his accomplishments. Neighbors, customers, and business acquaintances were always congratulating him on his son's heroism. "The war is the perfect place for him, Horatio. He'll be the town hero when he gets home," they all said.

Horatio would smile and thank them for their kind words. However, in his heart, he knew Harry would never return home.

Chapter Nine

"RIVER OF BLOOD"
CHICKAMAUGA

SEPTEMBER 17, 1863

Since the catastrophic defeat at Vicksburg, the morale of the Confederate soldiers dropped to its lowest point; however, they didn't completely feel the war was at its end. The 18th, 36th, 38th, and 58th Alabama Regiments had joined up with the Army of Tennessee outside of Chattanooga. There were 43,000 Confederate troops ready to recapture the city. The only problem was the 60,000 Union troops dug in and ready to keep it at all costs.

Tom had done a good job whipping his men into shape. His

unit knew they could count on him in a pinch; in return, he got their respect and loyalty. Desertion had become a big problem throughout the army, but all of his men were present and accounted for. Colonel Inge ran a tight company and loyalty ran deep with his leadership. That's not to say there weren't problems. When Tom got promoted to sergeant, there were those who wanted to "test the waters" and see how far they could go before pushing the line. Tom was not beyond whacking someone upside the head to get their attention, or on the other hand, showing some firm compassion when necessary. In a short period of time, it became clear who was in charge and discipline began to return.

Not long after Tom became sergeant, a soldier by the name of Bob Bateman got drunk and fell asleep on sentry duty. Tom had been making his rounds, checking on the various guard posts, when he saw Bateman passed out in a rifle pit. Tom reached down, grabbed him by the collar of his jacket, and literally snatched the drunken soldier to his feet. He slapped his face hard to bring him out of his drunken stupor. He'd known Bateman since childhood. He was a good man, except for one thing. He drowned his demons in the bottom of a whiskey bottle.

"You drunken coward! You dare to get stone-faced drunk when your comrades are countin' on you to keep 'em alive! Alert them if the enemy calls!"

Bateman shook his head, trying to clear the fog that filled his brain. "Tom, I swears! Please don't bust me! I ain't never doin' it again! The boredom, the camp life, I can't take it no more! I wanna go home!" He pleaded.

"Go home? Hell, who don't?" Tom spat. "Don't lay no crummy excuses on me, Bob Bateman. You're a good man in a fight, Bob, but I can't depend on you anymore. You're a drunk, plain and simple. What if a Yankee patrol had come marchin' up here? You'd be dead and so'd your buddies that're countin' on you."

"I know, Tom. Just give me one more chance. Don't tell the boys. I can't get drummed out like 'ol Luther did. I promise you Tom, I won't let ya'll down again. If'n I do, I'll cut my own hair and let you drum me out yourself." Bateman's eyes were blood red and pleading; spittle sprayed from his mouth as he cried for mercy.

Tom looked him over, head to toe---hard, in disgust. "Bob," he said, then hesitated to think about what to do with his former neighbor. Morale was low enough and another drumming out would only make matters worse. "Are you awake enough to finish your duty?"

"I am, Tom. I am!" Bob's eyes showed hope.

"When you're done, in---two hours, you go down to the creek an' clean yourself up before comin' back to camp. Get some rest and then come to see me." Tom poked him in the shoulder hard to get his attention. "Me an' you are gonna have a real "Come to Jesus" meeting. Do – you – under – stand – me?" Tom said, speaking the words slowly and deliberately, continuing to poke his finger into Bob's chest accenting every word.

"I do, Tom---I promise to---" Tom cut him off before he could finish. "That's Sergeant Durrett---an' don't make promises. Just do it."

That morning, Bob Bateman returned to camp. He looked rough and worn, but a changed man. No one ever saw him take another drink of whiskey, and he was never asked why.

Morale was not a problem on Thursday, September 17th.

Letters

Staying alive was all that occupied every man's mind. General Bragg had given orders for Clayton's Brigade, including the Eighteenth, to move up close to the Chickamauga Creek and secure the position. Colonel Inge made sure the Eighteenth was not spread too thin and continued to encourage his troops as they marched forward. The air was electric and saturated by the smell of war.

Regiments of the Union Army were encamped on the north side of the creek. The terrain wasn't ideal for warfare; it was heavily wooded and hilly. "I don't like this, James," whispered Tom, as the march continued. "You won't see those bluebellies 'til they're in your face." He turned to his cousin. "Henry, are you listenin'?"

Henry hadn't said a word since their march to the creek began. "Yeah, what is it?" He answered back nervously.

"When this gets started, you an' James stay close to me. Try not to get separated. I'm 'fraid we're gonna get into some hand to hand stuff. I hope it don't come to that, but be ready."

"I've got a bad feelin' 'bout this place we're going, Tom," Henry warned.

"Henry, just fight like a wild man, focus on what you're doin'.

What you've been trained to do. This ain't your first dance. Just like Shiloh. Remember?"

Henry kept his eyes forward. "I'm tryin' to forget Shiloh, Tom, but it's not me I'm worried 'bout. It's you," he said flatly.

"Me?" Tom answered in surprise, then laughed. "Don't worry 'bout me, Cousin. You just keep your own head down, you hear?"

James listened to the conversation, keeping quiet. He knew that Henry sometimes had premonitions about things. But, Tom always laughed it off, saying it was a bunch of hogwash.

"Henry," James finally spoke, "you know, the Durretts came in this war together, and we're going to leave that way."

Tom didn't have time to listen to Henry and his feelings about the future and left to check on the rest of the platoon. He glared left and right as he marched through the ranks, making sure there were no stragglers or loafers. Occasionally slapping a soldier on the arm, giving him encouragement. Adjusting another's knapsack, even if the need wasn't there. It was his way of letting them know he was right there beside them. He turned to look over his shoulder and saw Bob Bateman a few steps behind him.

"I've got your boy's backs, Tom. Don't worry," Bateman stated.

Tom nodded once to let him know he understood.

Darrel Giles, a short stocky soldier from Tuscaloosa County, caught up with Tom as he continued to make his rounds. "You know what the Cherokee Injuns call this creek, Tom?"

"No, Darrel. I'm not really worried 'bout that right now. I heard Colonel Inge call it Chicka-somethin' or other."

"Yeah, Chickamauga. But, you know what the Injuns called it? The River of Blood, that's what they call it, Tom. Don't that bother you none?"

"Darrel, I got a whole lot more on my mind right now, than to worry 'bout the name of this place. But---if I do end up dyin' here, it'll be a comfort knowing you told me the name of it." Darrel's short legs were having a hard time keeping up with Tom's long, quick strides, and he was getting short of breath; he was almost jogging to keep up.

"Let's just make sure it's Yankee blood an' not ours. Ok, Darrel?"

"Alright, Tom. I just thought you should know."

Tom stopped and put a hand on Darrel's shoulder. "Now I know. Drop back, Darrel. Catch your breath an' keep your damn head down." Tom knew that some men just had to talk and jabber about nothing in particular, trying to manage or get rid of nervous energy before a battle. Some were dead quiet, into themselves. Letting each man deal with the possibility of dying was part of the game. To each his own.

The regiment finally stopped a few miles from the Chickamauga Creek. Officers gave orders to dig in for the night. The noises and voices of Yankee camp life could be heard across the creek. Each side knew of what was to come.

The passing night was cold, but campfires were not allowed. Even though the woods were thick and Clayton's Brigade was far enough back from the creek to be out of sight, no one wanted to give the slightest hint of their location. A cold, frosty dawn arrived and camps were stirring up and down the line. Colonel Inge rode up to Company E's location and brought his horse to a gentle stop. He looked calm and ready to do his duty. He set the tone for his men. "Tom, we'll be crossing the creek sometime today. The Eighteenth will be in a reserve status for a spell, but I suspect we'll still get our shoes wet in the upcoming encounter."

"We're ready, Colonel," Tom answered. "It sounds like there's gonna be plenty of bluebellies for everybody. I'm not worried 'bout runnin' out. Matter of fact, when we run them Yankees outta Chattanooga, I'll buy you a steak dinner in town."

Inge tipped his hat. "You're on. See you on the other side of the creek, Tom." The Colonel saluted, spurred his horse forward and continued on down the line.

Tom made his rounds again, making sure all his men were ready and staying busy. This was no time for idleness. Give a man too much time to think and he might think about running. As the sun began to rise, sounds of sporadic gunfire erupted. Some men whooped in enthusiasm; some dropped their eyes to the ground and began to pray; some involuntarily took a step backwards in retreat.

All day the Eighteenth and other reserve units heard scattered gunfire, and at times they heard the large thunderous volleys of rifles as hundreds of men strung out in seemingly infinite lines cut loose with fire; they faced their enemy, sometimes less than one hundred yards apart, trading volleys. There were endless streams of wounded soldiers being brought back to the rear positions for treatment. Some staggered back by their own power, dazed, with lifeless eyes staring nowhere. Some were carried, cradled in the arms of their comrades as though they were sleeping babies in their mother's arms. Some were on their feet, but unable to walk alone, and had to be helped by others who were also wounded. The effect on the men watching this parade of the wounded was not one of defeat. To the contrary, it was one of pride and vengeance. The wounded spoke of pushing the enemy back. Victory was at hand, not defeat. One soldier, with wounds to his arm and head, winked at the reserves as he proudly marched of his own accord. "We've warmed 'em up for ya', boys. They's all yours now!" He called loudly. The entire unit cheered and waved their regiment banners and flags in response.

Friday night, September 18th, the Eighteenth took up position on the Chickamauga. About dark, Colonel Inge ordered them to wade the creek and set up camp and sentries on the north side that was the Yankee side. The temperature had dropped. The officers still ordered for no campfires to be lighted. The men didn't need to be told.

Letters

James sat huddled next to Henry and Tom, all three shivering in the dark. "Damn Tom, I'd be willing to let the Yanks shoot at me if I could light a fire," he chattered.

"Well little brother, you light a fire an' you won't have to worry 'bout a Yank getting a bead on you. I imagine one of our own boys'd do it for you."

"How much longer to sunup do you think?" James asked, keeping the conversation going.

"Less than an hour, little brother. Be patient."

"Oh, I'm patient alright. No hurry here."

Everyone could hear the Yanks cutting trees and building breastwork defenses in anticipation of the upcoming assault. "That's a bit unnervin'," shivered Henry. "Why ain't we building some defenses of our own?"

Tom looked at Henry with a deadpanned expression, "Henry---we're doing the attacking---not defending."

James laughed softly, then Henry, then Tom joined in. It was a nervous reflex laugh---each attempting to make light of a dark situation.

Before long orders started being passed down the line. "Prepare to move!" Colonel Inge rode the line back and forth, encouraging, prodding, and motivating.

"That man sure can stir up a bunch of people with guns, can't he, Tom?" Henry joked.

"Yeah, he can, Henry. Well, I guess we can't just turn 'round and go home anymore. We've stirred up those Yankee boys pretty much, by now." Tom turned to James. "You ready little brother?"

"Yeah, I'm ready," James answered. "They're in my way to get home."

The thick forest limited visibility to one-hundred-fifty feet in any direction, less than the range of a rifle; cannons exploded in the occasional field that broke the heavy forest. Battle lines didn't exist and enlisted men made tactical decisions along with their commanders. It was impossible for the officers to command their units when they themselves were involved in hand-to-hand combat. Shrapnel from cannonballs and large splinters from exploding trees crippled and killed men by the dozens. Generals on both sides realized that neither army would come out a clear winner under such conditions. The field on which the men fought was not the choice of generals, but the choice of fate.

Now that the time had finally arrived, the fear had subsided. The mechanics of battle shot through James's mind. Move. Be sure of your shot. Shoot for the body. Take cover. Reload. Move.

They stepped lightly and cautiously through the woods. "I see 'em!" yelled Henry. The sight of the enemy scared him so bad, his first shot misfired from his hip, not even getting a chance to shoulder his weapon.

"Dammit, Henry!" Tom screamed. "Calm down an' aim! The one you miss might be the one that kills me!" That thought alone jerked Henry back to reality.

Blue and gray uniforms alike hugged the ground, hid behind trees, rifles ready, waiting, afraid that the next shot will be the end for him. The moans and screams of the wounded blended in with the frantic sounds of battle. Tom made sure his men were moving forward, not retreating. "Shoot an' move!" he shouted, "we're gainin' ground!" He saw Henry was to his left---in a rhythm of moving, shooting, reloading. Tom's eyes scanned the landscape for James, but he was nowhere to be seen.

"Henry! Where's James?" Tom shouted.

Henry waved his arm forward. "He's ahead! He saw Giles go down! He's tendin' to him!"

"Damn that boy!" Tom ran zigzag through the trees, searching out James. He spotted him running back towards him, with Darrel Giles slung over his shoulder like a sack of potatoes. Tom heard the dreaded whistling sound of cannonballs that had started overhead. "Down, James, Down!" Tom shouted, still running towards his little brother. The first explosion was about fifty yards off to the left, but the second one was closer. The concussion blew James off his feet, hurling Darrel and him through the air, both landing yards away with a bone-crunching thud. The blast from a third explosion knocked Tom's legs out from under him as he tried to keep his balance. He was stunned and senseless, ears ringing. He felt a strong hand yank him up by the collar of his jacket.

"Hurry, Tom! More's in-comin'!" It was Bob Bateman. Henry ran up and grabbed Tom under the arms, and the three stumbled forward to James and Darrel. They saw their crumpled bodies in a heap, one on top of the other. Tom ran with all his might, sloughing away the arms of Bob and Henry. He saw a large splinter, the size of an axe handle, sticking in the back of either James or Darrel. He wasn't sure which. The cannon fire didn't let up its relentless bombardment. The surrounding trees shattered and splintered from the cannon shot, hurling wooden missiles through the air as dangerous and deadly as the shrapnel itself.

"James!" Tom screamed. He slid to his knees and turned over the body with the large splinter protruding in the back. The blank, dead eyes of Darrel Giles stared back at him. James lay face down in the dirt. He moaned and slowly turned to his side.

"James! Are you hurt?" Tom cupped his brother's head in his own rough, callused hands. James's face was smeared with dirt, with moist streaks smearing his cheeks.

"I'm okay," James gasped. "How's Darrel?" he croaked, looking around dazed and unsure of his whereabouts. "Th-the explosion knocked us down and his weight knocked the breath outta me."

"He's dead James. He saved your life when you was savin'

his," Henry whispered softly. "You're a lucky man, James." For this one isolated moment, it seemed that the war was standing still in time. Silent. The four of them were oblivious to the rifle shots whistling by their ears, explosions in the distance, and the men charging to the front around them. For the Durretts, this was the closest any of them had come to losing one another. Tom shuddered at the thought.

Suddenly, the time capsule ended, and the sounds of war erupted again. "Tom! Come on!" Matt Rupert shouted as he ran towards them. "The Yanks are runnin'!" He stopped in his tracks, staring down at the man beside James. "That Darrell?"

"Yeah," answered Henry.

Rupert nudged Tom with the butt of his Enfield. "Damn. Too bad. Come on Tom, he won't be the last either. We got 'em on the run an' we need you now!"

Tom got to his feet and barked out his orders. "Henry, take James to the rear of the lines an' stay with him." He grabbed Bateman by the crook of the arm. "You're with me."

Tom and Bob ran low, hunched forward, dodging trees, bodies, and retreating wounded, trying to catch up with the unit.

Fellow soldiers were falling like leaves from a tree in the fall as a result of the fierce volleys of firepower and the snipers fixed on their killing zones from hidden nests. "Look Tom, daylight! There's a clearin' up ahead," Bob shouted, pointing to their right.

"Stay low, Bob, it ain't over yet!" As the clearing appeared, they saw Yankees running scattered and unorganized through the open pasture, searching for cover and sanctuary in the woods. Some ran straight into the arms and fire power of Rebel soldiers as they exited the woods. The Confederate units became more organized as more officers and soldiers emerged from the heavy forest. Companies were reforming and order was retained. Tom saw Colonel Inge and he waved to get his attention.

"Sergeant Durrett!" Inge responded. "Assemble your men, we need to cut off all avenues of escape, and keep these Union ruffians from returning to Chattanooga." Sweaty, white foam covered his stallion's breast and neck; Inge's face was streaked with bloody scratches from tree branches that had slapped his face as he'd charged through the woods earlier. His uniform was disheveled, but he stood proud, unafraid in the stirrups. "There's word of the enemy

approaching from our left flank and we gotta stop 'em at all cost!"
Inge noticed the absence of James and Henry. In a voice of dread, he
asked, "Tom? Where are they? James and Henry?"

"They're fine, Colonel. James got his senses knocked outta
him by an explosion. Henry took him back to the rear. They're good."

"Good.   Form up your men---now.   We're going to
Chattanooga, by God!"

As the Eighteenth began to reorganize itself, it was obvious
that it had taken a heavy toll. There were too many known faces
missing. Inge took his position at the front of his men and began the
march northeast, towards the woods. Other companies fell into order
behind their commanders, and there was a new spirit in the regiment.
Within a hundred yards of the tree line, all soldiers quickly became
aware of movement and noise, apparently made by a large number of
soldiers approaching from the northeastern direction of the woods. A
line of blue uniforms suddenly appeared before the Eighteenth and
with a sudden and deadly volley of rifle fire, they laid down on the
unaware Rebels. Colonel Inge was among the first to fall, a Minie
ball shattering his right knee. His horse reared, throwing off Inge, and

then ran wildly through the field as his master lay wounded on the ground. Without hesitation, all units charged forward directly into the face of the Yankee fire. The Yanks were surprised and caught off-guard by the resolve and courage of the Rebel army; they broke ranks and retreated in haste, leaving their weapons and pride behind in the grassy field.

Rupert called out, "Look at 'em Tom! You ever seen a more beautiful sight? We're gonna run 'em plum outta Tennessee!"

"I know, but the Colonel's down," Tom said pointing in the downed leader's direction. He saw several officers with him, tending to his wound. "Corporal Bateman! Get this damn unit in order. I'm gonna check with Lieutenant Cohill about Colonel Inge. Now get to it!"

Bob Bateman looked on in surprise. "Excuse me Sergeant Durrett, but did you say *Corporal* Bateman?"

"Look around, Bob. Pickings is kinda slim right now. I need somebody I know and trust to help me right now. You're the man--- now get busy!" Tom turned and trotted away to check on Colonel Inge.

A small group of men had gathered around Inge, and as Tom edged his way into the center, he could tell the commander was in excruciating pain. His knee was completely shattered with a hole replacing what used to be his kneecap. He was losing too much blood, too fast, and the palor of his face was a sickly gray. Inge glanced up and saw Tom. "It looks like that steak in town will have to wait a few days, Tom," he managed to say between gritted teeth. "We're winning this one, don't let the men think otherwise, Tom."

"You don't worry none 'bout that, Sir. You just get well so you can get back on that fine horse of yours. And get us outta this damn war."

Inge gave a weak smile, but grimaced in pain at the same time.

"Get the wagon up here on the double!" Dr. Armstrong ordered. "Let's get this man to the hospital immediately."

Tom turned and walked slowly back to his company. "Too many good men are gonna die in this damn war," Tom said, but no one heard him.

Chapter Ten

"THE SLAUGHTERHOUSE"

SEPTEMBER 19, 1863

James and Henry threaded their way through the thick forest, avoiding the dead and dying of both armies. Hundreds of walking wounded made their way back to the rear lines for medical help. "Meat wagons" were loaded with soldiers unable to retreat by their own power and slowly maneuvered their way towards the field hospitals. Occasionally, a wagon would stop to help those who fell in their tracks and could go no farther on their own, but wounded soldiers who had no chance of survival were left behind.

James felt guilty. "These men are in serious need of attention, Henry. I don't think half of them will make it to the hospitals. I've got a headache and a bloody nose. I don't deserve to be falling back with the wounded."

Henry kept his hand pressed against the middle of his cousin's back, urging him forward. In spite of his words, James was still unsteady on his feet, his balance off. "Shutup, James. You hadn't run backwards in one battle, and every man here knows you're no coward. You caught the backside of a cannonball tryin' to save Darrell's life. Weren't thinkin' of yourself. They's not a man here that'd try to shame you for goin' back. Now shutup and come on."

James could tell that Henry was put out with him, so he dropped the subject, watching the men around him. "Talk is that we're winning this battle, Henry. Sure doesn't look like it, does it?"

"Nah, but It's gotta be just as bad on the other side too. Wonder how many we lost this time? Hope it's not as bad as Shiloh."

"I really don't need to go on to the hospital, you know. They're going to be so busy, they won't have the time or patience for me. Look at 'em, Henry," James said, nodding at the walking wounded around them. There was a distinct sadness in James's voice.

"It'll just make me feel better if we at least have a orderly look at you," Henry said, slightly relenting. "Don't argue with me 'bout it. Then, we'll go back to camp. Tom and Bob'll be comin' in soon," Henry answered flatly.

He didn't want to admit it, but he was also as shaken as James by the carnage around him, but he had to put on a brave front. He was afraid James was injured more than he was letting on. Concussions from those explosions could knock a man senseless. He'd seen it before. As of yet, James hadn't said anything about Darrel. He knew that would come down on him later like a ball-pin hammer. Henry still envisioned the large sliver of tree stuck in Darrel's back like a spear. He wouldn't be forgetting it anytime soon, either.

Both teenagers moved slowly in silence, trying to imagine themselves anywhere else but here. "James," Henry said quietly and with unusual affection and hesitation.

"Yeah, Henry," James answered.

"I wish I was as brave as you."

Neither boy turned to look at the other. "You're the bravest of the three of us, Henry. You're the heart, Tom's the soul, and I guess I'm the conscience of the group, maybe. I don't know. But, you bring humor and spirit where there is none. You're brave, Henry. You just don't realize it. You've already proved it."

They walked in silence and gradually saw the regiment encampment appear through the trees. From the distance, it seemed peaceful, with campfire smoke spiraling lazily into the air; however, the scene belied the surrounding carnage.

"How's your ears? They still ringin'?" Henry asked.

"Yeah, pretty much. Sounds like a bunch of bells in my head."

Straight-faced, with a gleam in his eyes, Henry asked, "Would you like me to hum a tune to go along with those bells?"

James smiled weakly.

The light moment between the boys faded quickly when they approached the field hospital grounds. Large tents with tops, but no sides, were set up in small clearings among the trees. Wall to wall rows of cots in straight lines were filled with wounded soldiers. The sound of pain dominated the woods. Scattered around the tents, men were slowly dying; lying on the ground, leaning against trees, waiting for someone to free them from pain. Orderlies dashed from patient to patient, trying to determine who was in most need, who could wait, and forgetting those that it didn't matter anymore.

Surgery, as it was, was performed in a smaller tent, isolated from the recovery area so the overworked surgeons could perform their gruesome duties out of sight from the others.

"My God, Henry, I can't go in there. I don't care what you say. These men are dying. I can't do this. Let's go back to camp and I'll rest there."

Henry knew he was right. He remembered this same scene after the battle at Shiloh. Most of the men stayed clear of the hospitals, unless the need truly arose. The sight and suffering was unbearable to watch.

"The Pit" was the area most avoided. This was where the hundreds of amputated limbs from surgery were discarded, burned, and buried. The stench of burning and rotting meat permeated the area; everyone recognized the large, black plumes of smoke as they billowed in the air. The surgeons were so overwhelmed with casualties, lack of proper medicine and equipment, and fatigue that amputation was the most convenient and expedient form of surgery. Anything short of a flesh wound was removed. This weighed heavily on the consciousness of the doctors trying to do their duties. Educated men, those who had been dedicated and trained to heal, were transformed and reduced into the equivalent of butchers in a slaughterhouse for cattle. When one passed by the surgical tents, the screams of patients and the horrible sound of the handsaws grinding back and forth across bone stayed with even the most hardened veterans.

"Let's go, James," Henry said, pulling his arm. "I think I'd rather be on the front line getting shot at than be here."

As they left the hospital area, another meatwagon rolled by, passing those in the way. Henry saw Colonel Inge in the bed of it, lying on his back, his head being steadied in the lap of Major Hunley. Henry could tell that Hunley was encouraging Inge to hold on. He was obviously in severe pain.

Peter Hunley and Richard Inge had been friends since childhood and even attended West Point Military Academy together as cadets. They joined the Eighteenth when the war started and had served as officers since its original organization. Both men had distinguished themselves as brave and respected officers and gentlemen.

"You hang in there Rich, don't you dare die on me," Hunley chided. "It's only a leg wound. Do you hear me?" Hunley said sternly to his best friend.

Inge fought to stay conscious, in spite of the excruciating pain in his shattered left leg. "Don't let them take my leg, Pete. I'd rather die than go home half a man. My career'd be over---no way to make a living. Is it bad? I can't tell."

Hunley knew the leg was useless; the Minie ball had completely shattered the knee, almost severing the leg. Even if the surgeon didn't amputate, it would be totally useless. But, what concerned him was the loss of blood his friend had sustained. He feared that Richard would bleed to death before he could make it to surgery. "Now, you just don't worry 'bout that, Rich. You'll be dosey-doeing in no time." Hunley's attempt of encouragement was weak, his voice betraying him.

Inge turned his head so he could see his friend's face and clasped his hand. "You always were a terrible liar, Pete. You're a good man and the best friend a person could ask for, Peter Hunley.

Watch over my men, they're a good and brave regiment. There's not a coward in the bunch."

"Never you mind that now, Richard F. Inge. You'll be back and you can lead them into hell yourself." Both men knew it was not to be, though.

James and Henry ran to catch up with the wagon. "Colonel Inge!" James shouted. Hunley saw and recognized them, but waved them off, not wanting to stop the wagon or further hinder his friend.

"Who's that?" Inge groaned.

"The Durrett boys---James and Henry."

"Thank God, I was afraid they'd been hurt. Call them over, I want to talk to them," Inge urged. Reluctantly, Major Hunley motioned for the boys to come ahead. The wagon had slowed down to a walk and was easing to a stop in front of the surgical tent.

"James, I'm glad to see you and Henry are okay. Tom's at the front. I saw him after I went down. He's safe."

James feared for Colonel Inge. His face was pale and chalky. He was dying and he knew it. "Thank you, sir. They'll take care of you here. Captain Rutland is a fine doctor," James encouraged.

Letters

"Thank you, James. Give your brother a message for me," Inge croaked, attempting to smile. "Tell him I said to charge to the front and take no prisoners." Then Colonel Inge gave the boys a weak wave of the hand as the orderlies carried him into the surgical tent with Major Hunley following close behind.

Colonel Richard F. Inge died on September 28, nine days later from loss of blood and infection after his leg had been amputated; his best friend was at his side. Major Peter Hunley was promoted to Lieutenant Colonel and took over his best friend's command.

The Confederate forces won at Chickamauga, but at a loss of 18,000 men. The Eighteenth lost twenty-two out of thirty-six officers and three hundred out of five hundred men were killed and wounded.

Chapter Eleven

"THE SIEGE"

NOVEMBER 22, 1863

The siege of Chattanooga had been going on almost three months. The cold, rainy weather, low rations, and a general disgruntled attitude about victory turning into defeat made camp life miserable for all concerned. Enlisted soldiers were losing confidence in their officer's competence; in addition, insubordination and open defiance had become a regular order of the day. It was common knowledge that General Bragg made a critical mistake when he decided not to follow through with his attack on the Union forces as they retreated into Chattanooga, but instead, he relied on questionable advice to lay siege and starve them into surrender.

Letters

Confederate forces took up positions on the two most strategic vantages overlooking Chattanooga: Lookout Mountain standing at 2200 feet and Missionary Ridge at 800 feet. Side by side, the mountains gave the Confederates an advantageous view of the surrounding countryside and enabled them to cutoff any attempt to resupply the trapped Union army. However, unbeknownst to General Bragg and his officers, General Grant had built pontoon bridges north of the city, crossed the river, and reinforced the besieged city with fresh troops and supplies. This was the beginning of the end of the siege for Chattanooga.

James was hunkered down around the campfire in front of his tent, wrapped in the greatcoat his mother had sent Tom and him. The war began to weary him to the bone. The weather, the cold, and the doubts about what they were doing here started to breakdown the just causes he had so heartily believed in. *I guess miserable weather brings out the worst in a man.* He got up, trying to move closer to the fire, as the sticky Tennessee clay stuck to his hands and feet like a paste. The ground was damp and the clay dirt stuck to everything it touched; the fire crackled, giving little warmth, fighting the cold the same as the man hovering over it. James's breaking point of frustration was about to explode when Henry and Matt Rupert walked up, put their hands close to the fire, and stamped their feet in unison, trying to stimulate the circulation in their bodies.

"Hey, James. You look warm and cozy," Matt teased.

"Oh yeah, never had it so good. How about you?"

Matt shrugged. "You know, just tryin' to stay warm. Don't guess I could beat you outta that coat, could I? Looks warm."

"It is and you can't," James grinned.

"Your mama's good 'bout sendin' those care packages, ain't she? Wish my folks'd send me somethin' sometime."

"You know we share what we can, Matt. Except the coat, of course."

Matt and Henry sat by the fire next to James. "Where's Tom?" Henry asked.

James shrugged. "You know Tom. He can't sit still. He's out there checking on sentries and supplies, what little there are, and trying to keep up spirits while we sit here and freeze."

"Yeah, well, I could use some spirits in the liquid form m'self,"

Matt grumbled. He stood up and started pacing around the fire in a circle. James knew he was about to cut loose on some triad about camp and wanting to shoot somebody.

"Dammit all James!" Matt started with a wave of the arms, "How can you be so damn calm 'bout everything all the time? Ever'body knows ol' Gen-er-ral Bra-ag-g is crazier than a bedbug. We coulda' jumped on them Yanks after we whupped 'em at the Chickamauga – or whatever the hell it's called, and be sittin' fat n' sassy in Chattanooga right now. 'Stead, we're sittin' here on two big hills freezin' to death, an' dyin' of boredom!"

James stared at the fire. He knew Matt was right, he'd been thinking the same thing. He knew things were getting bad if he and Matt were having the same thoughts. He grinned at the thought.

"Now, Matt," Henry chimed in, "You know these are highly educated gentlemen runnin' this here war, an' I'm sure they know what's best for us. If'n they knew you was so unhappy, I'm sure they'd change their plans. Don't you think so, James?"

James stood up and looked Matt straight in the eye. "You know what you need, Matt?"

"Yeah, I need to start shootin' some damn generals, that's what I need. Theirs or ours, don't make no difference to me," he grumbled.

"That's not exactly what I had in mind, however, you could probably get a few medals if you shot the right ones."

Matt relaxed a little bit and eye-balled James. "What's on your mind?"

"Well, Sam Evans has got a little bacon left over, and we're going to fix it up with some biscuits and have a little feast tonight. Then, we thought we'd mosey on down to Gambler's Paradise and try our luck. You're welcome to join us."

"Food, gamblin', and Sam Evans! I don't know if my mama would approve of the bad company I'm keepin' 'round here. How'd you hook up with Sam Evans? That rascal's wilder than a march hare and can make me laugh harder than anybody I know."

"He's been coming over here a lot from Company I. He said they're a "bad luck unit" and doesn't want to have anything to do with them. So we've been doing a few things together. He's a likable sort, and I trust him, mostly," was all James said.

"Well, it all sounds good to me, but I ain't got nuthin' 'cept that hardtack garbage they hand out at the commissary."

"Well, don't bring none of that," Henry joked, "we've been using that stuff to patch the holes in our tent and start fires."

Matt nodded. "I hear that," he said. "Anyways, sounds good to me. Say James, does Tom know you're goin' down to Gambler's Paradise tonight? I didn't think ya'll took up with that kinda stuff much."

"Well, I'll admit, it was Sam's idea, but Tom jumped on it in a minute. You know---us Durretts don't have anything against having a good time. I think you'd be quite surprised to know that we make a point of trying to laugh at least once a day," James said with a dead-panned expression. "Besides, Sam knows every crooked and straight game in the valley."

Henry laughed, "Yeah, an' he's probably got a cut off the top from all of 'em. Did you know that boy goes down to the killin' field a couple of times each week, an' trades with the Yanks! He'll take coffee, sugar, and such and trade those boys outta some of the damnest things. It's hard to believe, but he says the Yanks are worse off than us, an' they're cold, tired, hungry, an' wanna go home, too. Just like us."

James stared at his feet, "I knew he was trading."

"Yeah," Matt added, "well they may act like us, but don't forget, we're fightin' those bluebellies 'cause they's tryin' to tell us what we can and can't do. My family's too poor to have slaves and probably wouldn't if they could, but I'll be damned if they's gonna tell me I can't have 'em if I want 'em!" Matt preached. "Whatcha' think, James?"

He shrugged. "My family's fighting right beside you, Matt. We don't take to slaves either, but we have our rights. I wish they'd just leave us alone, and let us mind our own business." Then James smiled. "Now I'd probably let them have the state Mississippi, but I certainly don't want them in the Holy Land of Alabama!"

"You're a strange one, you know that, James?" Matt said flatly.

"No stranger than anyone else," James defended.

"Oh yeah you are. You're quiet, you don't complain, you read all the time, an' in two years I ain't ever heard you state an opinion 'bout this stinkin' war. But damn it all, you're one of the deadliest, straight-shootin' boys in the company. I'm just glad I'm fightin' with you an' not against."

"I think that was a compliment and I'll take it, Matt. I'm just protecting what's mine, that's all," James stated. "Now, do you want to join us for supper and a few crooked card games tonight?"

"Damn straight. I wanna see what you Durrett boys are like when you're not readin' or killin' somebody."

The boys feasted on their bacon and biscuits, feeling as though they had eaten a home cooked meal. Tom brought Bob Bateman with him, and he contributed some cornbread he had left over from his own care package from home. After stuffing themselves, they all leaned back against the fallen logs arranged around the fire, arms behind their heads, and legs stretched out to warm them up. A full stomach, a crackling campfire, and friends seemed to take the edge off the cold and thoughts of the war temporarily.

James looked across at Sam Evans. He was a tall, lanky young man, and probably the most likable person he'd met since joining the army. Sam could inject humor in any conversation, regardless of the seriousness of the moment; his comical imitations of other soldiers and especially officers were uncanny and requests were constant. The real claim to fame for Sam, among the soldiers of the Eighteenth, was his dexterity with cards and obsession with gambling.

One time, while trudging through the mud on their way to sentry duty, Sam spotted two robins sitting on a branch together. "James," he said, "I'll bet you a cup of coffee that the bird on the right takes to flight 'fore the one on the left."

"Now what kind of fool bet is that?" James questioned.

"It's only a fool's bet for the one that loses," Sam grinned. "You game?"

"Sure, what have I got to lose."

"A cup of coffee, of course. Now watch!" Sam reached down, chose a twig and then snapped it in half. The birds immediately flew skyward off the branch; the one on the right was the first to liftoff. Sam laughed, "I'll come by an' get that coffee after duty tonight." When they walked off, James just shook his head and chuckled.

James had also seen Sam wipeout a month's pay from two men in a poker game one night. After taking all their hard earned money, he gave each of them half of their losses back so they wouldn't be broke for the rest of the month. James figured Sam was more about the thrill of the game than it was the money that motivated him so much. But now, Sam was stretched out, cap on backwards on his head, and a homemade toothpick waving up and down between his two front teeth. He couldn't help but start laughing at the comical looking figure who was quickly becoming a close friend and confidant.

Tom looked over at him, pretending to be angry, "Well, I want to thank you kindly for interruptin' my peaceful thoughts I'm having over here, James. What's so dang funny all of a sudden, anyway?"

"Sam is," James laughed.

Sam looked up and flashed his bright white teeth, "What?"

"Oh nothing," James grinned, "you just seem a little stressed out, that's all."

Henry jumped in, "Yeah, he's just thinkin' 'bout Gambler's Paradise an' who he's gonna skin tonight."

"All's fair in love, war, and poker, boys," Sam said, sitting up, warming his hand against the fire. Ya'll ready to go? I don't want ya'll gettin' too rested and comfortable here. Pigeons are waitin' on us!"

James got up first, "Let's go gentlemen, time's wasting!"

Matt got up and stretched his arms and arched his back, "Damn, James. I've never seen you so anxious to lose your money before. I'm gonna keep my eye on you tonight, an' make sure you stay outta trouble."

Sam stood, turned his hat around, buttoned the top of his tunic, and finally rubbed his fingers back and forth across his front teeth, as though polishing them. "I feel lucky tonight, boys. Gotta full stomach, good friends, an' a hot hand of poker waitin' on me. Let's do it!"

The group headed down towards the valley and Gambler's Paradise.

The six of them strolled through the various pockets of company camps as they made their way towards the valley. The sounds and routines of camp life never seemed to change. Activity centered around the spotted campfires where debates about the war, stories about home, and somebody was always singing a southern tune, while another played the spoons, all of it echoing throughout the forest. The noise of one camp faded and the voices of the next grew louder as the boys from Company E laughed and joked their way to Paradise.

Tom had noticed a subtle change in James the past month. He seemed to be trying extra hard to cope with day-to-day routines. Sometimes keeping to himself and reading all day, and then other times talking his fool head off about anything and everything. He'd been spending a lot of time with Sam Evans lately, and he appeared to have a calming influence on James.

Tom worried about his little brother. He was the baby of the family, the most intelligent, and by far the most serious minded. James was an accepting young man who thought through everything, and didn't judge others for being foolish in their own ways. The burden of keeping James alive was his, but he couldn't be at his side every minute of the day. Sam, Henry, and Matt were filling the void for him. Tom considered himself a good judge of men, and he liked Sam. He'd seen him in action at Chickamauga, using his wits and common sense, instead of just charging forward into gunfire without a sensible thought. He'd have a talk with Sam later. James didn't need to know.

Tom quickened his pace and sidled up next to James. "How's it goin' little brother? We haven't had much time to talk lately. Colonel Hunley keeps me pretty busy tryin' to keep these boys outta mischief."

"You mean how's it going even though there's a war going on?" James could tell his big brother was beating around the bush about something.

Tom smiled. "We've done okay, you know. We're alive, we've dodged the measles, dysentery, and bullets, an' we're better off than most."

"Yeah, I know. But better than most, just means getting by around here."

"This war's changed ever'body, James. It has a tendency to bring out the best and the worst in a fella---nobody goes home the same," said Tom.

"I know, I'm just trying to hold it together for now. I'm beginning to feel guilty," James answered in a hushed whisper.

Tom gently took James's arm by the elbow and pulled him to a stop. He motioned to the others. "You boys go on up ahead," Tom called, "James an' me are gonna sit for a spell. We'll catch up."

"We'll wait for ya'll at the bottom of the hill," Bob called back. "We wanna make an entrance an' let 'em know who we are!" He knew that Tom had some concerns about his brother lately. He'd keep the group moving and give them some space.

"Sit a spell, little brother," Tom said, pointing to a place. The brothers stepped off the path, found a dry spot under a big oak and sat down. They each stared straight ahead, not looking at the other. There was an unusual awkwardness between them.

"Feelin' guilty 'bout what?" Tom started, picking up where his little brother left off.

"Killing."

Tom sat silent. He knew James was compassionate about his fellow man and cared for others, but he'd seen him kill as many Yanks as any other man in battle and never flinch. Maybe, it was all coming to a head.

"We all feel some guilt 'bout that, James."

"Not me," James said flatly. "Oh, I've felt bad about killing those boys---but I never had any guilt about it. They were shooting back, you know."

"So what brought on these pangs of guilt all of a sudden?" Tom asked quietly.

James hesitated. "Well---you're not going to believe it, but I've been down to the killing ground with Sam and did some trading with the Yanks." He lifted his back from the tree and turned to face his brother. "Tom, I met one kid that was not older than sixteen. He was from Massachusetts, but he's also got some family in Texas. He gave me a letter and asked me to mail it to Fort Worth for him. The poor kid was afraid to let anybody in his own camp know that he had family in the South. He's also got cousins in Hood's Texas Brigade and wanted to know if I knew where they were. I told him I didn't."

"Hood's bunch is over on Missionary Ridge," Tom said.

"I know, but I didn't want him to think he might be shooting at his own kin. The poor soul was scared to death as it was. I also know that if I see the same boy in my sights---I'll have to kill him."

"And what does Sam think 'bout all this?" Tom asked.

"He's just like me," James answered. "It bothers him, but then he said something that's typical Sam."

"And what's that?"

James grinned and tried to do his best Sam imitation, "Ya' know Jimmyboy. War is an argument an' the best way to win is to kill the other fella! I wanna go home a whole man, get a good woman, raise a big family, an' lie to my grandkids 'bout how I won the war singlehanded. I'll do whatever it takes to do it, too. I'll out trade 'em---then I'll out shoot 'em. I'm scared Jimmyboy---not strong like you--but I'm a survivor."

Tom laughed softly. "Not a bad imitation, little brother."

"Why do people always think I'm so strong, Tom? I'm not, you know."

"Well, you are, James. Folks know you're smart. You think things out 'fore you act, and you don't complain 'bout things going on. Most of these boys are uneducated, an' don't have a momma that knows the importance of books and education. There're so many idiots in this army. So, somebody like you stands out. You may think it's a curse, but it's not---it's respect."

"Sometimes, I think I'd rather be an idiot."

Tom chuckled, "Nah, plenty of those to go 'round. Matter of

fact---a bunch of 'em are officers."

"Yeah," James smiled, "and sergeants."

"Lookout, private! I can still pull rank you know," Tom teased, elbowing his brother off balance. Then, Tom laid a big hand on his sibling's shoulder. "Sam's right though, this is a fight for survival. There'll be plenty of guilt to hand around for all of us when this war's done with." Tom slapped his knees and stood. "Now! Let's go play some poker an' beat some of those boys outta their hard earned I. O. U.'s!"

James rose to his feet, and brushed the leaves from the seat of his pants. "I'm ready---and Tom..."

"Yeah?"

"I don't think I'll go back to the killing field until it's time. Know what I mean?"

"Yeah, I do."

Unknown to James, he would be going back to the killing field in less than forty-eight hours, and he'd be trading bullets instead of coffee with the Yanks.

Chapter Twelve

"GAMBLER'S PARADISE"

Gambler's Paradise was nestled in the valley between Lookout Mountain and Missionary Ridge. The founders, whoever they were, erected the first tent in a two acre clearing surrounded by trees, blocking its view from outsiders and the cold northern winds that constantly chilled the air. Rather quickly, other creative entrepreneurs began setting up their own makeshift gambling halls, and before it was over, twenty gambling establishments were offering opportunities for games of chance. The original houses of chance were closest to the trees, and therefore had the ideal locations protecting them from the elements of the weather. "Main Street" was a fifty-yard strip of muddy road with ten makeshift poker parlors on each side.

"Hawkers" cajoled and connived in front of most tents, trying to convince hopeful winners and hapless losers to try their games. "No cheatin' allowed here, boys!" "Get your money back here!" Each one pronounced an honest game and fortunes to be made, with a circus atmosphere. A few places provided dice games, blackjack, and stud poker, while the rest provided tables and dealers to play the games of choice and charging two-bits per head to enter.

A private's pay in the Confederate Army was $11.00 a month, however, when payrolls were late in delivering the cash, "Promise to Pay" notes were issued. Each soldier was promised payment of Confederate notes when and if the notes were ever delivered to camp. Few counted on the worthless paper to arrive, but at least the notes provided something to be used as trade and barter, substituting for cold, hard cash. It was not unusual for soldiers to carry trading goods in their knapsacks to use in place of money when they entered the gambling tents. In most cases, tangible goods like coffee and sugar were more valuable than money.

The existence of Gambler's Paradise was not condoned nor condemned by the generals. They knew the men needed an outlet for their restlessness and boredom, so it was ignored. The consensus was, gambling and an occasional drink of homemade hooch was better than mass desertion.

This particular evening, the crowd was large and rowdy; it was similar to a cow town on Saturday night when the cattle drivers arrived after being on the trail for three months. Soldiers were milling from place to place, fistfights broke out and were mostly ignored by passersby searching out their lucky spot. Hawkers were vying for everyone's business with promises of riches and a clean game.

"Stick with me, boys---don't let nobody pull ya'll astray, an' for Pete's sake keep your hands on your money pocket. There's plenty of pickpockets and thieves 'round here that'll get your cash before you get the opportunity to lose it honestly," Sam advised.

Tom looked on with amusement; he was looking forward to a night without worrying about tomorrow. Tensions were running high all throughout camp, and everyone, including himself, needed a break. There was a smell of battle in the air, and that's why he suspected there was such a big crowd tonight. James, Henry, and Matt walked with their mouths slack-jawed, eyes wide open, and hands on their money pockets.

"How long has this been here, Sam?" James asked, amazed at the circus-like atmosphere.

"'Bout a month. Keeps getting bigger ever'day too. Started off with a couple of honest games, but now all the shysters have moved in and turned it into a fleece market. If you don't know where to go, a man can end up goin' back to camp bare naked, if he ain't careful."

Several of the hawkers acknowledged Sam with a wave and a smile, but he just nodded and kept walking with his guests. "So what's your pleasure, boys? Twenty-one? Stud? Dice?"

"I'd like a straight game of stud, if it's possible," Tom answered.

"Stud it is, gentlemen! Follow me!"

James leaned over to Henry, "Why do I feel like a sheep being led off to slaughter?"

Henry laughed, "Who cares, James. What's there to lose? Money?"

"No, my coat."

"Then, don't bet it!"

Sam led them to a tent at the very end of the road, next to the trees. A giant of a soldier stood at the entrance flap, arms folded across his chest. He even towered over Tom in size. Standing silent at his post, not a sound of promises or clean games came from his mouth, just a greeting of, "Welcome."

"You ever seen him before, Tom?" James asked, mesmerized at the man's size.

"Yeah, he's a corporal from Company I. Good ol' boy from what I understand, but I wouldn't want to tangle with him."

"Oh really?" James said sarcastically.

"Evening, Sam," the giant spoke.

"Evenin' George. Any good games tonight?"

"Always, Sam."

"I've brought some friends an' I wanna make sure they're taken care of this evening. Think that can happen, George?"

"You know us, Sam. Best game in town."

As the boys from E Company entered, eyes lifted from various players to scope out the new gamblers. Tom was immediately struck by the neatness of the room and the welcomed warmth from the makeshift stove in the center. Six tables circled a large crude metal bucket filled with burning ambers of wood heating the entire gambling parlor. Each table accommodated six chairs, one for the dealer and the rest for the players. Everyone played against the dealer, and he took a percentage of the winnings, the rest going to the house.

"Dang!" Henry exclaimed in surprise, "I'd been here more often if'n I'd known there was a warm spot like this 'round here!"

Sam stepped up to the front of the group. "I'd suggest splitting up---don't all bunch to one table. That way you'll be takin' the other boys' money and not each others." The boys hesitated at first, feeling like strangers who had walked into someone's house uninvited. "Don't be shy boys, jump in there an' find a seat."

They began to spread out, each finding a spot that suited them. Sam strolled to each table making sure his friends were getting settled in, like a mother hen watching over her chicks. It was obvious he was in his own element.

Matt noticed Sam talking with the other players, slapping them on the backs, and making jokes. He seemed to know everyone in the room. He finally made his way over to Matt's table. "You gonna play any, Sam?" Matt asked as he checked the newly dealt hand. "Cards are fallin' just right!"

"Nah, not just yet. I like to get the feel of a room. Ya'll just enjoy yourself." Then, he moved on.

By the end of the night, every member of the group from Company E walked away from Gambler's Paradise a winner. Promise to Pay notes, Confederate money, a little extra coffee, sugar, and tobacco filled the pockets and knapsacks of the players. Sam led the way down "Main Street" and then stopped when they reached the edge of the woods with the paths leading back to camp. "Well boys, it looks like ever'body made it out alive, an' nobody seems to be shoeless."

"Sorry, you didn't get to play, Sam. Looked like the place stayed full all night," Henry joked as he flipped the wad of bills in his hand.

"You know, Henry---come to think of it, since you boys are leavin', I just might go back down there an' see if I can find some of that same luck you boys were soakin' up."

"Thanks for the evenin', Sam. I'm sure Lady Luck will still

smile on you. We'll see you tomorrow," Tom said. He waved the rest forward. "Come on, gentlemen. The sun'll be risin' soon."

Sam twisted his hat around backwards, turned, and waved. "See you boys later this morning."

"Dang, it's kinda late to start playin' cards, ain't it? It's almost 3:00 o'clock by my reckonin'," Henry yawned.

As the group sleepily plodded up the angled path to camp, Tom and James lingered behind the others. "You know why he went back, right?" Tom asked as they strolled side by side.

"Yeah," James smiled, "he's gonna win back what he let us win tonight."

"You figured that out too, huh?"

"George told me. He said Sam informed him earlier in the day that some special friends were coming tonight, and he wanted them to leave with full pockets."

"Yeah, then what?" Tom asked, already knowing the answer.

"He said it was okay with him, since it was Sam's place." Both men walked in silence for a moment. Finally James spoke up, "It feels good to be alive tonight, Tom. It's good to know there's still decent people wanting to do good for others in the midst of fire and brimstone. Why do you think he did it?"

Tom shrugged. "I don't know, Jimmyboy. Just wanted everybody to have some fun before all hell breaks loose, I guess. It's gonna break soon, I'm 'fraid."

"Yeah, I know."

"Yeah."

The brothers walked back to camp side by side without another word spoken.

Chapter Thirteen

"BATTLE OF THE CLOUDS"

NOVEMBER 23, 1863

"Gather 'round boys," Tom instructed. "It's black bean time. Things are starting to get stirred up at the perimeters, and each company's picking twenty additional boys for picket duty." Moans of dread emerged from the throats of the men. "What's the matter? You boys've been gripping 'bout nothing to do. Well, now you're 'bout to get plenty to do."

The Eighteenth, along with several other regiments were posted about four hundred yards above the base of Lookout Mountain, the first line of defense, or offense, depending on which came first. Observers atop the mountain spotted increased troop movements and new artillery placements around Chattanooga and on the killing field, indicating a major action about to happen; it looked like the Confederate line was going to be a defensive position.

Picket duty was the most dangerous and least desirable assignment because of its close proximity to the enemy's front lines. The picket line for the Confederates was about two hundred yards down the mountain from the Eighteen's position. Rifle pits and breastworks were strategically placed and manned to stop or at least slow down any enemy advancement. It was also the prime target area for enemy snipers and sharpshooters; the boys called it "picket murder." Along with constant pot shots, the Yankees lobbed intermittent cannon fire into the lines for an additional softening-up effect. In weeks past, there had been a picket truce between both armies, and this was more by the soldiers stationed at each front than the commanding officers; however, as of late, fire from snipers and sharpshooters had been unusually fierce and frequent.

The preferred method of choosing soldiers for picket duty was the black bean "volunteer" drawing. A sergeant would take a sack of white beans and then add the appropriate number of black beans for the duty roster. Soldiers withdrew beans from the sack, and those, who choose a black bean, "volunteered" for picket duty. Selection for the most hazardous duty was then put into the hands of fate.

Tom held the sack open, allowing each man to draw a bean. Moans of dread versus sighs of relief echoed down the line as he passed the bag from soldier to soldier. Among the twenty "volunteers" were James, Sam, and Matt, with Corporal Bateman in charge.

"Don't worry boys, Bob'll take of ya'll, and I'll be down to help if it gets too rough," Tom offered. "We're gonna be spread out thin, so everybody needs to stay at your best. Word's out that those bluebellies are getting ready to make a big push our way. General Bragg's been shifting units around all over the place, and our position's been weakened. The rest of ya'll hold your places here in case the pickets break. So, don't be cozying up to the campfire feelin' fat an' sassy up here. If we don't hold the line, you picket boys skedaddle up the hill to the summit. We'll have to hold 'em there. We could be in a bad way here, boys, I'm not gonna lie to you."

"You think it's that bad, Tom?" James asked with concern.

"Just be ready for anything, James."

"Well, it's 'bout time Sarge," Louis, one of the older soldiers said. "We've been sittin' on our duffs too damn long. If the generals had let a private or two run this outfit we'd already be done. As long as we've been sittin' here, we coulda planted a new crop of cotton, if it'd been spring time."

Tom nodded. "Well, the time's come Louis, so put your plow in the barn, and get your gear. You're getting your wish."

Weather conditions increasingly worsened with temperatures dropping into the low forty's; the rain and drizzle chilled a body deep to the bone, especially for those who didn't have proper winter clothing and supplies. A ring of fog circled the mountain peak about halfway up, blocking visibility for the troops on the summit. This made it impossible for the companies on top of the mountain to have any idea whether their boys were winning or being overrun below. Muddy ground, constant rain, and poor visibility didn't make for ideal fighting conditions, but there was a sudden urgency and an anticipation that prevailed throughout all the camps. Sixty days of boredom, cold weather, empty stomachs, and lack of confidence in commanding officers had deteriorated morale again. All of that was forgotten now. Activity stirred the spirits. Weapons were checked and double-checked, the quartermasters dispersed ammunition, and men grabbed tobacco, food, and water from their tents to sustain them for the engagement ahead.

"James, keep your head down, you hear?" Tom warned his little brother. "Them snipers are busy, and the picket lines are weak as it is. We're in for a battle, again."

"James smiled back at Tom, "You know me, I'll be careful. It's the Yanks that need to watch out. Can't much happen with the terrible trio on the front line."

"Just the same, little brother. Be careful."

Henry stayed behind with Tom, and he didn't like the matter of being separated from James and the boys, "Sam, you watch after my cousin, now."

"You kiddin'?" Sam answered. "I'm stickin' to him like molasses on a flapjack. He's my good luck charm! I'm takin' him back to Gambler's Paradise tonight after we wup up on the Yanks!" He laid an arm across James's shoulder, "Come on James. Let's go to

Letters

Chattanooga."

Matt stood by acting as though his feelings were hurt. "Well, what the hell am I? Chopped liver? Ain't nobody gonna look after me?"

Bob Bateman cuffed the back of Matt's head, "Come on little baby, I'll rock ya' in a cradle when we get there."

The picket line fire had been intense all morning, but it had increased as the new reinforcements arrived. Even though the Southern forces were spread thin, their accuracy of return fire was deadly. The constant sound of Minie balls zinging close by and sometimes finding an isolated target unnerved many of the front line soldiers. The firepower of the Yanks was now superior since Grant had reinforced the Union side with fresh recruits and heavy artillery. James and the rest of the Eighteenth curled into human balls as shrapnel from exploding grapeshot torpedoed through the air.

"What the hell stirred them Yankee boys up so much to make 'em so irritable?" Matt screamed over the incoming fire.

"I know one thing for sure," Sam yelled back, "I ain't doin' no more tradin' with them boys if they's gonna act this way!"

After close to an hour of back and forth exchanges, the tumultuous sounds and explosions of conflict ceased. The Union guns went silent. After a few moments, cautiously, James, Matt, and Sam lifted their heads above the dugout rim to scope the situation. "Look out for snipers," James whispered. "They know we'll be sticking our heads up for a look see."

"Then, why are we stickin' our heads up?" Matt cracked as he spat a wad of chewing tobacco from his cheek. "This ain't good. Sumthin's up."

"Yep, they's up to something, an' I don't think we're gonna like it, either. I think I'd reload, boys," Sam said.

The silence was deafening. After a few minutes, even the birds started to sing and chirp, sensing the carnage had stopped.

Then the reason for the sudden cease-fire came to light. "My God," James said in shock. "Looks...," his words trailed into silence.

Thousands of Union troops began marching, as if on parade, onto the plain of the killing ground. Their numbers swelled and covered the entire area; masses of regiments by the thousands were being positioned to the center, additional sections rolled on the field like a patchwork quilt unfolding onto a bed. In unison, the left and right flanks of the moving blanket encircled the base of the mountain like the horns of a bull.

"…bad," James finished.

"Yeah," croaked Sam, "but you know what? It's just gonna be easy pickins' an' target practice, the way they's all linin' up for us."

"Have you noticed how we're a little outnumbered here, Sam? We haven't got enough ammunition to kill 'em all," Matt grumbled.

"No, but I'm sure as hell gonna take a bunch of 'em with me."

Matt put a fresh plug of tobacco in his mouth, licked his thumb, and ran it over the sights of his rifle. "Aim, fire, and load boys. That's all ya' gotta do."

Bob Bateman paced back and forth, behind the line of soldiers. "We ain't runnin', boys. We paid a high price for this piece of mountain. Hold your ground---remember who you are."

"Damn right," mumbled Matt.

Movement and the sound of approaching Rebel reinforcements from the rear positions brought the chatter of the birds and men to a halt; additional troops arrived to help secure the inadequate defenses of the picket line. Tom appeared at James's side. "Looks like you got 'em stirred up, little brother. They look kinda pretty, don't they? All lined up, drums a tappin', and flags a wavin'."

"Yeah, but they'd look prettier in New York or somewhere else up north, instead of here in our backyard."

Tom squatted down beside James and laid a hand on his shoulder. "Now I want you to listen to me, James. I'm tellin' you this, and I want you to listen hard. General Bragg has weakened our positions bad by sending other regiments over to Missionary Ridge and then sending 'em to God knows where, but they ain't here. There's no way we can hold these boys back, but we have to buy extra time for our troops on both hills. Do you hear me, James?"

James nodded, keeping his eyes on the unfolding masses of Union soldiers below him. "I'm listening. Go ahead."

Tom continued, "We've been caught with our draws down, boy. Them so-called commanders wasted too much time a sitting and tryin' to figure out the Yanks next move. Now we're gonna pay the price. We'll lose this here line for sure, but we gotta slow 'em down. Which means runnin' like Texas jackrabbits at the last minute. Don't take no chances, and don't try to play the hero on me. When I give the order to retreat---do it. And, don't look back. Henry and the boys'll give ya'll cover as they can. I know you---and I know you'll try to be the last one out---but don't. I'm gonna pass the order down through the ranks, and you let Sam and Matt know for sure. Understand?" Tom's voice was stern, and the concern for his brother's welfare was obvious.

"I understand, but you have to understand something too, Tom," James said, still keeping his eyes forward. "I'm not going to step over somebody that needs help, or leave Sam or Matt behind, just so I can be the first up the hill." Then, he smiled. "But then again, I'm not the captain of this sinking ship either, so I don't have to be the last one to go down with it."

"I figured that'd be 'bout the best I'd get," Tom grinned back. He gave James a final slap on the back. "I'll see you at the top, little brother."

Soon after Tom's departure, the Union troops started their forward advancement. Cannon bombardment was fierce and constant, intending to keep the Rebel forces in disarray, inflict maximum damage, and ultimately cause a massive retreat. Even though the Rebs were outnumbered, a high death toll for the Yanks had to be calculated due to the location of the Southern defenses. Grant knew the Rebels wouldn't just throw down their arms and run. There'd be a stiff price to pay for victory. And a stiff price it was. Wave upon wave of the blue army surged towards the gray line, and time after time it was repulsed. The Rebels held their ground on the picket line as best they could and poured as much firepower as humanly possible into the advancing enemy from the North.

"Damn!" Sam yelled. "What got these boys so riled all of a sudden?" He swung his rifle up to his shoulder, took quick aim, and fired. "That's one less bluebelly for dinner tonight!"

"They probably started lookin' closer at the crap you's tradin' 'em!" Matt called as he fired off a round of his own. "Bingo! Can't hardly miss, but they do seem to be gettin' closer!"

James reloaded; the barrel of his rifle was red hot from the rapid and repeated firing. He looked to his right and noticed that the right flank of Yanks was advancing quicker to the bottom of the mountain than the center position the Eighteenth was defending. Tom was about twenty yards to his right, firing his pistol, pacing the line in a crouch, yelling at the top of his voice, urging his men on. Bateman was to his left yelling and driving his men beyond their limit.

"Matt! Get Tom's attention!" James screamed over the overpowering musket fire. He pointed, "The right flank!" Matt checked and saw the situation and crawled his way to Tom. They exchanged words and then Matt made his way back to James and Sam. "He said to drop our knapsack an' get ready to run before we get cut off! Time's gettin' close!"

Cannon fire finally began zeroing in on the Eighteenth's position. James watched the pattern of the explosions coming closer and closer, left, right, center. "Move back!" Tom yelled repeatedly in the mayhem around him. "Back to the ridge! Now!"

Men started running, dropping everything, including their rifles to lighten their loads and made a hasty retreat. A cannonball exploded not fifty yards from James's spot; explosions started stair stepping their way towards him. James was reloading when Sam stood and grabbed him by the arm, "Let's go, James! We'll hold 'em at the ridge!"

Matt continued to hold his ground, "Damn Yankees, can't fight fair, man to man!"

James and Sam simultaneously reached down and grabbed him by his tunic, dragging him to his feet. "Let's go Matt! We can't hold 'em anymore. Cannon fire's wipin' us out! We're gonna be overrun!" Sam yelled.

They literally pulled Matt from the trench as shells exploded all around them. "Damn it all, I'm gettin' real tired of runnin'! We're givin' this damn war away!" Sam spat in frustration.

Soldiers ran haphazard in all directions, trying to avoid the cannon blasts and rifle fire. Friends knocked and pushed each other down and out of the way to find cover from the zing of Minie balls. Dead bodies were strewn throughout while wounded lay crying for help. Few concerned themselves for others. Past companions were left behind along with the rifles. The right flank collapsed before all of the Eighteenth could fallback safely; Union soldiers closed in and cut off most avenues of escape. Scattered pockets of brutal and fierce hand to hand combat broke out as a frenzy of bayonets, rifle butts, and fists choked the air, and men fought in desperation for survival.

James, Sam, and Matt slipped and skidded through the mud and weaved between the trees, struggling to make their way to the ridge and avoid the oncoming rush of the opposition. They didn't throw themselves into the battles of the blue and gray uniforms splattered with red that went on behind them; they wanted to live to see another day. All around them the brutal chess game intensified as soldiers fought to the death.

The steep grade of the hill slowed their progress. Gulping in the cold air as it burned their lungs with every breath, they clawed their way upward. James led the trio as Matt lagged behind, his feet finding no traction in mud. He stopped beside a tree to catch his breath and suddenly felt himself being jerked violently backwards, and a sharp burning sensation, like someone shoving a red hot poker into his right side.

"Arr-r-r-g-g!" He screamed in pain, knowing he was about to die. A Yankee soldier had attacked Matt from behind, thrusting a bayonet through his back. He fell to the ground, writhing in agony, trying to rub out the fire in his side.

The Yank, an obvious veteran of more than one battle, stood

above Matt, bayonet gripped in both hands over his head, ready to make the final death thrust, "Die ya' Rebel scum!" In his lust to kill the Rebel soldier at his feet, the ambusher didn't see James and Sam scrambling back down the hill, fury and hate fueling their purpose as they sped to Matt's rescue. James sprang forward, hurling head and shoulders first into the chest of the startled soldier. Their bodies tumbled down the hill as one, head over heel. James's fury far outweighed that of his opponent; his momentum carried him on top of his enemy on the final roll. James pounded his fists into the man's face, about his head, and shoulders, paying no attention to the pain to his scraped knuckles. A fury consumed him, wanting nothing more than to murder the man with his bare hands.

Matt lay on the ground, holding his hand on the wound trying to stop the flow of blood, "Kill the sum' bitch that killed me, James!" He called weakly.

Sam slid within seconds, quickly kneeling beside Matt, checking his wound. "Hold tight, partner. I'll be right back." He stumbled, losing his balance as he slid down the hill, desperate to reach James, hoping to stop another friend from getting killed.

Finally at the scene, Sam dropped his rifle and wrapped both arms around James's waist and physically jerked him off the beaten soldier. James's arms and legs flailed as he fought Sam, trying to get back at the ambusher and finish what he'd started. Sam had never seen his friend in such a lust to kill like this before. He was stunned by his savagery.

"Let me at him! He murdered Matt!" James screamed.

"He ain't dead yet. Now, dammit, stop kickin', James! He twisted James away, throwing him to the ground, then pointed back up the hill to Matt. "Go back and help Matt. He needs ya'." Then, Sam returned his attention to the Yank on the ground. "I'll take care of this murderin' coward. He's mine now. You've done your part," Sam said, his own fury building in his gut.

The Yank lay on his side, knees pulled up to his chest in a fetal position. "Don't hurt me no more! I give up! Take me prisoner, I give up!" He begged.

Sam turned to James and pointed towards Matt again. "I said to go, James. I've got this."

James blinked and rubbed the muck from his face. He turned

and scrambled up to help Matt without looking back.

Sam slowly took a few steps towards the cowering soldier, bent over to pick up his rifle, never taking his eyes from the prey. He straightened, pulled his own bayonet from his belt, fixed it on the rifle barrel slowly and methodically with a twist and a click. Eyes fixed, just like the bayonet, never wavering from his target.

"Please don't! I beg you. I give up!" The man pleaded, now on his knees, holding his arms out straight as though praying.

"Sorry fella," Sam said softly with a poisonous venom his voice. "I don't see no white flag wavin'. But, I'll make you the same sweet offer you gave to my dying buddy over there. You can die…"

In a blink of an eye, before he'd finished the sentence---Sam thrust the bayonet directly into the heart of the Union soldier, then pulled it out slowly from the punctured chest with a sucking sound.

"…ya' Yankee scum." He leaned over and wiped the wet sticky blood from the bayonet across the pants leg of the dead soldier. A shiver ran through his body as he replaced the death blade back in his belt. "Damn," he shuddered.

James and Sam avoided eye contact with each other as they

tended to Matt. The adrenalin rush of their fury had vanished, and now they were left to deal with their own consciences. They were feeling the shame of their deed.

"How's he doin'?" Sam asked, struggling to find the words.

"Hell, ask me, not him," Matt whined. "I ain't dead yet ya' damn fool."

Sam grabbed Matt by the scruff of his jacket, his temper exploding. "Look, I just killed a man for you an' I don't need none of your smart mouth right now, Matt," he snapped. "Understand?"

"I'm sorry, boys. I'm thankful for what ya' done, I really am," Matt apologized. Just get me outta here, okay?"

Sam let go of Matt's tunic and slid an arm under his shoulders. "Let's lift him up and get the hell outta here, James. We'll be completely cut-off if we're not careful. Come on, let's go." Both boys cradled their arms together like a chair and started up the hill with Matt.

"Did either of you ever see Tom coming up the hill?" James asked, checking back over his shoulder.

"Been a little busy the last few minutes, James," Sam said as both boys struggled to get Matt up the hill. "Last I saw him, he's gettin' everybody out at the right flank when we took to runnin'. He's probably on the ridge waitin' for us now, James. Don't worry, he can take care of himself," Sam responded.

"I hope so," James said. He had a bad feeling in the pit of his stomach, though.

Chapter Fourteen

"TOM'S CAPTURE"

Tom and Bob scrambled desperately to get the last of the Eighteenth off the picket line and back to the safety of the ridge. "Run boys! We're goners if we don't beat the Yanks to the top!" Tom yelled, urgently motioning for them to get moving.

Less than fifty men remained, and Tom was determined not to leave one living soul behind. The going was tough. Rebs hurdled over dead bodies, weaving through the woods attempting to escape the onrush of the enemy. Tom, Bob, and ten others brought up the rear. Minie balls whizzed by their ears, thudding into trees like sledgehammers into a log.

Amos Bishop and Bob Bateman ran low, crouched over, side-by-side, zig-zagging their way through the maze of trees. "We're gonna make it Amos! Stay low!" Bob called out. Suddenly Amos stumbled forward and dropped face first hard onto the ground. Bob skidded to a stop to help him up and saw that the back of his head was gone. Nothing but bloody pulp remained. "Damn, I hate this war!" He screamed. He gathered his wits and ran to catch up with Tom and the others, not wanting to suffer the same fate.

Out of nowhere, a blue line of soldiers appeared from the right flank, rifles and bayonets drawn, separating Tom, Bob, and the last of his men from the main group. Further up the hill, a thunderous volley of rifle fire shattered the air, as Yankee muskets discharged simultaneously into the group ahead of Tom.

"Stop where you are, or you'll meet your maker the same as your comrades just suffered!" A Union officer commanded from his horse, raising his saber to skyward.

"Halt you Johnny Rebs or we'll shoot you where you stand!" A sergeant added, reinforcing his lieutenant's words and aiming his rifle directly at Tom's head.

The last eleven men to leave the picket lines, stopped in their tracks, dropped their rifles to the ground, and raised their hands slowly above their heads. "Don't shoot!" Tom called back in a firm voice. "We ain't aiming to die here just yet." He turned to his men, "War's over for us boys, don't give 'em no cause to shoot."

Pacing his horse back and forth before his men, trying to make a show of his authority, the young lieutenant glared at the gaggle of prisoners, relishing the coming praises he'd receive from his commanders.

"Sergeant! Search this bunch of cowards running from the field of battle and prepare them to join the rest of their dirty rabble. I'm taking a squad of men to round up more of the running devils. Be ready to march when I return!" With more drama than necessary, he ordered a corporal to enlist twenty of his men to follow him.

"Yes sir-r-r," the sergeant mumbled under his breath, showing an obvious dislike for the flashy, inexperienced lieutenant. He lowered his weapon and cautiously approached Tom and his men, exhibiting no fear or apprehension. "My name is Sergeant McAnally. Who's the leader of this bunch of Johnny Rebs?"

Tom stepped forward, "My name is Sergeant Thomas Durrett

of the Eighteenth Alabama Volunteers, Sergeant. And I'd appreciate it if you and your lieutenant wouldn't refer to these brave men as cowards. We may be on opposing sides, but we're none the less braver than your own men." At that, the other ten Southerners subtlety straightened their shoulders, standing upright, and stared eyes forward.

McAnally faced his adversary, regarding and judging him carefully. "Done," he said. "I hear what you're saying." His eyes took in each individual prisoner and nodded his head. "Okay then, Sergeant Durrett, form your men in a sharp line and instruct 'em to empty their pockets and prepare to be searched. We ain't interested in personal effects, just weapons." He twisted around sharply, took five steps forward and reversed himself again to face Tom and his men. Respectfully and with military courtesy, the sergeant gave Tom the space to deal with his own men.

Tom turned. "You heard the man, Eighteenth. Form a line and empty the goods from your pockets. Don't hold anything back." Each man to the last followed Tom's orders soundlessly, giving the Yankee guards no cause for alarm.

Satisfied with the search, Sergeant McAnally ordered his prisoners to sit cross-legged on the ground, hands behind their heads in two equal rows. "No talkin', or the price of punishment will be execution. Be sure to pass that on to your men, Sergeant."

Soon after, the arrogant lieutenant returned, but without any new prisoners. Seeing Tom and his men sitting cross-legged on the ground, his dissatisfaction erupted. Red-faced---words literally spitting from his mouth, he screamed at the top of his voice. "Sergeant! What the hell is going on here?" He yelled, pointing at the prisoners on the ground. "Have these men been searched? Why aren't they on their knees and tied according to protocol?" All the men, Union and Confederate alike turned towards the officer. "Tie them now or I'll shoot them myself!"

Tom raised his eyes with a death stare at the lieutenant. He'd have the pleasure of killing him if he came within arm's reach. It'd be worth the price. He noticed that McAnally had a disgusted look on his face, as well. Veterans who'd fought in wars and were battle experienced had no use for "banty rooster" officers who thought of battle action as a game and a means for advancing their careers. Men of this caliber were blind to the needs of others, only their own self-interests were served.

McAnally snapped to attention and walked briskly to the lieutenant's side. He knew he needed to calm down the situation before it got out of control, and he didn't want the death of defenseless prisoners on his conscience because of the foolish whim of an egotistical idiot.

McAnally stepped up to the officer's horse, holding it by the bridle. "Sir, can I speak to you a minute? I think we've come across some extraordinary prisoners here, sir. I suspect the sergeant in this group is a carrier with field operation instructions for their generals." He nodded in Tom's direction. "That Rebel sergeant is a step above what we've seen before in these Rebs. He ain't dumb, Sir. I'm tryin' to butter 'em up, be nice, an' get some valuable intelligence from them."

McAnally stopped and stroked the horse's neck, letting his words sink in. "You know, you'll get a lot more bees with honey than vinegar, Sir. We don't want them to just clam up on us. Now, do we?" He could tell the lieutenant was listening closely to every word. "And sir, we both know this could be quite a feather in your cap with headquarters if the Rebs are favorable to spill what they know."

The lieutenant twisted one end of his handlebar moustache. "I see your point, Sergeant," he said, just above a whisper. "Perhaps you're right," he said confirmed, sitting up erect in the saddle. "So, do you think I should try to make amends to the scum and play along too?"

McAnally shook his head. "No sir, I believe it'd be best for you to proceed up the hill and engage the enemy. That's where your leadership is most needed," the sergeant said, hoping he'd get his fool head shot off.

The lieutenant straightened back his shoulders even more so. "You're right, of course. Carry on here, Sergeant and keep me informed with a runner of anything that develops. Keep these men separate from the rest of the rabble we've captured. I'll inform command of the situation, and of course, put in a good word for you and your astute observations. Detach with twenty men to escort the prisoners back down the hill, and I'll take the rest with me to engage the enemy."

"Thank you, Sir. Excellent idea." McAnally softly patted the horse's rump. "You better go now."

The lieutenant gave a brisk salute to the sergeant, twisted the ends of his moustache again, and then spun his horse around to face his command. "Alright gentlemen! To your feet! First and second squads with me, and spread your line across the face of the hill! The rest of you stay with Sergeant McAnally and guard the prisoners until relieved." With that said, he waved his arm forward for the troops to advance and he fell in behind them.

McAnally felt sorry for the poor souls ordered to follow such an inept leader, but he knew there were enough experienced men in the companies to follow their own instincts when it came down to survival.

Sergeant McAnally shook his head and stepped up to Tom, relieved that the lieutenant had finally left. "You got any of them ninety-day wonders in your army, Sergeant?" He asked Tom, still shaking his head.

"'Fraid so. Ya'll killed off most of the good ones."

The Yankee sergeant nodded in confirmation. "That's 'cause

the good ones are up front with their men, where they's supposed to be, not in the rear like the one you just met."

"What'd you tell him to get him to leave?" Tom asked, gaining new respect for his captor.

McAnally grinned. "Told him you's a bunch of carriers an' had special information for the generals. Said it would make him look good to the commanders. That's all it took."

Tom frowned. "Carriers? Did he ask to see any papers or anything?"

"I didn't say he was smart. Just ambitious."

"We've got some cut from the mold, Sergeant."

"I'm sure you do." McAnally gave Tom a hard look, then turned to make sure the lieutenant was out of sight. "I like you Durrett. Any other time we could probably cozy up to a bar somewhere and have a beer together, but for now, I don't trust you a bit. Just stay with your men 'til we catch up the other prisoners. Then, you can just blend in with the crowd. The lieutenant will never know the difference. I'm not even sure the dang fool will make it back. Now, tell your boys to keep their hands in their laps an' sit quietly." McAnally doubled the guard around Tom and his men.

With the lieutenant gone, Tom felt more at ease now, as he sat cross-legged and cold on the wet ground. But he couldn't get his little brother out of his head. He knew James was going out of his mind with worry. Maybe someone saw his capture and would let him know he's okay. He didn't want James thinking he was dead. That would be too much for either of them to bear. Even though McAnally allowed the prisoners to drop their hands from behind their heads and keep them rested in their laps, there was no talking allowed, but faint whispers were heard among his men. The guards let it pass.

Tom and Bob made eye contact. Each read the resignation in each other's face, and the knowledge that the war was over for both of them. Watching the guards carefully, Bob spoke softly, "Can't think of 'nother man that I owe more to than you, Tom Durrett. It's been an honor fightin' with you."

Tom smiled back at him. "Shuddup, Bob."

A young soldier with an ill-fitting uniform that looked a size too big for him, came walking towards them. They figured they were about to be told to be quiet, so they stopped their conversation. He didn't seem to be a threat and actually gave them a crooked little grin, "Either of you men know anything about the Texas Brigade? I got a cousin in that outfit, and I was wondering if you might know where they are?"

Tom's earlier conversation with James popped in his mind. It was eerie knowing that he was talking to the same young soldier that James traded goods with and mailed letters home for just a few days before. "Young man, you go about two-hundred yards up that mountain and through that ring of fog up there, and you'll be able to shake hands with your cousin." Tom saw the life literally drain from the young boy's face.

"You mean we been fighting each other this whole time?" He stammered in dismay.

Tom wanted to ease the boy's conscience as much as possible; he wished he'd never said anything. "I doubt it, young man. Unless you've been fightin' above the clouds there. You ain't laid a finger on him---yet."

This seemed to ease the boy's discomfort a little bit. He nodded. "Much obliged, Sergeant," he whispered and slowly trudged back to his post.

"Tom felt as though he was sharing the same sense of dread as the young Union soldier. The boy was worried about killing his cousin, and Tom feared for his brother. The depth of the sadness that engulfed the boy affected Tom; he now understood why James had changed.

A loud rumble of men coming down from above alerted the guards and prisoners alike. Blue soldiers thought it might be another assault by the Rebs from the rear; gray uniforms prayed for rescue. Hopes of the grays were dashed as hundreds of Confederate prisoners, conversing the hill with their hand interlocked behind their heads, carefully made their way down the slippery mountain. Yankee guns trained on their every move. Tom craned his neck, trying to see if he could spot James in the crowd.

Chapter Fifteen

"RUNNING THROUGH THE CLOUDS"

The retreat to the summit of Lookout Mountain was massive and chaotic. Rebel soldiers dropped their knapsacks; even rifles were tossed aside to lighten their loads. Loud and repeated volleys of sporadic gunfire surrounded James and Sam as they struggled to carry their wounded friend to the security of their own lines. Despite the lateness of the evening, the fog still hung like a wreath of moss around the peak of the mountain.

There had been no time to stop and tend to Matt's wound, and he grimaced with pain and held his side to staunch the flow of blood as they threaded their way through the sparse wreckage of trees. He saw a large red patch covering the left side of his shirt. "You know boys, I think I'm gonna be okay. Set me down a minute and let me get my feet under me."

"We don't have a minute," Sam panted, "but I'll gladly sit you down." They lowered him onto an outcrop of rock and gingerly set him down.

He grinned, putting on a game face of relief to let the boys think he was okay. "If you boys'll just let me put my arms 'round your shoulders, I'll make it fine. I feel kinda silly being carried like an old woman." Matt lifted his shirt to examine his wound. "Looks like the blade went plum through, but I don't think it hit any of my vitals, just skin." He closed his shirt and made motions to get up. "Let's get the hell outta here 'fore we're run over by them bluebellies again."

James shouldered him down. "Since when did you become a doctor?" He asked, squatting down to examine the wound. He saw the vertical punctures in his side, front and back. Matt was right, the bayonet pierced the fatty part of his side, just above his hip, and the flow of blood had made it look worse than it really was. The bleeding seemed to have slowed down, but his coloring was pale and chalky. "You're going to live, Matt. We just gotta make sure you don't bleed to death."

"I'm for that," he said weakly.

James took off the heavy greatcoat and his tunic. "Sam, take your pocketknife and cut off the sleeve of my shirt here and then cut one side of it down the middle. We've got to wrap it around his wound or else we'll never get the bleeding to stop."

The chill of the north wind raised goose bumps on James's upper body as Sam deftly cut the sleeve from his shirt. "Now wrap him up and let's get the hell out of here," he said putting on his shirt and coat. "We can't stay in one spot too long. I don't want to get stuck in some Yankee prison for the rest of the war."

"Amen to that," said Sam, as he wrapped the makeshift bandage tightly around Matt's waist.

Matt gritted his teeth as Sam knotted the sleeve snug and tight. "Come on, let's quit jawin'. That gunfire's getting closer, an' we need to make our way up to the top. I don't wanna be holding you boys back."

"The fog's 'bout fifty yards up," Sam said. "Let's move---our boys are up there waiting on us."

"Yeah, if they ain't already run and left us behind," Matt mumbled.

"James!" A familiar voice echoed above them. Henry was sliding and scrambling his way down the hill towards the beleaguered band. "Come on!" He said, waving them up. "We're holdin' the line above the fog!" He slid within a few feet of them and saw Matt's blood-soaked shirt. "Jesus, Matt! What happened?" He asked, staring at the bloody wound.

James's face lit up. Henry's arrival was like an angel sent from God. "Have you seen Tom yet, Henry?" He asked first thing.

"No, but it's crazy up there. Units are scattered everywhere, and most of the officers are dead or captured. We're trying to hold the line, but we're run over by our own men as they come scamperin' through us like a bunch of scared jackrabbits. Is he okay?" He asked, pointing to Matt. "He don't look too good."

"Yeah, but we need to get him to a doctor. He'll be whining for a month if we don't."

"I heard that," snapped Matt.

"Come on," urged Henry, "we don't have time for all this

foolishness. We got a bad situation up there. Ya'll take Matt an' I'll lead the way up so we don't get shot at by our own men," he hesitated and grimaced, "like what happened to the Nineteenth." Then, he shook off the memory. "Come on, we've only got 'bout fifty yards to go."

James and Sam hefted Matt to his feet and the four of them started the climb upwards. The going was rough, but with Henry leading the way they made good time, picking their way through the devastation. The haggard and exhausted band finally reached the edge of the fog, carefully inching their way through the thick soup.

"How far we gotta go in this stuff, Henry? I'm starting to get a little nervous 'bout getting shot by our own boys," Matt complained as he struggled to keep his feet moving.

"Hard to tell, might not be a bad idea to start shouting, let 'em know we're coming," Henry answered.

Henry cupped his hands around his mouth and yelled, "Hey boys! Eighteenth comin' up with wounded! Don't shoot!" Layer by layer the fog began to thin, as they inched their way forward. "Anybody there? We're comin' up! Don't shoot!" He repeated.

A coarse and scratchy voice suddenly called out from the misty clouds, "Identify!   An' you better be true, else you're a deadman!"

"You don't reckin' that's God speaking outta them clouds do you, Sam?" Matt asked.

"Hope so," he answered, "that'd mean he's rootin' for the South. I hope."

"Company E!" Henry shouted back to the voice. "Durrett, Evans, and Rupert! We got a wounded man with us!"

"Who's your sergeant?" The voice returned.

"I'm losin' my patience with this fool," Henry mumbled, then yelled, "Thomas Durrett, you dang fool! Now don't shoot, we're comin' up!"

"Slow an' easy, boys. They's a hundred muskets trained your way."

"I'm sure," said Sam doubtfully.

"Let's hurry it up, boys. I think I might be dyin' after all. Starting to feel kinda weak," Matt moaned. "My stomach don't feel right."

"Would you make up your mind. One minute you're dying, the next it's just a flesh wound. If I'd known you were gonna bellyache this much 'bout a little 'ol scratch, I'd have left you down at the bottom of that hill," Sam shot back, struggling under the weight of his friend.

"Well damnation, if I don't die Evans, your gonna have the pleasure of me dogging your sorry butt so I can repay you for the way ya'll jostled me 'round, trying to agitate my wound."

"Your wound is on James's side, not mine, you dang fool."

"Don't even bring me into this," said James. "I've got more to worry about than you two fussing like a couple of old women. I've got to find Tom when we get to the top." He shifted his shoulders to get a better grip on his burden. "But there is one thing going for you, Matt. At least they won't amputate anything like a leg or something. Unless they get you mixed up with some other fellow."

"That makes me feel better."

"Nuthin's gonna happen to any of you. I'll make damn sure of that," Sam said, the joking gone from his voice.

"I see's you boys! Come on up!" The same scratchy voice called. As they made the crest of the hill and the fog cleared to gray skies, the hope of rescue and sanctuary the boys expected died with bitter disappointment.

Carnage was the single word that came to James's mind. Wounded soldiers bent forward, trudging onward up the hill, comrades unable to climb under their own power helped by friend and stranger alike. The landscape of a once beautiful mountain was now destroyed. Trees were splintered like so much kindling wood and the dreary background of gloomy, gray skies gave the whole mountainside a surreal and overpowering picture of death. Small pockets of wounded soldiers huddled in groups, attempting to give aid and comfort to those dying around them. Battle weary warriors lined the trenches, the last line of defense, shivering from cold fear--- anticipating the next assault.

"Damn, this is bad boys," James stated. "We'll be giving this mountain up, too, I reckon."

"Yep, an' you boys is lucky," said the same soldier that led them through the fog. "Looks like more than half our boys been caught or killed by the Yanks. We got the blind leadin' the blind 'round here. Nobody knows who's in charge of this man's army."

"Great," James mumbled, "that's all we need." His eyes searched up and down the picket lines, desperately trying to find his brother. "Any of you boy's know Tom Durrett? He's a sergeant for Company E," James called out to those they passed.

A lifeless voice mumbled from behind him, "You're his brother, right?"

James turned and saw a small group of battered men sitting back to back, fighting off the cold of the late evening and the pain of their wounds. All three faces told the story of their day. Defeated, lifeless, wanting only to go home.

"Have you seen him? He's alive, right?" James's voice cracked, expecting the worse.

The same soldier who spoke first hesitated, chose his words slowly, as though thinking and talking was a challenge. "I seen him, an' 'bout ten or fifteen others get captured by the Yanks. Bateman was the only other one I recognized. They's throwin' up they hands an' givin' up when I seen 'em last. Sorry fella, but leastwise he's alive. That's better'n some those poor devils left out there to die, bleedin' to death." The soldier cast his eyes down and then bowed his head. The dialogue seemed to drain what little energy he had left. "Them Yanks killed the last of our boys down on the pickets. Didn't even try to take 'em prisoner."

Despite his wound, Matt stood unsteadily to his feet and pointed a finger at the haggard trio on the ground. "Why didn't you try to help 'em you damn cowards! Where's your muskets?" He yelled, pointing to the empty ground around the trio. "You cast 'em aside so they wouldn't slow you down? You sorry bastards!"

"Stop it, Matt," Sam chided, firmly grabbing his arm and pulling him away. "Look at 'em. They did their part today. Leave 'em be."

Not one of the emotionally spent trio reacted to the venomous triad against them.

As James watched to the side, a sudden flood of grief swept through his body like a tidal wave, draining him of all feeling and strength. Sweat broke out on his face in small beads in spite of the cold, and blackness encompassed his sight, and he felt his legs give way like limp rags attached to his body. He became vaguely aware of hands catching him as he folded to the earth.

"James!" Dammit boy! Snap out of it, we can't do this now!" Henry's voice was firm, but sounded distant and hollow to James.

"James! Do you hear me?" Henry snapped, shaking his cousin's shoulders.

Gradually the sounds of war in the distance came back to James. Cannon fire above and below him, musket rounds, and someone shouting in his ear. Darkness gave way to light and the tragedy of it all was before his eyes once again. He blinked, sudden realization popping into his brain. "What happened? Why...?"

"Sam, get Matt up an' let's get the hell outta here. I've got James," Henry said. "This whole damn thing's fallin' apart."

"I told you before," Sam said, determination rife in his tone, "I ain't letting anything fall apart, Henry. We're sticking together, and survivin' together. Get your cousin and let's go."

"Where we goin'?" Matt asked, stumbling to his feet.

"Up," Sam answered, pointing to the peak.

The weakened picket lines entrenched above the clouds courageously held back the Yankee advancements, time after time. It was at a high cost though, and every gray clad soldier knew it was lost cause. Cowards and heroes alike showed their true spots. The cowards ran. The heroes held their ground. Companies were disorganized and scattered helter-skelter all over the mountainside. More than half of the Confederate officers had been captured or killed, leaving few competent leaders to rally the troops. Eventually, under the cover of darkness, the remainder of the Confederate forces retreated in mass from their final stronghold of the summits on Lookout Mountain and Missionary Ridge. The next morning, as the sun rose, Union soldiers defiantly planted the American flag atop Lookout Mountain declaring their victory for all to see.

The Confederate Armies of Tennessee and Alabama finally regrouped in Dalton, Georgia, less than twenty miles away and prepared for the harsh winter ahead. There'd be no fighting ahead for either army. Until spring, that is.

The passing of the following week was most miserable for James. The retreat was brutal. Desertions were heavy, casualties were high, and morale was at its lowest ever. All James could think about was Tom and how he must be suffering. Tom's capture was a double-edged sword for James. Capture was preferable to death, of course, but a huge cavern of emptiness took home in his heart. He couldn't fathom finishing the war without his brother. Sam, Matt, and Henry were there for him, but Tom was his brother, his mentor and confessor. Past rumors and stories about POW camps filled him with worry and fear for his brother's safety; however, he had small comfort in knowing that if anyone could survive the death camps, it'd be Tom. He just prayed nothing happened to the rest of them. He couldn't stand another loss.

Even though the family may have already been notified about Tom's capture, it was time for him to inform his mother and sister in his own words. Thinking of home sparked his memory back to his enlistment in '62. The bands. The parades. The hero's sendoff. How stupid and naïve they were.

James pulled the greatcoat snug to his body and sat cross-legged in front of the roaring campfire, and started his letter home.

December 2, 1863

Dear Sister,

I suppose you have heard the sad news of Tom's capture before now. I know that a wise Providence has and will direct all things to be as they are, but I sometime wish that I had been permitted to have had this fate. I know that if alive, a long and tedious captivity and exile from home and all that is dear to him awaits, but he can feel that he has done his duty, and that will sustain him in captivity or death if need be. I will tell you all I have been able to learn about him. When our Brigade went into battle, it went into an ambush, they weren't prepared and the first notice they gave of themselves was to pour a deadly fire into our Brigade from three directions. This threw us into confusion and a great many seeing that they were flanked and nearly surrounded started to run, but being rallied by the officers, stopped and fought until the officers also seeing the danger of being cut off, gave the command to retreat. Tom with eleven others of our company either not hearing or not wishing to obey such an order, stood their ground and while the rest made their escape were surrounded. The rest is left to conjecture whether they continued to fight and were killed at their post (which I do not think probable) or seeing they were surrounded and no chance of escape, surrendered. But if the worst happened and God in his mercy saw proper to remove him from this world of sin and troubles to himself in heaven, where there is no war, no sad partings, then we should not grieve as those who have no hope, for though there is nothing perfect in this world, I believe Tom lived as pure and godly a life as man can live under such circumstances, though all the vice and wickedness incident to camp life, he was a uncontaminated as when he left home, now nearly three years ago. What I lose even by his absence God only knows, for he was to me brother, friend, protector, counselor, and all that I could ask for. But it has pleased God to remove my earthly stay and support that I may learn to call on him in the hour of adversity and need. I came very near being captured, so near that I was obliged to throw away my knapsack and haversack and run about five miles but I suppose I had better not tell that part of it as it is not military to throw away baggage on a retreat. I will close for tonight.

Thursday morning, December 3rd,

Dear Jane,

I am well this morning. The weather is very cold here, and as we have no shelters to sleep under, the frost is in a thick coat on our blankets every morning, but it is a great deal more pleasant than wet weather, though a great many of our men are barefooted and you can imagine that is not very pleasant in itself. I have a right lonesome time of it without Tom now. But camp is a bad place to be lonesome, for no matter what happens, everything goes on the same joking, trifling away a good serious conversation, but no such thing ever takes place between two soldiers. You must write often to me, for you know Mamma does not write often and Papa not at all. You must remember that every day when the mail comes, how anxiously I look for a letter.

I will write as often as I can, remember me to Mrs. Peak. Kiss Becky for me. I have not time to write anymore.

Remember me in your prayers.

From your affectionate brother,
James A. Durrett

Chapter Sixteen

"NOTCHES"
HARRY

NOVEMBER
LOUISIANA

Harry was comfortable sitting cross-legged behind a small outcrop of boulders, positioned about a hundred yards up the hill. He had perfect protection with tree cover and an open view of the plain below. The scope of the Sharps scanned the edges of the woods, left to right, searching out a target in the midst of the Rebel troops on the opposite end of the field. Occasional exchanges of picket fire from each side disrupted the day, providing just enough stimuli to keep the troops alert and uneasy. More show than results. Harry on the other hand was aiming for results. His bird's-eye view opened opportunities of accuracy not afforded the shooters in the valley. He picked his targets methodically and with reason. As he scanned the tree line, a face flashed across his lens. Without a blink, Harry brought the scope back to the large oak shielding the Reb.

Harry's habit was to talk it out to his targets. It gave him a sense of---comradeship. "Don't have no sympathy for some coward hiding behind a tree when your buddies are up on the pickets doing their jobs." He adjusted the scope as he continued to ramble on, "I'm gonna give you a number, fella. Twenty-seven."

Harry played a game with his hidden target, as he did most of the soldiers that fell victim to his rifle. Always talking to them, defiling them, encouraging and coaxing them. His only intent was to quicken their meeting with Saint Peter. "Are you gonna peek 'round to the left or right? I think...Right side this time. Tell you what, if you go left, I'll let you live," he giggled. "To the right, and you're heaven bound." He waited patiently, not flinching an inch, licking his lips in anticipation of the kill. "About time for you to come round, now." As if on cue, the cautious soldier poked his head around the left side of the tree, unaware of the dangerous game he was playing.

Harry's nerves were calm, hands steady; his heart rate stayed the same. A slight adjustment with the scope, with a full frightened face magnified in the lens, a gentle squeeze of the trigger, ---then the loud report of the Sharps. The unsuspecting Reb's head snapping back violently as the lead projectile entered just above the bill of his gray woolen cap and another notch for Harry.

"Sorry fella. I cheat."

Harry leaned back, satisfied with his day's work and the additional notches he added to the stock of his Sharps. He retrieved the pocketknife from his trousers and carved in the final notch of the day. "Twenty-seven." The sun was close to setting in the western sky, so he gathered his knapsack and rifle and started his trek back to camp. "Time to eat."

The sniper unit of the 96th Ohio stayed apart from the other companies in the regiment. They were not the most sociable group of individuals and preferred to associate with their own kind, which suited the regulars just fine. For the most part, they were an elite group of individuals who shunned outsiders, trusted no one, and became suspicious of anyone attempting to join their exclusive unit.

Harry was so anti-social to begin with, that he blended in immediately and was accepted by the expert riflemen quicker than most. He asked no favors or advice, and his kill ratio spoke for itself. Each sniper was unique in preference of rifles, cover and positioning, timing, and their own trademark "kill spot." In the beginning, Harry shot just to kill, using heart and headshots. Once realizing his brother snipers "trademarked" their kills, he developed his own. One shot in the cap, between the bill and the band.

The day's work done, Harry stretched out in front of the campfire, flat on his back, fingers meshed together behind his head. He gazed at the clear, dark sky above him and counted the multitude of stars in the coolness of the night.

Mac Furgeson, another member of the sniper unit, sat across from him sipping coffee from a battered tin cup. "Thought much 'bout what you wanna do after the war's over, Harry?"

"Nope, hadn't thought that far ahead yet. Reckon we still have a ways to go before this one's done," Harry answered flatly, not wanting to engage in conversation with Mac.

"Know what bothers me, Harry?"

Harry waited a few seconds before answering, "No, but I'm sure your gonna tell me."

Mac ignored the remark. "I'm gonna miss it. Miss it all."

There was another noted silence between the two before Harry finally gave in. "I know, but I'm sure there's always gonna be a place for men like us, Mac. It's man's nature to fight and war against each other. Somebody's always wanting to eliminate the competition. They just don't wanna get their own hands dirty, but I ain't gonna worry 'bout that now. I worry more 'bout getting shot in the back by one of our own, than I do a Reb. The Rebs are better shots than our own damn infantry."

Mac nodded in agreement. "Know what you mean, but I kinda like makin' our own boys feel a might uneasy, you know. Nobody messes with us unless they's either drunk or just plain stupid. Sure as hell don't hafta' worry 'bout them stealin' from us, like they do from each other."

An evil little grin came across Harry's face. "Yeah, they don't know if they're getting shot by the Rebs or us." Both men chuckled, ideas dancing in their heads.

"Wouldn't matter to me either, a target's a target. Ain't that right, Harry?" Mac propped himself up on an elbow. "Say, you still goin' for that kill spot in the cap?"

"Yeah, it makes it more interesting, you know. Body shots are too easy."

"Cuts down on your numbers, don't it?

"Nah, just like shootin' ducks in a pond, Mac. Ducks in a pond." Harry closed his eyes and decided to get some shut-eye.

Chapter Seventeen

"OUT OF CONTROL"
HARRY

The six-member sniper unit threaded its way through the main encampment, ever alert to the hostile surroundings. Their aloofness towards their fellow regiment members and a justified reputation as the killer squad, failed to endear them into the hearts of their own comrades. The squad rarely strayed away from their own territory without the company of someone from their own unit. Brief glances from busy soldiers followed their procession as they made their way through the numerous campfires and company positions; most soldiers avoided eye contact with anyone in the ragged looking troop of marksmen.

Attitudes among the infantry and cavalry varied about the

loners from the "Devil's Brigade," as it was dubbed. Many envied their prowess with a rifle and were even thankful for their existence as unit, but few, if any, wanted any association with them. They were considered mercenaries and bounty hunters, thrill killers and outcasts who couldn't co-exist in a normal society. Their observations were correct.

As expected, the members of this elite squad were totally indifferent to the opinions or attitudes of their fellow comrades-in-arms. They could care less. Sergeant Edward Bowie commanded his special group of marksmen with an iron fist and levity alike. He was fully aware of the volatile personalities and quirks of each man in his squad, and it was his job to keep them in line and satisfied. As for the squad itself, none of the members particularly enjoyed the company of the other, however there existed a mutual respect for each man's ability as marksmen. They had a job to do and loved it. They often fought and argued among themselves, but grudges didn't linger. There was an unspoken code to save bodily harm for the outsiders, whether it be a blue or gray uniform. It didn't matter.

The Devil's Brigade made their way to the commissary to

stock up for the ongoing siege. Unless an officer gave orders, this was their only foray into the main camp as a unit.

"Wel-l-l, looky here who crawled out from under their rocks, boys!" A rival sergeant of Bowie's proclaimed loudly, as he stood by the commissary wagon.

"Back-off McKinney," Sergeant Bowie ordered, holding up a hand. "We're here for supplies an' don't need any of your stupid lip." Bowie squared his shoulders and dropped a hand to his waist gun to make his point.

"You back-off, Bowie," he growled back. "I don't take orders from you, an' I don't want your scumbag unit down here dirtyin' up my camp. Matter a fact, none of us do. You boys just get back to where you come from," he snapped, dropping a hand to his own pistol.

Alvin Shucks, one of the original snipers of the 96th, stared hard at McKinney. "Seems to me your boys is the ones that's doin' most of the runnin', Ho-o-mer." Alvin spat on the ground, grinned, then casually glanced at Bowie. "I'll shoot him if you want me to, Sergeant Bowie."

"Shut up, Shucks," he snapped and turned back to Sergeant

McKinney. "We ain't here for trouble. We're fighting the Rebs not each other. Remember?" Bowie stated between gritted teeth. He just wanted to get his men's supplies and leave. He was tired of others hassling his squad for doing their job, but that didn't matter right now. Things were about to get out of hand real bad.

"I ain't afraid of you, Shucks," McKinney shot back. "You wouldn't know how to fight a man if he weren't three hundred yards away."

"That right, McKinney?" Mac piped in. "The way I hears it, you stay mostly behind your boys 'stead a'front them. Say it ain't so, Ho-o-omer," he taunted.

A crowd of McKinney's men began to gather and stepped up to face down the sniper squad.

Trouble was brewing and a fight was imminent, so Harry brought his rifle up, resting the butt on his hip, barrel pointed skyward. He didn't say a word, but his actions spoke loud enough and brought a silent stillness to the mob. The other five sharpshooters raised their rifles in kind, standing back to back, covering the angles.

Bowie stepped in front of his boys, arms out. "Now, look what you've done, McKinney, you damned fool!" He barked. "I thought we were fighting them Johnny Rebs, but you're making a hell of an effort to get your own men killed. Now, back down!"

Before McKinney could answer, a rustle of sabers approached from behind the sergeant and his men. "What's going on here?"A stern voice shouted in the background, as a group of four officers made their way through the crowd, shoving soldiers out of the way. "What the hell's going on, I said!" The captain shouted pointing at Harry and the others with his sword. "You men lower those rifles now or you'll be standing before the court! Do it now!"

Harry and the others reluctantly lowered their rifles in slow motion. Bowie snapped to attention and addressed the veteran captain he'd served for years, "Sir! There's nothing goin' on! We're here to draw supplies for the upcoming engagement and we're just shootin' the bull with Sergeant McKinney and his men, Sir. Just a little aggressive jawin' 'tween units, Sir!"

"I'm no fool, Sergeant," the grizzled captain responded, pointing a finger at Bowie and McKinney. "I suspect there's more going on than conversation. If you boys want to kill each other, you can do it after the war. Right now we have a common enemy that's trying to kill you on a daily basis. I suggest you and Sergeant McKinney keep that in mind, and I'm sure you can find somebody to kill that's not in your own army."

"Yes Sir!" Both men shouted simultaneously.

"McKinney," the Captain said, "prepare your squad for tomorrow's encounter and then report to my tent. Your men are taking the point position in the morning," he instructed.

"Yes Sir!" McKinney barked, but the bravado had dropped from his voice. Point units were suicide and he knew it.

Bowie smiled with satisfaction. He knew McKinney was all talk and a coward at best.

"Sergeant Bowie!"

"Yes Sir!" He jumped.

"You take that rabble looking bunch of men you call soldiers and get their supplies. Then, take positions post haste. I want to hear shots fired and bodies dropping as the sun peaks the horizon! You hear me, Sergeant Bowie? Sunup!"

"Yes Sir! Perfectly clear, Sir!"

It didn't take long before the camp buzzed with stories about the confrontation between the two sergeants. In the meantime, men stepped aside and gave up their place in the commissary line, so as to hurry the exit of Sergeant Bowie and his band of outcasts.

Mac nudged Harry playfully in the ribs, grinning as they moved ahead. "Hey Harry, what you tryin' to do back there, start a war? Raisin' your rifle like that? Man! Ol' Homer was shakin' in his boots! Did ya see him?"

"Yeah, Mac. I saw him."

"What were you gonna do if the Cap hadn't shown up?"

"At first, I was gonna kill him," Harry remarked dryly. "But I've changed my mind. I've got other plans for the sergeant now."

"I bet you do," Mac giggled.

The next morning before dawn, Harry had maneuvered his way to the high ground on the left flank of the Union forces. He moved in silence like a predator, cautiously quickening his pace through the trees, continuously referencing his location with the Southern position. His dark civilian clothes made him invisible in the twilight of the morning, and a change of clothes to blend with the daylight hours was in his knapsack along with his other essential supplies for the day. He carried no personal articles, keepsakes, or clothing that identified him as either Yankee or Rebel. One never knew when it might be necessary to switch allegiances for survival. Today though, Harry had a new game in mind for his Rebel friends.

He settled into his new vantage point about two hundred yards above the Rebel encampment. Checked his Sharps, arranged ammunition for easy access and fast loading, canteen and food close by. Everything within arm's reach. Targets always in plain view. No obstructions. He kept mobile, constantly changing location, eliminating the possibility for Southern snipers to home in on his position. Rebel sharpshooters were deadly accurate and their reputation preceded them. He admired their skills and their notoriety as marksmen was far greater than the North's. With no qualms at all, Harry would switch to the Confederate side if he thought they had a chance to win the war, but he knew it was unlikely at this point.

Settled in now, Harry was secure in his new post. He had plenty of camouflage from the trees, a clear view to his targets, and an escape route in place if he deemed it necessary to do so. All good snipers have an exit plan; they never leave anything to doubt.

On the Southern part of the plain, campfires glowed like fireflies in the morning dawn as sounds of camp life echoed in the valley. Harry moved around, getting himself situated, scanning the tree line for his morning targets. He was midway between Confederate and Union lines, the killing field lay in the middle like a large brown sponge, anxious to absorb American blood.

This is the damndest war. A gentleman's war, Harry thought. Everybody wants to have breakfast and shave before lining up to shoot at the other side. Why the hell don't we attack 'em whilst their eating breakfast? Oh-h-h no! That'd be ungentlemanly! Not the rules of war. Harry chambered the first shell of the day. "Well boys, as soon as it's first light, I'm gonna have some fun with the gentleman's rules!"

The sun crept above the eastern sky like a large orange ball, bathing the valley in gradual sunshine, and taking the edge off the cool, brisk morning. A beautiful day for battle, thought Harry, planting the stock of his Sharps firmly against his shoulder and taking aim at his first target for the morning. Three soldiers sat around the campfire, warming their hands, talking and drinking coffee. He zeroed in his target and squeezed the trigger. The tin coffee pot, that seconds before brewing hot scalding java, suddenly exploded before the three startled men. They fell backwards, throwing coffee and food in the air, scrambling for cover from the unseen coffee pot assassin.

Harry turned and laughed, enjoying the moment. "Mornin', boys!"

The Confederate lines came alive. Muskets snatched, knapsacks clutched, bodies searching for cover. Pot shots from Harry's unit started peppering the tree line on Harry's cue. He watched the handy work of the Devil's Brigade and watched the bodies fall.

He gathered up his gear. "See ya'll on the killing field, boys. I've got another score to settle first."

Harry adjusted his position about fifty yards back towards the Union lines, keeping his high vantage point. He knew the major push was organizing and waited patiently for the point unit to appear, waving the colors of their company flag. "Fools."

To his left, the Rebel companies were falling into formation as he waited for Sergeant McKinney's company to take the point position. "I'm gonna knock you down a notch, McKinney. You're bad for morale," he smiled.

Time rolled by slowly, but time was something Harry had plenty of. He watched the amazing precision of both sides as regiments and men by the thousands organized their companies, forming into their ranks. "Line up for the slaughter, fools."

He observed the officers galloping back and forth on magnificent steeds, barking orders and encouragement. But, Harry wasn't interested in them, at least for now. Using his scope, Harry scanned the front lines for McKinney and spotted him, standing erect, musket slanted back against the front of his shoulder, eyes straight. "Well boys, why don't we start this little skirmish a tad early today."

Harry aimed, squeezed the trigger, and felt the comforting kick of the Sharps against his shoulder. He watched McKinney fall, grabbing his right knee, thrashing around on the ground in pain. "Guess you'll have a small limp from now on, Sergeant McKinney," Harry giggled.

The Union troopers assumed the shot that felled McKinney came from the Rebel lines and all hell broke loose. Both armies charged the other and mayhem began. Harry watched in amusement for a few minutes and returned to his original position. Slowly and methodically, he settled in and started choosing new targets for the notches on his Sharps.

Chapter Eighteen

"PRISONER OF WAR"
TOM

DECEMBER 10, 1863
ROCK ISLAND, ILLINOIS

The trip to Rock Island Prison, in Illinois, was brutal for Tom and the four thousand captured Confederate soldiers from the Lookout Mountain and Missionary Ridge engagements. Tom and Bob were captured on November 25th and arrived at their final destination on a cold gloomy day, December 10. For almost two weeks, the prisoners traveled by train, packed into cattle cars so tight that there was standing room only. No privacy, no food or water. Nothing but a thin layer of moldy straw and a hundred men packed into a boxcar big enough for little more than half that size. The wounded and sick received no medical attention, temperatures inside remained near freezing the entire trip. With no energy or will to endure the inhumane conditions of the trip, many collapsed and died at the feet of their comrades.

Scheduled stops were made to refill the water tanks of the train, and it was only then that the cars were emptied one at a time to remove the dead or near dead to make room for the living. Survivors in each car were responsible for unloading the corpses of friends and relatives and stacking the bodies in huge piles beside the tracks like so many cords of firewood. No military eulogies, salutes, or proper burial for the deceased. Only silent prayers as prisoners returned to the train for the balance of what lay ahead of them. The boxcars were never cleaned at the infrequent stops, and prisoners were forced to return to the filth of human waste and the smell of death that permeated throughout the cars. This was a journey for the strong of mind and body. The weak perished.

"You think this is it, Tom?" Bob asked, shivering and gazing through the narrow cracks between wood-slated walls, as signs of civilization sped by. The expanse of the Mississippi River on one side with farms, military camps with regiments of soldiers marching and on duty, tent cities, and stockyards full of cattle and horses filled the countryside. "Can't take much more of this, Tom. If we stop again, then I'm runnin' for it cuz I'd rather die by a Yankee bullet in my back, than as a frozen pork chop in this stinkin' death car. I'm tired of being treated like an animal, Tom."

Tom stood to the side, his legs spread to keep his balance against the never-ending swaying of the boxcar. "I reckon this is it, Bob," Tom answered, his voice empty. Even Tom's proud stature had taken a beating on this ride from hell. "That's what the Yankee sergeant said last night. We're gonna be on some kind of an island on the Mississippi. So, unless you know how to swim, escape'll be kinda hard. I don't hardly reckon they're gonna hand out furlough passes for town, do you?"

The back and forth motion of the train seemed to lessen and large billows of steam escaped the funnel of the laboring engine as its speed slowed down. Heavy sporadic jolts jerked the occupants as the brakes screamed metal to metal. Men scrambled to the sides of the cars, peering through the cracks, trying to get a glimpse of their final destination.

"What's out there, Tom?" See anything?" Bob asked, his view now blocked by the others.

"Not a damn thing," he answered. How 'bout you?"

"Nah, too many people in the way," Bob said, stretching on his tiptoes.

"Relax, Bob. We'll be outta here soon. Then, you'll get to see everything there is to see."

The train jolted to a final stop, billows of smoke and steam rolling down the sides of the cars in cumulus clouds, giving brief waves of warmth to the freezing men in their wooden cages. In the station, hundreds of Union soldiers lined the length of the death train, muskets at the ready, as additional men ran along the rows of cars throwing the bolts, opening the sliding doors, and preparing for the exodus of prisoners. Orders were issued and shouted down the line by the officers in charge of unloading the massive numbers of men. The disorganization was obvious. Rock Island was a new prison and the prisoners from Chattanooga, Lookout Mountain, and Missionary Ridge were to be its first guests.

Finally, the guards started unloading two cars at a time; prisoners were formed into marching blocks of ten rows, twenty men deep. Guards formed parallel lines along each block front to back, eliminating any possibility of escape.

"Makes lots of sense don't it, Tom?" Bob commented as they lined up in the first block, shivering from the cold wind coming off the Mississippi.

"What's that?"

"Well, we're way the hell up here in Yankee territory, no weapons, no food, and no decent clothes, and freezing to death, and they're afraid we're gonna try to escape." Bob shrugged. "Now just where the hell they think we're gonna run to?"

"Home, Bob. And you know damn well we will, if we get the chance."

"Can't swim, Tom," Bob deadpanned.

"No talkin'!" Yelled a burly guard, pointing his rifle at them, "or you'll end up eating a piece of this here musket, an' be bait for the fish!" He jabbed his bayonet at Bob, the point stopping inches from his nose. "You hear me, Johnny Reb?" He snarled.

Bob stared back at the guard, holding his tongue.

The guard laughed, "Yeah, that's what I thought," then moved on down the line.

"You handled that just right, Bob," Tom whispered out the side of his mouth.

Those that had been unloaded and hustled into their formations were forced to stand at attention, exposed to the forces of nature, waiting for the other cars to be unloaded.

Bob kept his eyes the guard that had threatened him, as he moved down the line to pester another poor soul. "Plan on seeing that ol' boy in camp one day when he ain't got a hundred of his buddies with him."

Tom nodded. "Yes, sir. I can see that happenin'."

As they waited for the remaining cars to be unloaded, the prisoners shivered uncontrollably in the cold morning drizzle. Many of them had no shoes, coats, or hats. Hobo soldiers protected from the December winds by thin, deteriorating pants and shirts that were torn and worn through. They stood shoulder to shoulder, absorbing as much body heat as possible from the man next to them.

When Tom last saw James, he let him wear the heavy greatcoat his mother had sent them. He regretted it now. *Poor James.* He thought. *I'm, okay, James. I'm alive. You'll find out, jus' hold on, boy.*

When the final soldier disembarked from the train, the yelling started up again. "Straighten up there! Form your lines! You remember how to march, don't you, boys? For'ard march!" The close-quartered guards spat orders to Tom's group first and moved down the line. In succession, every block of prisoners thereafter started its first step towards a new stage of war that was about to begin for all of them. The first formation of soldiers marched sluggishly and out of order, no military bearing, just defeat in the cadence of their steps, moving at a snail's pace and staggering, feet shuffling, eyes cast down. Yankee guards taunted the already shamed Confederates, degrading their manhood and pride; Confederate dogs under the thumbs of their new masters.

"Hey, look at them scraggy buckets of scum, Joe! How many these boys you reckon have some pretty Southern Belle sittin' on a plantation porch, wondering where their beau is?" One guard taunted.

"Hell! I bet Sherman's already burned down them white cotton farms, freed the slaves, and on his way to the sea!" His buddy laughed.

"Can't believe we's ever scared of these boys. Look at 'em! Just a bunch a dirt farmers and squirrel hunters! Pitiful!"

The taunting continued with every step they made, rolling back and forth from the first block to the last.

Tom had had enough. "That's it, dammit," Tom mumbled in anger. "I'm not giving these boys no more quarter, Bob." Then, he called out orders, snapping his shoulders back. "Follow my lead, boys!" Determination filled his voice. In a motion that stood out among the slumped and defeated Southerners, Tom stood erect, shoulders squared back, and his eyes forward. "All right Eighteenth! Ya' ain't outta the army yet! Straighten up an' march with your right! Your left! Your right! Eyes for'ard! Pick up the pace, an' remember who ya' are!" Tom bellowed.

Hundreds of Rebel eyes jolted from staring at the ground to Tom's direction, ears strained in disbelief at his defiance. One by one and in groups, soldiers fell into step. Right, then left. Officers took command again, remembering who they were. Sergeants shouted orders to the squads around them, demanding order. Gradually, like a rolling wave on the ocean, the cadence of their steps were simultaneous and in order. Pride overtaking defeat.

If nothing else, then it silenced the Union soldiers' insults momentarily.

The citizens of Rock Island, Illinois, were abuzz with giddy anticipation at the arrival of Confederate prisoners of war. Many didn't know what to expect; Southern devils with tails and horns wouldn't have surprised anyone. Every townsperson planned to attend the upcoming parade, as the prisoners were marched to the ferries that would take them across to the newly built prison on the Mississippi.

The twelve-acre island was one of the largest arsenal depots for the Union Army. But, with the large influx of Confederate soldiers taken prisoner the past two years, it was necessary for the U. S. government to find safe and secure locations to build new prisons, accommodating the critical overflow problem. The existing prison camps were bursting at the seams and were breeding grounds for disease and starvation, costing thousands of unnecessary and cruel deaths.

As the parade of marching prisoners approached the main street, the Rebels saw and heard hundreds of spectators shouting and lining the main street, three to four rows deep, gawking at their approach.

"What the hell kinda deal is this?" Bob exclaimed from the side of his mouth. "Is there a circus in town?"

"Yeah, it's us," Tom said in disgust.

The jeering crowd made the prisoners nervous. They were defenseless, marching through hostile numbers of gloating Northern citizens. They refused to show their true fear to the crowd, though. Now, Tom knew how Luther Megs felt when he walked the gauntlet when he was drummed out of the Eighteenth.

"Just keep your eyes forward an' don't give an inch, no matter what," Tom instructed. "Pass it down," he ordered further. He was coming out of his depression, back in his comfort zone of leadership. If this was the hand he was to be dealt, then so be it.

Disappointment masked the faces of the townspeople of the approaching opposition army. This ragtag, starving bunch was the pride of the South? These are the ones who've been killing our brothers, fathers, and sons? These are the disciples of Satan that casts

fear into the hearts of the Union? Frustration and confusion turned to

anger as citizens hurled insults and curses; they spat in their enemies'

faces as they passed by. Not one soldier flinched or removed his eyes

from the back of the man before him. Marching. Eyes forward.

Then, the most amazing incident occurred that was the subject

of conversation for months to come. As Rock Island citizens

continued to hurl insults and rotten fruit at the parade of Rebel

prisoners, an angel from the South appeared in their midst. A

beautiful young woman, oblivious to the abusive shouts of anger,

stepped bravely into the street before Confederate soldiers, waved a

laced handkerchief high in the air to attract their attention, and shouted

loud and clear, "I'm from Kentucky! I'm a friend!"

Faces of the prisoners within earshot were at first shocked and

glowed in glory with the knowledge that one of their own was among

them. Word of the young lady passed quickly from mouth to mouth

through the ranks about the woman from Kentucky. As each

marching block passed by the fearless Southern Belle, she continued

to wave and shout encouragement, telling them to be brave and trust in God. Marching with even more pride than before, each line of men in unison doffed their hats and nodded to her as any Southern gentleman would when paying respects to a lady. Little did these men in gray know: this very lady patriot of the Confederacy, at her own peril, would assist forty-two prisoners escape from the Rock Island Prison in the next two years.

The docks became overcrowded with Southern boys who had fought their last battle for the Confederacy. Thousands were ferried across the Mississippi River to the place they would either die or finish out the war.

Onboard the ferry, Tom watched the shore and firm ground inch away from him. *I'm alive, James. Don't fret, little brother.* Then, a weak smile creased Tom's face.

"I wish I'd kept that damn greatcoat, James."

Chapter Nineteen

"THE RETURN OF LUTHER MEGS"

FEBRUARY 1864
DALTON, GEORGIA

Time dragged on forever for James as the Eighteenth settled back into the camp routine after the South's retreat from Chattanooga. Tom's capture was heavy on his mind and plummeted him into a depression that took him spiraling emotionally into a bottomless pit. The absence of his brother made him feel totally useless, no purpose, no direction in his life; his dependency on Tom, during this war was much deeper than he ever suspected. The boys had done their best to boost his spirits, but there was little cheer in camp, as far as he was concerned. He was put-off by the non-stop joking and razzing of soldiers as they found obnoxious ways of dealing with their own demons. It seemed that even death could not fend off the vulgar and contentious behavior of his fellow soldiers.

The winter in Dalton had been the most severe they'd ever experienced. To make matters worse, the misery of the cold was compounded by the confusion throughout the assembled regiments. General Bragg was scrambling to replace and shift around remaining officers to fill the voids created from the disaster at Chattanooga. Lack of organization and capable enough men to give orders left many units fending for themselves.

"This is the biggest bunch of idiots I ever seen," Sam mused. "These boys ain't got nobody to tell 'em what to do, and they just fall apart!"

When it became apparent that the unit was going to wait out the winter in Dalton, orders were given to the soldiers build their own shelters. This exercise served two purposes: keeping the men busy, thus reducing idle time for mischief and an attempt to cease the hundreds of men dying from exposure, pneumonia, and frostbite. The work was difficult and time consuming, but the final results was an instant makeshift city of crude log cabins spotted throughout the woods.

The heavy number of dead and wounded to the Confederate forces was beginning to take a heavy toll. In addition, another situation emerged compounding the already critical problem of depleted recruits: Desertion. Many of the enlisted men decided that three years was much too long to dedicate to the cause; the personal costs just weren't worth the effort to many of them. Regiments were losing large numbers of infantry and non-commissioned officers who stole away for home under the cover of darkness. The penalty for desertion was death by firing squad, and there was no lack of volunteers to carry out the gruesome task.

James couldn't fathom or even consider taking the life of one of his own---regardless of the crime. It was bad enough losing friends and relatives in battle, but now the army was killing their own. No one from the Eighteenth had made the dash for home yet, though he'd heard talk of some who'd considered it; he hoped and prayed they'd change their minds. If Tom were here, he knew there wouldn't even be talk about desertion, let alone doing it.

Letters

For the past month, James had stayed holed up in his cabin, stoking the fire, reading by firelight, coming out only when necessary or under orders. Henry, Matt, and Sam shared the same cabin with him; the space was cramped, but it provided the welcomed warmth from the cold and brought the four young occupants closer together than ever. They spent many hours talking and confiding with each other about past disappointments and triumphs, and future hopes and dreams. In spite of their closeness however, James chose to stay aloof and alone.

James heard footsteps approaching the front of the cabin. He knew it was probably one or all three of his roommates returning to cajole him from his spot in the corner of the cabin. All three had done their best to help him rise above his depressive mood, but he resisted all of their attempts. Even the gregarious Sam failed to lift his spirits.

Knock! Knock! Two hard raps on the door shattered his miserable vigil in the dark and dank room. It wouldn't be either of the boys, he thought. They wouldn't knock, they'd just come on in.

"Hey Jamie Boy! Don't cha' wanna come out an' see your ol' buddy?" A familiar voice taunted from the other side of the door.

James's eyes widened. It couldn't be, he thought. Rage and disgust surged through his veins; his temples pounded to the memory of a past drumbeat. Slowly, methodically, from his squatting position, he scooted upwards his back scraping against the rough bark on the logs, finally standing upright.

"What's matter, Jamie Boy? You too shy to come see your ol' buddy, Luther?" The taunting continued.

James pushed open the door.

Luther Megs stood about fifteen feet back, leaning against a tree with his arms folded across his chest, grinning like a cat who'd just killed the family dog. "Ain't you glad to see me?" Luther asked and leisurely glanced around their campsite. "Looks like you boys been gittin' whipped regularly since I left. Well---that's okay. Luther's here to get you boys back on track." He croaked, obviously pleased with himself, smiling and waiting for James's response.

"What's trash like you doing here, Luther? You come to get another ass-kickin' by the Durretts again?" James said in an emotionless monotone.

Luther's grin dropped a fraction, taken aback by James's

uncharacteristic remark. "Yeah---well---I heard that Big Tom got himself caught by the Yanks at Chattanooga. Ever'body at home's talkin' 'bout it like he's some big hero or sumthin'. I think he was just too stupid to get outta the way, myself." He straightened his posture regaining back some of his courage and pointed at James wiggling a finger. "Now, don't mess with me, boy. You ain't got no big brother watchin' your back no more, and I told you before---I'd be back. You need to be r-e-e-l careful from now on, Jamie. Just came by to warn you that I'd be around. Know what ah mean?"

Luther hitched up each side of his baggy pants in an over dramatic attempt of contemptuous bravado. As he moved to leave, he noticed a grim smile spread across James's face, catching him off-guard. Then, he froze in his tracks. A cold and hard object pressed forcefully against the back of his head. The unmistakable sound of a cocking pistol deflated any bravado that might have remained.

"Ya know, Luther," a calm voice whispered next to his ear, "I didn't know a dead man could talk." Matt kept his pistol trained on Luther's head as he circled around to face him. "I ain't a Durrett, but might as well be. Know the difference 'tween me an' them, Luther?"

Matt hesitated, waiting for an answer that never came. "Okay then, I'll tell ya. I'd shoot you in the back at the drop of a hat just because I don't like you. They wouldn't. That's the difference right there."

"Luther's top lip started to quiver, as he fumbled for words. "I-I ain't got no call with you, Rupert. You ain't no better'n me, you know," Luther said, keeping his body still and his hands dropped down to his sides.

"Oh, that's where you're wrong," Matt answered. "I never have, an' I never will be as low of a scumbag as you, Luther."

"Yeah, well---" Luther started, but his words froze in mid-sentence as he heard the sound of another pistol cocking behind him.

"Hey boys! We havin' a party I didn't know 'bout?" Sam piped in as he nudged Luther's head with the barrel of his Navy Colt.

James finally spoke up, deadpanned, "Sam Evans---meet Luther Megs."

Sam snorted. "This the white trash got drummed out last year? What're you doin' back here, boy? This is a fightin' unit. We don't allow cowards and thieves 'round here." He nudged the barrel of the Navy Colt hard against Luther's skull.

Luther's head bobbed forward, but he kept his eyes straight ahead, not looking either youth in the eye. "You don't have to worry, I ain't in this lousy outfit," he mumbled. "I'm with a 'nother one that needs real fightin' men," he answered back, trying to sound unmoved by the two pistols pointing at his head.

"Can I kill him, James? It'd be my pleasure," Sam offered, nudging the barrel tight against Luther's head again.

James slowly budged from the spot he'd been glued to the last two minutes. He reached over and lowered Matt and Sam's pistols. Getting nose-to-nose with man before him, he spoke sharply, "You need to know something, Luther. I'm different now…and the thing you need to worry about is that Tom's *not* here to protect you. He's an honorable man that wouldn't allow you to die in an unfair fight," James whisper, his eyes narrowing, "But I will." He backed up a half-step. "I want you to leave now---go to whatever unit you're with and stay real close to them. They're your only protection, now. Leastways till they get to know you like we do. And, if I see you again---you're a dead man, Luther. Hear me?"

Luther looked into James's lifeless eyes. "You, you don't scare me, Durrett. None of you little pups do," he snarled, squaring his shoulders. "I'll be back an' you can count on it."

James nodded once. "Then, I look forward to it, Luther. See you soon," he said matter-of-factly.

Luther hitched up his pants, ran his fingers back through his long, greasy hair, and slowly backed away, still eye-balling his adversaries. When he was, what he thought, a safe distance, he stopped. "Hey, Durrett!" He called, pointing his finger at James, imitating a gun. "Know what I mean?"

In a reflex move, Sam pulled the Navy Colt from his belt and pointed the pistol at Luther, "Hey, Megs!" Luther twisted around to confront the voice and Sam fired once, the bullet thudding into the tree next to Luther's head. "Know what *I* mean?"

Luther flinched and jumped a good foot off the ground and then turned and ran into the woods for cover.

"That boy won't live to see the next battle," Henry said as he stepped from behind the cabin, cradling his rifle.

Chapter Twenty

"CONVERSATIONS"

"I owe you boys an apology for the way I've been acting lately. I haven't been pulling my weight around here," James stated, with very little emotion showing in his tone or features. "Seeing Luther made something snap though. He made this war personal---and I'm afraid you're all in it too, now."

Sam stretched out on his pallet, enjoying the warmth of the stove in the middle of their room. "No problem, we carry each other's weight 'round here. You know---I just met Luther today, an' that boy really rubs me the wrong way already. I figured if I could put up with Rupert---everybody else would be a breeze, but that boy takes the cake."

"What do you mean by that?" Matt quipped, fending a hurt tone. "Puttin' up with *you* is the challenge. You're dangerous, Sam. Livin' on the edge all the time."

"Gotta live on the edge 'round here," Henry added. "We just don't wanna go over it, that's all."

James's eyes took in everyone in the room, one at a time. It was good to be back, he thought. At least he was making the effort to get back in the run of things. "Say, ya'll have any suggestions about Luther? It won't be hard for him to gather some of his own kind out there and start up trouble. Plenty around camp just like him, and things are gonna be hard enough without looking over our shoulders, waiting for some unknown fella on our own side to ambush one of us." James didn't like the fact that he'd involved the others in his feud with Luther. But, he supposed it was inevitable. He'd thrown down the gauntlet, challenging Luther to a duel of wits...no, a duel to the death.

"Well---," Henry said and paused as if in thought. "We know he ain't the sharpest knife in the drawer. We can probably count on him doing something stupid. He's his own worst enemy when it comes to using his brain, you know."

"I don't see the problem," Matt interrupted with a shrug of the shoulder. "Let's just shoot the no-count next time we see him."

Henry smiled, "I think there's laws against that kinda thing, Matt. 'Sides, no matter how tough we talk---we ain't that way."

"I'm just thinking out loud. You know how it is."

Sam stretched his legs out closer to the stove. "I'm just glad to hear you're thinkin' at all," he mumbled.

Matt pretended not to hear the wisecrack.

James continued along the same track, "I don't think any of us should be alone---always in pairs, at least until this is all settled. He's not brave enough to do something alone." He glanced over Sam's way. "What do you say, Sam? You've been kinda silent on the subject."

Sam didn't answer right away, pondering silently, flicking a toothpick back and forth in his mouth. No smile, no sparkle in the eyes. James had seen the same look on his face back on the ridge at Chattanooga when he killed the Yank that stabbed Matt. "I'm not waitin' on him to come to me. I shot at him. Just to get his attention, you know, but he ain't gonna forget that. He'll come back after me first, I figger." His lips finally broke into a crooked grin. "But...I ain't in the habit of waiting for somebody else to kill me first."

For some reason, that brought the conversation about Luther to an end, and the silence hung uncomfortably in the air like the fog that circled the peak of Missionary Ridge.

Sam sat up and playfully slapped Matt across the leg. "Come on, Matt. Me and you are gonna go to the commissary and get somethin' to liven up this here little party. I'm going to call in a favor." He winked at James and motioned for Matt to get up and follow him. He'd heard about some goings on about to take place and wanted to get a jump-start on the rest of the unit.

"I didn't know hardtack could liven up a party," Matt remarked. "Far as I know, that's all ol' Iron Britches has got left anymore. 'Sides, it's cold out there, I'm stayin' here."

"No you're not, you're coming with me. Remember, we go in pairs an' I'm more likely to get shot at in the dark if one of them Durrett boys is with me than you," he joked, pointing to James and Henry. "This is an important mission that needs a man of your skill an' fortitude to make it work, Matt. Come on," he waved, on his way to the door.

Matt stood reluctantly, brushing off the seat of his baggy pants. "Damn you, Sam. You always got something up your sleeve, an' it usually leads to trouble," he complained.

Sam grinned. "Yeah, an' you love it, too. Now, get your scrawny butt moving an' let's go."

Matt grabbed his side feigning an imaginary pain from his wound, "I guess somebody's got to keep an eye on you. Might as well be me."

The two cousins sat quietly in the warm cabin, watching Sam and Matt close the door behind them. "What you reckin' Sam's got up his sleeve now?" Henry said, finally breaking the peace and quiet after the other two had left.

"No telling," grinned James. "That boy's a genuine piece of work."

"Yeah, but he's as good as gold." A moment of uncomfortable silence filled the room until Henry finally broke the ice. He'd decided it was time to finally approach the subject of Tom. The boys had purposely avoided mentioning his name around James up until this time, but his cousin had to get over it soon enough. Henry wasn't going to tiptoe around the subject for the rest of the war. "Any word from your Mama 'bout Tom?" He asked, hesitantly.

"She's heard from him," James said reluctantly, but kept talking. "She said he keeps griping about me having the big coat." He smiled at the thought. "He said it's cold, and a lot of men are dying from all sorts of diseases that carry from man to man, but that's not much different than what we got here. Some of the guards are pretty mean, but not all of them, he says. He's having a tough time of it, but seems to be in good spirits. At least he's alive. There's that, anyway."

Henry probed, "Anything else?"

James shook his head. "Nah, not really. Mama's planning one of her trips up North and says she's going to visit Tom. Take him a care package and some warm clothes."

"I wish she wouldn't take those risks," Henry said. "It scares sister Caroline to death. The rest of us, too."

"Yeah, me too, but you know how she is. Stubborn as a mule. She's doing her own part for the war. Every time she comes back from one of her *forays* up north, she brings back valuable information for the generals."

"Yeah, but I'm afraid it's all gonna be for naught. I don't think even your momma can save the South, now. We took a bad beatin' back at Chattanooga, and I don't know if we can snap back from it. Not with what we got left, leastways."

James stared at the opposite wall. "I know. Change subjects, Henry."

After that small bit of conversation on Tom and the war, the next thirty minutes was mostly silent with bits and pieces of trivial conversation, until they heard the boys coming back from the commissary. "About time," James said, glad of their return.

Sam and Matt stumbled in, laughing to no end, and almost forgetting to close the door behind them. "I swear!" Matt coughed as he tried to talk and laugh at the same time, "I ain't never seen nuthin' like it! This boy could connive a Baptist preacher into believeing that hell was going to be a better place than heaven, if he thought he'd get something out of it!"

"What the hell are you sputterin' 'bout, Rupert?" Henry asked, annoyed at their loud intrusion and letting in the cold from outside.

Matt pointed at Sam. "Show 'em! Show 'em what you swindled ol' Iron Britches Cohill out of!"

Grinning to high heaven, Sam held up two one-gallon ceramic jugs of moonshine. Homemade whiskey.

"Can you believe it?" Matt exclaimed. "Get this! Sam found out that there's gonna be a big push tomorrow to get the boys to re-enlist for those whose time's comin' up. So the generals decided to get ever'body drunk, and then get 'em to sign up! Ol' Cohill's been keepin' the whiskey a secret." He slapped Sam on the back. "Our boy here knew 'bout it, like he always does, and started blackmailing him. Sam told him he's gonna let ever'body in camp know that he's hidin' whiskey if he didn't let us have two jugs tonight! Can you believe it? I ain't seen nobody ever get the better of 'ol Iron Britches before! Not like that!"

"We probably ought to lighten this up with something else, like coffee," Sam suggested with a smile. "This stuff'll take the hair off a dog if you ain't careful."

Matt poured fresh, hot coffee into everyone's cup and then

Sam followed, topping them off with splashes of moonshine. Matt settled back against the wall, feet stretched out, both hands absorbing the heat from his tin cup, then taking a sip, "O-o-o-u-u, whe-e-e! That's gotta bite to it, don't it? Hey Henry, I've been meanin' to ask you something."

"What's that, Matt?"

"They say you get these feelin's about things that are gonna happen. That true?"

Henry shrugged. "Sometimes."

"What's it like? What're you feelin', now?"

Sam sprayed coffee through his lips in a fit of laughter. "What kinda fool, stupid question is that?" The cousins chuckled, watching their two comrades fussing at each other.

"Well? How the hell do I know?" Matt defended. "If you don't ask questions---you don't learn nothing." He turned back to Henry, "So? How do you tell? When you think something's gonna happen?"

Henry scratched his chin, a bit perplexed, "I really don't know, Matt. It just kinda comes---like a bad or good feeling." Henry kept his eyes on the toe of his boots as he spoke. "It happened with Tom at Chattanooga. I told him to be careful---not like you always do in those kinda situations, but I meant it. I had a bad feeling. I was really afraid something was gonna happen to him."

James sat up straight, all his attention on Henry now. "What'd he say when you told him?"

Henry kept his eyes down. "Typical Tom, you know. Something like, "You just watch out for yourself. I'll be fine," he said, mimicking Tom's deep baritone voice, and shrugged again. "You know, typical Tom. Then, he ran off to the front."

James pictured the scene in his mind, as if he had been there at the time. Tom would love this night of talk and sipping whiskey. He'd be right in the middle of it.

"So-o-o, you got any feelin's about me? Matt tentatively asked. "You know, like something's gonna to happen?"

"Not really, Matt. It usually happens with family---or people I really care about," Henry quipped. Except for Matt, laughter erupted among the group again, with the effects of the moonshine beginning to take hold.

"Well, that's not funny," Matt said.

After minute, Henry got control of himself in an attempt to answer Matt's question. "Well, Matt---I'll be honest---I have had feelings about you. Good ones, and I'm not kidding with you now. But, I'm not saying no more 'cause I don't wanna jinx it."

"Hell," Matt said after taking another sip of spiked coffee, "I don't know whether to relax or worry," he sputtered.

"Worry," said Sam. "It'll keep you on the edge."

"What about James an' Sam? Any feelin's 'bout them?" Matt continued.

Henry quickly sobered, "No more feelings, Matt. Not now."

The night waned on with laughter and serious conversation alike after the subject of Henry's premonitions was dropped so abruptly. After a while, James and Sam decided to step outside for some fresh air to clear their heads. They'd put a big dent in the contents of the first whiskey jug, and they knew they'd be paying for it with major headaches the next day. They stayed close to the cabin, as the brisk chill of the night seeped through their clothes and skin.

Sam leaned against the cabin, slapping his arms around him to stay warm, and asked, "You ever think much 'bout that Yank back on Missionary Ridge?"

The question caught James off guard because neither had brought it up since it happened, but he was ready to talk about it. "Yeah," James answered. "Quite a bit, but probably not as much as you."

"I ain't never seen you like that. Hell---I ain't never seen me like that," Sam muttered. "It's like it was somebody else stabbin' that boy, and I was just watching it happen. Know what I mean? It's different face-to-face like that."

"Why'd you pull me off him, Sam? The rage I was in, I'd a killed him with my bare hands. You didn't have to do that."

"I know. For some reason, it didn't seem right for you to be the one doing it, though. I can't explain it, but it was up to me to finish the job."

"Does it bother you?"

"Some, but I'd do it again."

"Maybe, the circumstance won't present itself again."

Sam smiled; he loved to hear James talk his fancy words.

Maybe, that's why he thought he'd been self-appointed by some higher authority to protect James, without him knowing it. He was too good a man to die in this stinking war. James had the smarts and, most of all, the compassion to pull the country back together when this thing was over. James was going to be somebody when this was all over. He just knew it. He felt like he was protecting the future. "Well, Mr. Durrett, the circumstances have already presented itself."

"Oh? How's that?"

"Luther."

James turned and faced Sam as his face took on a dark, ominous expression. "He's mine, Sam. Don't interfere."

Sam just smiled at the dark face staring him down. "Oh, I'm not, James. I'd like you to have the pleasure. I've no doubt you can take him. I'm just gonna watch your back, that's all. He's all yours. I know that." Sam kept his smile on and slapped his best friend on the shoulder. "Let's get back inside. It's colder than a ditch digger's wife out here. And besides, Rupert an' Henry'll finish off that hooch an' we'll be left high an' dry." Sam already had a plan worked out in his head for taking care of the future.

Conversations continued on through the night and didn't stop until the whiskey jug was empty. Then, there was nothing else left to say.

Chapter Twenty-One

"RE-ENLISTMENT"

DALTON, GEORGIA

For the first day in months, the morning sun shone bright and not a cloud marred the clear, blue sky. The air was brisk and cold, but the sun took the edge off the bone-chilling misery that usually started each day. Soldiers rolled out of their cabins basking in the long-forgotten light of the day. Even though the boys had pulled an all-nighter and were feeling the worse for wear, they weren't about to miss a morning of sunshine.

"Now, I know why we only do that once a year," mumbled Henry, holding onto his head with both hands.

"Do what?" Sam asked while stirring the ashes to start a new campfire.

"You can't tell me you don't feel bad after drinkin' all that hooch last night!"

"Maybe a little fuzzy 'round the edges---but it ain't gonna ruin my day."

Matt came stumbling out of the cabin, boots unlaced, shirt-tail hanging out, eyes as red as a rising sun. "Gawd almighty! Who did what to John Brown last night? No more of that homemade shine for me. I'll never feel normal again." Henry and Sam glanced at each other, grinning, and Matt saw their smirks and held up his hands. "I know---I ain't never been normal. I know, I know. Old joke. Coffee ready?"

"We ain't even got the fire started yet, Matt. Why don't you quit whining an' get some started yourself. I'll mix us up some biscuits," Sam ordered.

"Anybody seen James? He's already gone when I got up this mornin'," asked Henry.

"I heard him rustlin' 'round early---he's gone before first light."

"He shouldn't be alone, not with Luther roamin' 'round," Henry said, concerned.

"He's okay," Sam assured him. "He's with Sol Thompson from over at Company I. Ya'll know him don't cha'? He's from Tuscaloosa County, too."

"Yeah, he's a good man. Heard he made lieutenant. Wish he's over here with Company E. Say, how'd you know he's with Sol?"

"I followed him. We got any sugar left?" Sam asked as he kneaded the dough for their biscuits.

"I shoulda' known," Henry smiled. "Yeah, we've got some if Matt ain't trying to make coffee with it."

"Anything's possible with that boy."

Matt came returned from the cabin, coffee pot in one hand and a sack of valuable coffee in the other. "I'll go down an' get some more water after I get the coffee goin'---we're gettin' low on java, you know," he offered.

"Making coffee *and* getting extra water. That's a first!"

Right then, James and Sol Thompson came up the path, shoulder to shoulder. James had a Colt stuffed in the front of his belt and a new Springfield rifle cradled in his arms.

"Hey!" Henry shouted. "Where'd you get that Springfield?"

"Sam isn't the only one around here with connections," James smirked. "The whole regiment's getting new rifles later this month to replace those worn out muskets we've been using. This is going to help our firepower for sure." James tossed his new weapon to Henry so he could examine it.

"Oh man," he sighed, running his hands over the stock and barrel. "This is nice. When do we get our hands on something like this?"

"Hey Henry," said Sol. "Hadn't seen you in a while. Keeping your head down, I see."

"Hey, Sol. What's the word on the rifles? Is James special or do we get one too?"

"He told me 'bout ol' Luther, and I thought he might need something a little quicker than that ol' musket he's hauling around. So, I just made a command decision to issue his a little early." Sol pointed at James's belt. "Fixed him up with a Colt, too. Course, Luther's so popular, first man that kills him will probably be given a medal or made an officer."

Sam stood up from the fire, licking flour and raw dough from his fingers. "Hey Sol, like some breakfast?"

"Sam! You son of a gun! I didn't see you hunkered down over there. How's it goin'?"

"Good. You an' ol' Ed Jones 'bout the only two fellers I miss from I Company. Ya'll ain't the "Bad Luck Boys" anymore, I hear."

Sol grinned, "Nah, that's one reason they're giving us the Springfields early. They gave us every faulty musket ever made in the beginning, you know. Figgered they owed us a favor, I recken. You need to come over and visit. Need somebody to make me laugh, Sam. And, I need another scrounger like you. Ain't been the same around camp without you. Things are nice and quiet for change."

Sam shrugged his shoulders and gave Sol a mischievous grin, "You just let me know what you need, Sol. Anytime for you."

A few minutes later, Matt came up from the creek, huffing, puffing, and red faced carrying two large goatskin pouches of water, one looped over each shoulder, "Could use some damn help here, ya' know! A wounded man ain't supposed to strain himself this way."

Nobody moved to help him. "James, I thought you kept better

company than Rupert, there," Sol joked.

"He's a good water toter and his colorful language keeps us entertained," he answered.

"Biscuits 'bout ready. Y'all come knock the fur off your tongue with some hot coffee and we'll eat," announced Sam, pulling the Dutch oven off the fire.

"Hey Sol," Matt called, lifting up his shirttail, "wanna see the scar that Yank gave me at Lookout?" A "not again" moan cried out in unison from the boys. He waved them off, "Just ignore them," he frowned and, without waiting for an answer, lifted his shirttail the rest of the way up and turned sideways to show off his prized scar. "Look! That sucker went clean through one side to the other!" Matt poked his fingers in the front and rear puncture wounds demonstrating the projection.

"Does he do this often?" Sol asked, glancing Sam's way.

"Only if it's someone he ain't already showed it to on a daily basis," Sam snorted.

Once the food was shared out, talking ceased and everyone enjoyed the breakfast. After a few minutes, Sol finally broke the silence. "Well boys, I hate to be the bearer of bad news and put a damper on such good food and company, but I'm gonna give ya'll a heads up on the day. 'Bout ten this morning, you're gonna hear the all call bugle an' everybody's gonna meet on the parade grounds."

"What's going on?" Henry asked.

"Re-enlistment," Sol stated. "Most these boy're comin' up on the end of their three-year term. Command's worried about a big fallout and everybody scootin' on home."

"Can't blame 'em," said James. "It's been a hard three years---too many friends and family lost."

Sol nodded. "I know. I just wanted to give you boys some time to think it over. Colonel Hunley'll be by and let the regiment know soon about the all call. They ain't telling nobody what it's about, but I'm sure plenty already know."

Sam went ahead and asked what the others were thinking. "What're you gonna do, Sol?"

"I'm re-uppin'. I decided I'm in it for the long haul. I'm not putting you boys on the spot and asking what you're gonna do---but I'd hate to see good fightin' men leave. We can still win this---I think."

Matt stuffed a whole biscuit in his mouth and decided to speak up, "Well, as for me," he mumbled between chomps of biscuit, "I don't mind telling you what I'm doin'. I'm stickin' it out. I ain't never had many friends before, and I like the life. I'll be right beside you, Sol. You can count on it."

Sol smiled and got to his feet. "Now, I know I'm in trouble." He nodded at the small group. "Thanks for the biscuits, boys. I need to get back to my place and get things movin'." He turned to James, "---an' James---Company I's boys're keepin' an eye out for Luther, too. That bunch he's runnin' with ain't the smartest, but they are dangerous. Keep your eyes open and I'll be seeing you boys around." He snatched up his rifle, waved, and headed down the trail without another word.

James looked up at Henry, "What do you think?"

"Oh, I guess I'm leaning towards stickin' it out, too. Least ways I was 'til Matt said he was stayin'." He gave Matt a friendly shove as he was stuffing another biscuit in his mouth.

"Sam?" James asked.

"I'm thinking on it."

A stab of disappointment hit James. He'd made his mind up

to stay long ago. He wouldn't feel right leaving now---with Tom stowed up in a prison camp up north. He'd feel empty---like he was leaving things unfinished. He'd grown close to Sam and depended on his humor and companionship. He was the edge of danger and the risk taker that James never was; his alter ego. "Who's gonna keep Matt in line if you leave---none of us can take him more than a few minutes at a time," James said in an attempt to mask his disappointment.

"Playin' on my conscience won't work, James," Sam stated and got up. "Let's clean up and get ready for the dog and pony show."

Word about the assembly had already leaked out and some of the men made their way early to the parade grounds, curious about the goings on. There were no secrets in the army. When the all call was finally sounded, almost half of the units were already in place. If the grumbling and complaining that rumbled throughout conversations were an indication of the success of the re-enlistment rally---the numbers were going to be small.

Sam and James walked side by side while Matt and Henry sauntered ahead them. There lingered an uncomfortable silence between them before Sam finally spoke up. "You should go home, James."

James looked at him in surprise. "I can't do that, Sam. I'd be letting Tom down. I've got to finish this business. You should know that better than anyone."

"James, when this thing is over, and I don't have much hope of us coming out on top, it's educated and smart people like you that's gonna bring the South up from the ashes. The Yanks are gonna Lord over us like dictators and you know it. Winners take all the spoils of war; they always do. You going home will assure folks like me and Matt that somebody's still left to look out for what's ours. You end up getting shot by some Yankee bullet is a lot worse than something happening to me."

James was shocked at Sam's words and he grabbed his arm, pulling him to a halt. "That's crap and you know it, Sam. It's going to take all of us and I can't sit around at home tending to a damn farm knowing that Henry and you and Matt are here fighting. Not knowing what's going on. Hell, even my mother's doing her part for the South. And Tom, what about him?"

"Oh, I'm sure he'd agree with me."

James shook his head. "Yeah, maybe so, but he doesn't have any say in this now. You underestimate yourself, Sam. I don't think you have any idea how important *you* are," James lectured, pointing a finger at Sam. "Men like you will get more done in the shadows than anybody like me ever will."

Sam frowned. "Now listen, James, you aren't thinking right. People like me look out for themselves---you think about others before yourself. Always have."

James nodded to the path, indicating he was ready to walk again. "You're selling yourself short, Sam. You look out for me all the time. You're not as sneaky as you think you are. I knew you were following me to Sol's camp this morning. Watching my back. You weren't thinking about yourself and you can't tell me any different."

"All right, then," Sam conceded. "You go home and I will too. We do it together. We both know we can't win this thing anymore."

"I can't, Sam."

"Then I guess we'll both have to stay and try to keep Rupert outta trouble together."

James sighed, "I guess so."

Makeshift podiums had been quickly constructed all in a row before the assembled regiments. Each regiment was ordered to line up behind company colors, with commanders at the front. Speeches were made, designed to rouse the troops into a mass of patriotic hysteria, and thus firing up a burning desire to re-enlist for the good of the Confederacy and the families at home. As spirited as the speeches were, they fell on deaf ears. Infiltrators, who were loyal to the cause and had already signed up for the duration, were ordered, to mingle among the companies and heavily campaign for the cause. Finally, after hours of wrangling and cajoling, the final order was announced.

General Clayton, the commander of the Eighteenth, stood straight as an arrow before his regiment. "Men! Everything that could be said is done. Your own conscience and the future of the South are in *your* hands! If you don't feel it's your duty to stay and fight and defend your own farms and families against the murdering bluebellies, then the rest of us brave men will defend your wives and children for you---to the last man! Now---at my command, I want every man who wants to come with me, to take three steps forward for the South!" He paused for effect and shouted, "Ma-a-r-r-ch!" Less than one fourth of the more than one thousand men assembled stepped forward.

James, Henry, Sam, and Matt were among the few from Company E that took the three steps. They heard the guffaws and comments about being "crazy" and "glory boys" from men all around them.

Seeing the miserable response to their efforts, commanders all down the line dismissed their men, excepting those who'd volunteered to re-up.

"Well---it was more than I thought," commented Henry. "Looks like we're gonna be a bit short handed."

"Oh---don't worry, Henry," said Sam, his mischievous grin returning. "Come tomorrow---all them boys that're calling us crazy will be marchin' right beside you again when we finally head for another skirmish. Wait n' see."

"What makes you so damned smart, Evans? How come you know so much?" Matt snapped.

Sam turned, facing Matt. "You know that hooch we got last

night?"

"How could I forget? My head reminds me ever'time I blink my eyes."

"Well---they got enough rot-gut hid back in the woods to get ever man here drunker than Cooter Brown, fire up their patriotic spirit, and have a full course re-up by the end of the day."

"I'll be damned," Matt laughed. "You believe that, James?"

"Sounds just like the army to me. What better way to get a thousand men to do what you want than to get them drunk."

"Once a year's plenty for me," said Matt.

"Amen," moaned Henry.

True to Sam's prediction, another all call was bugled for assembly at 10:00 A. M. sharp the next morning. All but a few podiums were struck down, and in their places were wooden, twenty-gallon vats of whiskey. Once again, orators spouted forth calls of patriotism for defenders of the South, however, this time the speeches were shorter and whiskey was offered in place of patriotic browbeating. Officers ladled out the stout drink in generous portions, dropping the formality of rank and glad-handing privates as though they were best friends.

"Ain't this about the most disgusting thing you ever seen?" Matt commented. All four were stretched out in the shade at the edge of the woods, watching the fiasco and comedy of command trickery take place before them.

"I love it," laughed Henry. The fun part's gonna be the achin' heads in the morning, and most of them having no idea that they just signed up for three more years of hard labor."

"Payback," said Sam.

As the day dragged on and clear thinking dissolved to the bottom of the whiskey vats---false bravado and wild talk of "whippin' them damn Yanks" became the focus of the day. When the time was right, the command was given for all regiments to get in formation. Those who could stand, did. The rest leaned on their neighbor or just gave up and sat at attention on the ground, that is, those that could still stay awake. Company colors waved proudly in the evening breeze--- identifying each individual company. "Hope we don't get attacked right now," mused James.

"Yeah, be ashamed to waste a good drunk like this and get

shot," laughed Sam.

Once again, General Clayton, like the other commanders, took the podium before his regiment. "On the "Forward March!" men---I want every last one of you to follow your color bearer to glory! Sign up for your country!" In a dramatic move, Clayton reached his right hand across his body, withdrew his saber from its scabbard, and waved it in a circular motion over his head. "For-r-war-r-r-d 'Ar-r-r-ch!" He yelled. Color bearers charged forward with Rebel yells filling the valley. Soldiers who had already re-upped dragged, coaxed, and berated everyone they could, leading them to the paper of their future.

"Don't you just love the army," Sam chuckled. "Another three years of bliss an' hangovers."

"I don't think it's gonna last another three years," James predicted.

"It won't," said Henry. "I got a feelin' it'll be hardly a year."

Chapter Twenty-Two

"LUTHER"

Luther had taken full advantage of the free liquor being served out by the officers at the re-enlistment rally. The more he drank, the more his hatred was fueled for the Durretts and the pack that worshipped their every move. "Damn Durretts," he cursed under his breath as he stumbled his way through the dark moonlit woods. His new-made friends from his current unit decided to stay and finish off the last remnants of the free whiskey.

It was just as well, Luther wanted some time alone to brood and plot out his planned demise for James and Henry. It hadn't been too difficult getting accepted back into the service again. He'd joined a Texas unit that was unaware of his drumming out, and with the shortage of able-bodied men, he was able to sign up without any snags or holdups. In his mind, he had cleverly chosen a unit that was far enough removed from the Alabama regiments, but one that traveled and fought in the same campaigns. "Ol' Luther's smarter than they all think," he laughed, jubilant at his own sinister treachery. His sole purpose was to get vengeance on the Durretts; he didn't give a hoot about the cause for the South or anything else. They could all go to hell as far as he was concerned. "I'll take care o' them boys in my own sweet time, an' do it my way. Just gonna let 'em sweat a little. Let 'em wonder when ol' Luther's gonna do 'em in," he ranted in his drunken stupor.

Then without warning, Luther felt a forearm from behind wrapping around his throat, crushing against his windpipe, jerking him backwards, and cutting off his air. His assailant was shorter than him, forcing his back to be arched in a painful backwards bow. He struggled, grabbing and scratching at the arm that crushed his throat, but to no avail. Frantically, he clawed at the arm, trying to pry it loose, digging in the heels of his boots, trying to knock his attacker off balance. He felt the barrel of a pistol poked violently into his right ear. Next, he heard the unmistakable cocking sound as the hammer clicked into the firing position. He stopped struggling and dropped his hands from the choking restraint at his neck.

"Hey Luther," the voice whispered in his other ear, the lips and breath brushing the skin. "I don't want you to say a single word. Just listen. Now, nod your head once if you can understand me." Luther shakily nodded his head down once. The assailant felt Luther's body tremble as he increased the forearm pressure against his victim's throat.

"It's time for you to go away, Luther. As far away as you can get. Nobody wants you 'round here anymore. We know why you came back. There're bets goin' on 'tween the companies on who's gonna kill you first. Even got some officers to ante up a few bucks. Personally, I bet money that you'd turn-tail yeller and run, an' that's exactly what you're gonna do." He tightened the grip just enough to make Luther cough for his breath. "Look at it this way, Luther---I'm savin' your miserable, stinkin' life. Run. Tonight. Now. If you don't---I promise---you'll never see the sunrise in the morn'. I want your scrawny butt outta the state--- understand?"

Luther nodded his head once. In spite of the earlier warning, a garbled whisper croaked from his throat, "I-I know y-you." The dark figure increased the pressure again on Luther's throat and forced the pistol barrel deeper into his ear. "E-e-e-o-o-o-w-w!" Luther screeched.

"Ya' ain't too smart, Luther! I told you to listen! Not talk!" He withdrew the gun from Luther's ear. "I'm leaving now. Remember, it's up to you to decide if you want to see the sun rise again." Suddenly, Luther's body was twisted around and violently pushed against a tree, his assailant's hand, once again, wrapped across his throat in another death grip. Sam pressed his face nose-to-nose to Luther. "Remember this face, Luther. It's the last one you're gonna see---either now or later. Whichever way you want it is fine with me." Sam quickly withdrew his hand from Luther's neck and disappeared into the night before the troublemaker knew he was gone.

Luther's knees, weakened by fear and quickness of the ordeal, gave way. The rough bark bit through his thin shirt as he slid down the trunk of the tree and plopped to his seat on the ground. His whole body shook uncontrollably and his top lip quivering in a quickened nervous twitches. "Damn Durretts." He sat dead still beneath the tree, trying to control his nerves. At last on shaky, unstable legs, he stood upright, cautiously scoping out the shadows of the surrounding trees, scanning for other unknown assassins. "I didn't wanna be in this chicken outfit anyways." Luther dropped his wrist by his sides and hitched-up his pants. "Damn Durretts."

James, Henry, and Matt decided to build a big campfire and enjoy the crisp night air, instead of staying in the stuffy cabin for the night. All three lay flat on their backs, hands folded behind their heads, staring at the bright, yellow full moon that hung among the millions of stars.

"Hey, James," Matt said, interrupting the silence, "you recken ever'body 'round the world sees the same thing we do? Like the moon, an' that big dipper lookin' thing, an' such?"

"Wherever it's dark, I reckon they do, Matt."

"You know what they say 'bout the moon, don't you?"

"It's not made of cheese, Matt."

"I know that---I ain't stupid you know…looks like it, though."

"Too bad Sam isn't here to see this, he'd like it," James said, ignoring Matt's comment about cheese. "Where'd he go, anyway?

Anybody know?"

"Yeah," Henry said, "said he was gonna collect some bets from some boys over in the Texas camp."

"Nah, just one bet," Matt thought, smiling and staring up at the Swiss cheese moon.

Chapter Twenty-Three

"RUN TO ATLANTA"

MAY 1864
ROCKY FACE MOUNTAIN

The Eighteenth re-enforced its count to a strength of almost five hundred men during the winter and spring of 1864 during their bivouac in Dalton. Most of the new recruits were teenagers who had barely turned the legal age to join the ranks. A combination of enthusiasm and fear of what lay ahead was obvious on their fresh, young faces. In camp, the old timers reveled in telling stories of past battles filled with dark and disturbing humor about fallen comrades, embellishing their tales to the point of disbelief.

"Is that true?" One scared recruit asked after hearing one

particularly gruesome story about a soldier being speared by a shattered tree branch.

"We don't tell lies 'bout such things here, boy," the grizzled vet explained as he spat a stream of tobacco juice at the boy's shoes. "It's the gospel."

Matt and James strolled by casually as men from their unit expounded tales of war to their fresh-faced captive audiences. Matt shook his head as he heard snatches of gross exaggerations. "I hope these young whipper-snappers can shoot an' keep up with us when the action starts up again."

"It's a waste," James stated. "They're scared---just like we were. You can see it in their eyes. They'll be the first to run when the pressure's on and we'll be left high n' dry."

"Well, least ways we got some warm bodies 'round us."

Minor skirmishes had started again after winter broke and spring began to thaw the snow and nerves of winter camp. "Just like a bear comin' outta hibernation---he's just a little testy after being in a cave for so long and he wants to take it out on the first thing he sees," Sam said as he cleaned his new Springfield rifle.

Letters

The Dalton troops finally struck camp at the beginning of spring and moved north, taking up positions back close to Chattanooga at Rocky Face Mountain. The Confederate army had secured the south side of the mountain and the territory beyond. The Eighteenth had the plum and advantageous assignment at the very summit of Rocky Face. Below them was the Union Army, peacefully preparing for the day's fortunes. For James, the scene was reminiscent of last New Year's and brought back memories he'd buried inside for the past few months. Lookout Mountain was on the horizon only a few miles away; it was strange seeing a place that just a few months earlier had been the scene of death and mayhem. Never-ending explosions walking up the mountain. Tom's capture. Sam killing the Yank. Now, it all looked so peaceful and untouched, except for the scars of the wooded banks shattered by past cannon fire.

Henry looked out over the valley below and a ripple of fear shuttered through his body, unexpectedly. "You know, James---I'd kinda put this nervous feeling outta my mind over the past winter. That knot that sticks in the pit of your stomach. You know? I was anxious for action while we were cooped up in that damn cabin, but I ain't so sure now. That musky old cabin sounds mighty good right now."

"I don't think you're going to have much time to ponder on fond memories, Henry. I'm ready now for whatever comes our way. I have a feeling this'll all be over soon, you'll see."

"At least we got our new Springfields, now. I'm kinda ready to test it out---like having a new toy."

"See, all you gotta do is shoot something, Henry, and you'll feel better."

Matt and Sam came up from behind, red-faced and out of breathe. "O-o-u whe-e-e-e!" Matt crooned in the background. "We about to have some fun! Peace in the valley is gonna take on a whole new meanin' for them Yanks down yonder!"

Henry turned to Sam, a confused expression on his face. "What the hell is he blabbering 'bout now, Sam?"

Sam spoke up, "He's right! Look behind me---we gotta surprise for them blueboys."

James and Henry checked back down the hill and saw about twenty men with ropes, pushing and pulling to all get-out, maneuvering a cannon up the wooded and rocky trail of the mountain.

Matt grinned. "Sam talked that ol' crusty Tarrant into puttin' one of his precious cannons on the hill, so's we could blast the hell outta them Yanks whilst they're cooking breakfast and taking it easy!"

"What in tarnation is this?" Asked Colonel Hunley when he heard all the commotion stirring around the side of the hill.

A sergeant attached to the artillery division scuttled his way up the rugged terrain ahead of the cannon and presented himself, sufficiently winded, to Colonel Hunley. "Sir! Compliments of Colonel Tarrant!" The sergeant dropped his salute, still trying to catch his breath. "The Colonel figger'd you could use a little extra firepower to go along with them new Springfields ya'll got this month."

Hunley grinned ear to ear and bowed, doffing his Stetson. "My compliments to the Colonel, Sergeant. Tell him I'll return the favor by trying to keep those nasty bluebellies away from him."

"I'm sure he'd 'preciate it, sir. He's leaving some of his best boys to man it for you, sir. They's the second best artillery squad in Colonel Tarrant's company. Sergeant Riley's in charge, Sir."

Hunley smiled a knowing grin, "And who, am I to suppose, to

be the number one artillery man under the Colonel?"

"Well---me, of course, sir!"

"Very well, Sergeant. Good luck to you and God speed."

"Right, sir!" The sergeant turned on his heels and started his way back down the hill.

"Henry! James! Gather up some boys and help these hard working gents position our new toy so's it can do the maximum damage! Let's wake 'em up, gentleman!"

The boys from Company E helped maneuver the cannon at the very crest of the summit of Rocky Face, giving it a complete, unobstructed target of the Union camps below.

"Sergeant Riley!" Colonel Hunley called to the artillery sergeant manning the gun. "Am I to understand that you're the second best artillery sergeant under Colonel Tarrant's command?"

Riley frowned and bristled at the condemning words. "Sir! You must've been under the spell of that evil Sergeant Boruk! Ever'body knows he couldn't hit the broad side of a barn, Sir!" He retorted with a correct, crisp salute to the Colonel.

Hunley smiled. "That's what I want to hear, Sergeant Riley.

Now, point that big muzzle of a cannon at something and raise some hell!" He turned to his company, "Eighteenth! Form your ranks along the crest line and lay a volley of hell like they've never seen before upon their souls! Let 'em know we've returned!"

James and the boys looked down into the valley as the trails of smoke from hundreds of campfires spiraled lazily toward the clouds. Infantry and cavalry milled around like ants on the move, taking care of their daily routines and chores, totally being unaware of the impending doom about to crash down upon them.

"Kinda peaceful, ain't it Sam?" Matt crooned. "Too bad we're about to knock holy hell outta 'em!"

"Yep," Sam laughed, "a dirty shame."

After the artillery piece was in proper placement, Riley ordered it to be loaded, eye-balled his target, and ordered brisk instructions for adjustments. Once satisfied, he nodded at his men and held his arm high. Confederate eyes, up and down the line, watched his every move. "Fire!" He shouted at the top of his lungs. A Rebel yell pierced the clouds as the first shot scored a direct hit in the dead center of the Yankee encampment. Past defeats died from memories as blue dots scattered in all directions seeking cover from the deadly and unexpected barrage. With precision mechanics, the cannon masters reloaded, adjusted their aim again, and fired another round into the heart of the camp.

Hunley strutted among his men, wishing he had a full complement of artillery to shatter the ranks of the Union forces below, but if one gun were all he could attain, then he'd make due. Never look a gift-horse in the mouth, he thought. Then, raising his saber overhead, he shouted, "Show 'em how a Springfield works, boys! Lay down fire at will and give 'em hell!" The Colonel observed the valley below and reveled in pleasure as the explosions and rapid fire from the Springfields created chaos below and Yankee soldiers scattered in all directions, with mayhem rendering control, men dropping one after the other, trying desperately to dodge the deadly fireballs from above. This was exactly what his men needed after the humiliating defeat in the same spot just months earlier.

"Now, I can fight a war like this!" Sam yelled above the reports of the new rifles. The boys from Company E, up and down the line, picked off blue uniforms like contestants at a turkey shoot and rejuvenated vigor and enthusiasm consumed the whole regiment; hope had resurfaced once again.

James eye-balled some of the new recruits, watching them waste valuable ammunition as they fired haphazardly, caught up in the moment, adrenalin controlling conflicting emotions. "Look at those green recruits, Henry. They're probably not hitting half of what they're aiming at. If they can't hit anything when they've got a stationary target and out of the way of harm, what're they gonna do when the Yanks start shooting back?"

Henry reloaded quickly, keeping his eyes focused down below, and snapped, "Quit worrin' about them boys now, James, for Pete's sake. Just take care of your own targets and we'll worry about them later!"

As the morning droned on, the lone cannon on loan from Colonel Tarrant and the sharpshooters, unfortunately, were not enough to keep the Union forces in check for more than an hour. Yankee cannons reorganized their ranks and set loose with their own return barrage to the top of the mountain, zeroing in on the summit of Rocky Face and forcing the Eighteenth to take cover behind the crest of the mountain. "There they go again," yelled Sam, "getting all peevish and stirred up just because we're interrupting their breakfast!"

The Eighteenth watched as explosions from twenty-plus cannons stair-stepped their way up the hill, just as they did on Lookout Mountain, creating huge eruptions of dirt that filled the air as each man saw death climbing his way. Hunley had seen enough. The safety of his men was paramount over his reinjured pride. "Disperse and take flanking position left and right! Behind the hill! Now!" He ordered.

"Here we go again! Matt sputtered in anger. "Fall back! Fall back! What the hell's wrong with *Charge*?"

"Shuddup, Rupert! An' move or we gonna be looking for pieces of you all over the side of the hill!" Sam shouted above the sounds of nearing explosions. "We ain't givin' nuthing up---we're just adjusting our advantages!"

"How come we're always adjusting backwards?"

Another hour of relentless, ear-shattering fire exchanged between the two sides, while Company E held to their flank positions and rained down more deadly volleys of accurate, pinpoint fire, slicing up Yankee infantry before their artillery units was able re-position to the flanking targets. Back and forth, from both armies, the volleys of fire persisted, cannons against rifles. Rebels taking advantage of the high position; the Yanks dominating with superior cannon fire from below; neither side wanting to give or concede an inch, until finally, as the noon hour approached and the sun glared brightly from the center of the domed sky, an uncanny and simultaneous silence roared throughout the valley. Cannons and rifles stopped together. No ground gained, none lost.

The clicks of soldiers reloading their rifles, canteens clanking, and finally a chance to speak without shouting, rolled up and down the ranks. James stood his rifle between his knees as his back pressed against the hill, savoring the silence of cannons below. "It's strange how that happens, isn't it?" James whispered. "It's almost as though warriors have an extra sense that tells them it's time to stop. You ever noticed that, Henry?"

Henry laid back, stretching his legs and closing his eyes, savoring the quiet in his own way. "There're things that happen in war that can't always be explained, I guess. No sense or rhyme."

James closed his own eyes. "Yeah, I know. Good things happen to bad people, bad things happen to good people. Enemies stop firing at the same time."

Henry turned on his stomach, resting his chin on his arm as he stared down below into the valley, finally wiping the sweat from his brow. "Some people have premonitions they never had before," he whispers under his breath.

Surprisingly, the Eighteenth was able to hold its position on Rocky Face Mountain for a week before the tide of the engagement gradually turned against them. The Union commander in charge of the Federal forces, General Sherman, a brilliant and aggressive military tactician, knew a frontal attack against the rebel sharpshooters would be suicidal and costly in lives. But, he also knew that he had the advantage of superior manpower. When the Union general made his move, the Eighteenth observed masses of federal troops dispersed by the thousands, to the left and right flanks of Rocky Face, in an attempt to cut them off from the main body of their own troops in the rear to the south. The gray picket lines and the forces holding the mountain held no chance against the growing numbers of Union infantry that could overrun their tenuous positions.

"Hunley!" General Clayton shouted, getting his young Colonel's attention. "Prepare to evacuate the scene---now! Our picket lines along the base are falling like a house of cards! That clever devil Sherman's flanking us on both sides, and if we don't get the hell off this hill, we'll be spending the summer in a Yankee prison! Go!"

Hunley barked off the retreat orders to his subordinates, frustration in his voice. "Down the hill boys!" He shouted, making his way along the gray line. "We'll return to fight another day!"

Sergeant Riley's men were packing as much ammunition as they could on the pack mules when Hunley caught his attention amongst the mayhem of retreat. "Sergeant Riley, I'm afraid you'll have to leave your cannon and ammunition behind. There's no time to dally here. Set explosives and blow it to pieces. It's done its duty and we certainly don't want to leave it for our bluebelly friends to turn on us."

"Yes sir!" Riley nodded, recognizing the urgency of the situation and immediately instructing his men to prepare the charges. "Evacuate your men, Colonel! We'll blow her when you're ready!"

"Well, Henry---shall we?" James said theatrically, sweeping his arm in the direction of the bottom of the mountain. "We've done this before."

May through June of 1864, the Eighteenth and accompanying regiments retreated ever more south, constantly driven back by the overwhelming numbers of the Union Army commanded by General Sherman. Confederate forces threw up hastily built defensive breastworks, whenever possible along the way, to repulse the ever advancing army. In spite of their superior numbers, the Yanks incurred heavier losses than the Confederate forces due to attacking defensive positions in open ground; but, Sherman's constant flanking strategy forced the Rebels to pull up stakes and fall back each time. Straight through the heart of Georgia, they were driven until, eventually; their final stand was made in Atlanta. Though civilians and army made the greatest and bravest efforts alike, the great city fell to Sherman's forces with the Confederate army retreating again in haste. Losing Atlanta was a fatal blow to Southern pride and brought the realization to heart that the South was clinging to the edge of the final abyss of all out defeat.

Letters

Chapter Twenty-Four

"TRUE COLORS"
HARRY

NOVEMBER 1864
LOUISIANA

A sharp shiver bolted up Harry's spine as he sloshed on patrol through the murky, snake infested Louisiana swamp. It wasn't the cold that made him shiver---it was fear. He was out of his element and he didn't like it one bit. The night was surreal, as scattered rays from a full moon filtered through moss-covered trees. The forest looked like an army of cloaked witches descending on unsuspecting travelers who trespassed through their territory. Every witch provided protective cover for potential, deadly assassins.

His unit had been ordered to scout the swamps for any "night crawlers," Rebel sharpshooters attempting to infiltrate the scattered Union picket lines. The usual defenses of breastworks and dugouts were impossible because of the watery and soggy terrain. The 96th was fighting in the Southerners' own backyard and were getting picked apart a little bit at a time. There were no open fields to crush the enemy by sheer force of numbers. The sniper unit was given scouting duties since the usual covert tactics provided by high ground was eliminated. Close quarter fighting and murderous ambushes were the order of the day, hit and run tactics that kept Union forces on edge and unprepared. This was warfare by deception, and the Yanks were untrained and confused about such encounters.

"Harry," Mac called in a barely audible whisper, "I can't see a damn thing out here 'cept ghosts and goblins."

"Shuddup Mac, bad enough to be sloshin' in this damn soup with snakes an' who knows what---don't need you announcing our positions," Harry reprimanded. He despised relying on others for his safety. He was accountable only to himself. Six men sloshing laboriously through soggy, mud-sucking swampland sounded like a marching band on parade. If Harry were alone, he'd be invisible.

Suddenly, the night came alive as musket flints ignited the murky darkness like firecrackers, and long narrow sparks flew from rifle barrels illuminating the woods like a Fourth of July celebration. Minie balls zinged through the air smacking into trees like a sledgehammer against a stump.

Thumpf. "Ug-g-g..." Someone was hit. Someone close to Harry. Ruben Mendoza, maybe? Suspecting it was him, Harry heard the final breath exiting his lungs.

"Ambush!" Somebody screamed.

"Take cover!" Another yelled.

Moonbeams filtered through just enough for Harry to see shadows diving for cover. He jumped belly first in the soggy muck, landing on his elbows so as to keep his Sharps dry and free of mud.

"Harry! Where are ya', Harry?" Mac called, taking cover behind a tree stump that gave him scant protection from the ambush.

Harry stayed quiet, not giving away his position.

"Aim at their sparks when they fire," ordered Sergeant Bowie quietly to the man the next tree over. Pass it down!"

Harry crawled and scooted backwards from his original

position, watching shadows on the perimeter close in on his trapped mates, cutting off all possibilities of escape for the hapless sniper unit. He didn't care. He was looking out for himself. Fear cramped his stomach muscles again. He heard his comrades screaming out directions and cautions. "Over there Amos! To your right! Shoot an' move, boys! Don't give 'em a target!"

Completely covered in muck and slime, Harry found a tree, pressing his back against it, his knees scrunched up to his chin, keeping his Sharps between his knees, barrel pointing upward to the clear, starry sky. His body shivered and cramped uncontrollably. His eyes bulged with fear, staring straight ahead at eerie shadows moving in zigzags through the woods. Harry started wetting his pants, losing complete control of his bladder. He didn't try to stop. He didn't want to. He had managed to get far enough back to watch the skirmish, as though viewing a play on stage at the Community Center back home, but he was close enough to feel the vibrations of the attack that shattered his nerves. His unit was trapped, but he was outside the circle of sharpshooters. He didn't want to die. He didn't want to face the bullets. He wanted to be the unseen assassin. No danger from exposure. No one shooting back.

As suddenly as it began, the shooting stopped. Silence overtook the swamp. Even the insects and birds and frogs silenced their calls. Seconds ticked off like hours. Damage inflicted to blue and gray alike. Fearful, searching eyes darting from all quarters, waiting for the next shot. The Rebel's advantage was gone and both sides were on equal, uneasy terms.

"Go home, Yanks!" A mocking voice called from the night. "Ya'll only die if'n ya' come ahead!"

Harry's body began to calm in the silence. Raw, sensitive nerves began to desensitize. Control gradually returned. Nobody told him what to do. He shook off the personal humiliation of wetting himself---no one would know. Harry was back in his element. He lifted himself from the tree and slowly crawled to his left, circling behind the voices of the taunting Rebel ambushers.

After a few more moments of deadly quiet, Bowie called across the swamp waters, "We're backin' off now, Reb!" Then, he lowered his voice, "Slow an' easy boys, don't turn your backs," he cautioned quietly, "just back away and keep your eyes open." Four of the five remaining members of the sniper unit stealthily backed away, using the trees for cover, crouching low, getting ready for a counter attack.

Harry continued his way on undetected, circling left, watching his mates passing by him on their retreat. Finally stopping, he hid behind a tree, slowly cocked the hammer on his Sharps and waited. Sure enough, after only minutes, he saw the shadows and heard sloshing feet as the Rebs stalked his retreating unit.

"Creatures of habit," he thought to himself. He chose his target, waiting patiently, the moonlight providing for a clear shot. He had his target and took a bead on approaching figure. Slowly, he squeezed the trigger. "Bang!" His shot shattered the silence. Birds immediately took flight from their perches in the trees.

"Ug-g-g!" The sound involuntarily gasped through the victim's lips as the bullet entered the side of his head.

"Forty-nine," Harry whispered. He crouched, still moving left, circling behind his prey. Predicting their next move. The old familiar juices of the hunter versus the prey had returned. And, it felt good.

"Jessie! That you? Ya' okay?" A shaken Rebel voice called

out to his friend. He got no answer.

"Fifty," Harry whispered when he squeezed the trigger again. Jessie's friend joined his buddy face-down in the murky waters.

The sniper unit hit the soggy ground as soon as they heard the first shot, but they recognized the report of Harry's Sharps, distinguishing it from the outdated flintlocks of the Rebel ambushers.

"Harry!" Mac whispered. "You ruthless sum'bitch," he smirked.

"Stay your spots, boys. Don't move," Bowie ordered. "One of us is out there."

Harry continued to flank the Rebs as they retreated helter-skelter, run and hide maneuvers, trying to evade their unseen assassin. He remained invisible. He stood back against a tree, facing opposite the enemy. "You Rebs can go home now!" He called out. "We're done here tonight!" Crouching low, he moved silently tree-to-tree--- back to his own unit. He'd concealed his act of cowardice. "I owe nobody nothing, now," he thought.

"O-o-o-o Whee-e-e-e! Did you see my boy, Harry, out there!" Mac marveled as the unit huddled around the roaring fire back at camp, shaking off the cold and rubbing out the cramps from their aching limbs.

"We thought you was dead for sure, Harry. You never called out," Boris Kawalski, a big, over muscled killer from Poland declared. "We saw Ruben go down and figured you to be swimming with the fishes."

"Nope," Harry answered. "Just stayed low. That's all."

"Tell you what," giggled Mac, "I damn near peed my pants laughin' when ol' Harry said, "You Rebs can go home now!" You're sum'thin else, Harry."

"Yeah, Mac. Sum'thin else," Harry said.

The Ninety-sixth encountered some it's most fierce and costly campaigns fighting against Confederate troops as they continued their drive across the Southerners' home turf. Finally, at the end of November, Union forces turned eastward along the coast of the Gulf of Mexico.

During a lull in the action, Harry and Mac were alone in camp, sitting sat cross-legged in front of their tents, cleaning their rifles, when a Lieutenant Ramsey, an infantry officer, rode into their territory. Ramsey leaned forward on his mount, resting his forearms on the saddle horn. "Harry. Mac. Sergeant Bowie around?" He asked, checking out the deserted campsite.

Harry shook his head. "Nope. He's at the commissary--- should be back soon."

"Nope. Ain't here," Mac mimicked.

Ramsey watched the two as they continued breaking down their weapons in smooth, quick, and effortless motions, their eyes on him at the same time. He admired their skills, but their mannerisms and lifeless eyes made him uneasy, just like they did anybody else that was around them.

"What's going on, Lieutenant?" Harry asked, unafraid to question a superior.

Ramsey felt compelled to answer, "We're moving out, Harry."

"I hope it's drier than this cesspool. My feet ain't been dry for a month," he complained.

"It is, but it's not gonna be any easier goings, though. You can count on that. The Rebs know their losing and they're gonna be fighting tooth an' toenail to the last man before they give an inch. Just like a cornered wildcat."

"Where to?" Harry asked.

"Our final objective is Mobile, Alabama. There's a major push that way from the remaining forces here in the South. We're gonna end this mess once and for all. We plan to be there by February if it all works out right. We should have damn near fifty to sixty thousand troops there for the final push."

"Sounds good to me, Lieutenant. I ain't never been to Mobile before," Harry said with a smile, jacking a cartridge into his Sharps' chamber.

Chapter Twenty-Five

"FALLEN SON"

NOVEMBER 30, 1864
FRANKLIN, TENNESSEE

After the retreat from Atlanta, the Eighteenth was given orders to return up north to Tennessee, acting as a reserve unit for the Army of Tennessee, who was in a fight for survival to route the Yanks from Franklin and Nashville. The two cities were vital as future pipelines of supplies for the Confederate Army since the state of Georgia had succumbed to Sherman's march to the sea. Most of the Southern forces were surviving on whatever food and supplies could be foraged and scavenged from the countryside and desecrated farms. The folks at home had little more food and the basics of day to day survival than the army and were unable to send the valuable care packages to fighting relatives, as they had at the beginning of the war.

What was left of James's brigade and Company E was perched high on a hill, observing the Army of Tennessee as they charged the Yankee defenses of Franklin. Two opposing lines, stretched for at least a mile, throwing one vicious volley of rifle fire after another at each other; supporting artillery blew showers of dirt and human limbs skyward, as men charged and defenses held.

"Je-e-zus, James! You've ever seen anything like this before?" Matt exclaimed, watching the blue and gray lines of combatants engaged in a desperate fight in the lower valley.

"No, I haven't. I think it's scarier watching a fight like this, out of the fray, than being down in the trenches in the middle of it. I know what's going through the minds of every man down there. So do you. Heart pumping like crazy. Eyes darting every which way. Wondering if the next volley is your ticket to Saint Peter's Gate. It's hard to sit here and watch men die."

Sam lay next to James, listening to him talk as he observed the same deadly mayhem in the valley. He loved listening to James philosophize, even in such a disturbing time as this. James had a way of feeling something for any man, no matter what color the uniform. He spoke of compassion for all men, not just Southerners. And, Sam couldn't even recall James speaking out against the coloreds. Things were just the way they were, that's all. James had allowed him to read some of the letters he'd written home; they contained no bitterness or resentful spite, only concern for his family and comrades in arms. Most men complained of the bad conditions, lack of food and clothing, and sorry officers, but not James. He played the cards he was dealt and didn't complain. Sam preferred stacking the deck in his own favor. "So James, would you rather be down there fightin' or up here watchin'?" Sam asked, trying to give James a "damned if you do, damned if you don't" question.

He turned and looked at Sam with his knowing eyes and crooked smile, "I'd rather be home."

James and the boys had watched the carnage fly since noon that day, and now, as dusk began to fall, it appeared the Rebel forces were finally gaining ground. "Damn, fellas," Henry spoke, after he aimed a stream of tobacco spit at Matt's shoes, "I think them boys is gonna go at it all night. You ever seen 'em do full scale night fighting before, Sam? Like this? I ain't ever seen it."

"Nah, never have---don't make much sense to shoot at something you can't see cause of the dark."

"Just watch and be glad you're not in it. I don't think I could handle a nighttime fight like this," James added.

Daylight gradually faded, giving way to a cloak of darkness; gunfire died away to isolated pockets, each soldier vying to get in the last shot. Then, the night exploded again from a fierce barrage of artillery fire from the Confederate artillery line; evidently wise commanders decided not to give up their forces' momentum to the darkness. In perfect sequence, the long line of rebel cannons sparked their fuses, setting off fireballs that spelled death for the poor souls at the other end.

"Damn that's beautiful," whispered Sam, in awe of the continuous and deadly light show. "Reminds me of Tuscaloosa on New Year's Eve." The four of them watched, caught up in their own private thoughts. Finally, by ten o'clock that evening, the Yanks showed little or no resistance against the overpowering Rebel forces, quickly evacuating the besieged city and finally retreated under the cover of darkness.

At dawn, the next morning, Colonel Hunley made his rounds through his beleaguered troops, his heart sickened, as he observed the barely two-hundred remaining brave souls that had been part of the original 800, three years earlier. Now, they looked like walking death. The forced marches for hundreds of miles and constant fighting for most of three years had taken its toll. They were living pretty much off what they could scrounge from the countryside. Most of them were barefooted and wore threadbare clothes because the army had nothing left to give them. His men had been reduced to being grave robbers, picking through the bodies of fallen soldiers, plucking shoes and coats from the lifeless corpses. Survival overruled moral judgment. Every one of his men had a heart the size of a lion's, and he was proud to serve as their commander. Too proud to quit; too stubborn to die.

"Alright boys!" Hunley announced, putting on an enthusiastic bravado he didn't feel. "Those Tennessee boys have done all the hard work for you. Now we're gonna Tennessee Waltz into town and mop up! Form up and look sharp!"

Matt gathered up his meager belongings and dusted the dirt from the seat of his baggy britches. "Well---least ways we're going *into* town instead of runnin' *outta* it," he grumbled.

The advancement to town that early morning turned out to be a devastating experience for the men of the Eighteenth. They sidestepped and dodged around the dead and wounded bodies of Yanks and Rebels alike, making their way through the recent battleground. Moans and cries for "Mama" echoed all around them from the survivors holding on to a thin slip of life. James scanned the bloody scene; a chill ran through his body, causing him to shiver from head to toe. "This is like something out of an Edgar Allen Poe story," he commented.

"Nobody could tell a story like this," Matt whispered. "Who's Poe?"

"Never mind." James didn't feel like playing mind games with Matt right now, not in the midst of all this carnage.

The crisp, clearing morning stood in deep contrast to the bloody earth. However, not even the grotesque killing field prepared the Rebs for the grisly sights that lay ahead.   Haltingly, the men approached the breach on one of the deserted Union breastworks, high mounds of dirt engineered to stop the enemy's assault.

"My God!" Henry gasped, being the first to reach the crest of mound. Muttered sounds of disgust and shock came from the mouths of even the most hardened veterans as they viewed the ghastly sight. Body limbs and mangled, contorted torsos of dead Union soldiers by the thousands were stacked at least five deep---one on top of the other. A manmade work of art designed to fend-off attacks was now a ready-made grave for the masses.

"My God," James repeated, "there're thousands of them. How can we do this to each other?" He felt bile from the hardtack he had eaten earlier rise to his throat. He tensed his throat and stomach muscles, fighting the urge to throw up. He wished Tom were here. He'd know what to say, but then he thought better of it. No. He changed his mind. He was glad Tom wasn't here to see this human travesty. Some things you can't or shouldn't share with others.

Sam reached over and pulled James away from the scene by the elbow. "This way, James. Let's go up this road into town. Hey,

Henry! Matt! This way!" He called out, waving for the boys to follow him.

"What're we gonna tell the folks back home about this, Sam? How can we even explain it? They can't understand or comprehend what we've just seen," James moaned.

"We don't tell 'em, James. Like you said, they'd never understand it. This is something we'll have to carry to the grave on our own. Come on, it'll be better in town."

The four of them walked ahead slowly, dazed and unsure about anything anymore.

If the Eighteenth was expecting a hero's welcome when they marched victorious through the streets of Franklin, they were disappointed. The townspeople seemed as dazed and confused as some of their liberators. Crowds of civilians rushed forward to groups of soldiers, asking if they knew their sons, fathers, or brothers.

"What's your unit?" "Do you know Louis Countess?"

"Are there any Texas companies here?"

There were pleas for food as well. "The Yanks robbed us blind---took our food and anything that wasn't nailed down!"

"Sum'bitches took all my chickens an' killed my dog!"

"Can you spare some food?"

The boys kept moving on, either nodding or shaking their heads in acknowledgement to the civilian peas. They didn't have the words to respond.

"Hell---I thought we had it bad. Look how scared these people are," Matt commented.

"Wouldn't you be scared if your whole town was taken over by a bunch of Yanks," Sam answered. "Them boys weren't here for no tea party, you know."

They treaded slowly down the middle of a dusty neighborhood street strewn with debris. Magnificent two story homes lined each side; homes, that in the past, had dignified the street with manicured lawns and picket fences, now stood sadly with broken windows, brick walls riddled with bullet holes, and fences ravaged for firewood. James saw Colonel Hunley waving his way as he stepped from the porch of one of the fine homes. "James!" Hunley called. "You boys come over here. I need your help."

They made their way across the overgrown lawn to see

Letters

Colonel Hunley at the bottom of the porch steps. Keeping them out of earshot of the occupants of the house, Hunley said in a low voice, "The lady of the house is a Mrs. Hasson, and she's in a bad way. I need the four of you to keep guard and make sure she's not harassed or bothered by any riff-raff that's running around here, until I get back. Her husband was killed at Chickamauga, and she has a son serving on General Cleburn's staff. I just hope he didn't come to the same fate as the general."

"Cleburn took a bullet charging the breastworks yesterday, didn't he? That's what I heard," Henry commented.

Hunley nodded. "Yeah, damned shame too. He always insisted on leading his men into battle himself. Commendable, but not a very smart thing for a general to do. That's why they have majors and colonels. We tried to convince him he was more valuable alive than dead, but he wouldn't listen."

"Good to know generals can stop a bullet too," Matt smirked. "No disrespect intended, sir."

"Yeah, but it's always the wrong general," Sam added.

"Where are you off to, Colonel?" James asked.

"To look for her son, but I don't have much hope of finding him alive. He'd already be here with his mother if he were. Come on, I'll introduce you, then you boys stay out front and make sure nobody bothers her."

"You know her personally, Colonel?" Sam asked.

"Yeah, I was with Jack, her husband, at Chickamauga when he took a bullet in the chest." Hunley left them on the porch, went back into the house, and then brought Mrs. Hasson outside. James could tell she was a lady of stature and pride, but, at this moment, all her defenses were down. Her face and swollen red eyes told the whole story. Vulnerable, teetering on the edge of total despair. She clutched a dainty lace handkerchief in both hands, wringing it back and forth to calm her anxiety.

The Colonel held his wide-brimmed hat in his hands, nervously sliding it around in a circular motion as he faced her. He leaned over, speaking softly to the emotionally spent woman, trying to ease her pain. "Mrs. Hasson, these are some of my finest men---I'd trust them with my own life. That's why I'm leaving them with you. No harm will come to you while I'm looking for your son." Hunley attempted a smile, but it was weak. "I'm sure he's barking out orders to some poor private or non-com, Ma'am."

Mrs. Hasson looked up into Hunley's eyes. "Colonel Hunley---I appreciate your kindness and I know you're trying to give me hope about my son. However, if you had just rescued your mother's hometown from a bunch of murderous, low-class criminals---wouldn't you rush to her house to check on her safety?" Her voice was surprisingly strong and firm. Her frail, outward appearance masked the strong inner strength of the petite Confederate widow.

Hunley stopped fidgeting with his hat, stepped backwards a pace, and stood up straight. "Yes m'am I would, but I'm also a soldier, and I serve for my commander's pleasure. If it were his desire for me to wait---I would."

A sad smile creased her set lips as she raised her hand gently and affectionately patted Hunley's rough, whiskered face. "Colonel, we both know there's not a Southern gentleman officer alive that would deprive a son from seeing his mother in a case like this."

Hunley returned a slight smile, "Yes m'am, I know." He put on his hat, pulling the brim low over his brow and turned to James.

"Watch after this fine lady until my return."

Less than an hour later, James spotted Sol Thompson and Colonel Hunley carrying a stretcher between them. A young man with a bloody, bandaged head lay limp on his back, one arm across his stomach, the other hanging loosely off the side.

James alerted the others, "Look boys, the Colonel's back, ya'll help them with the stretcher and I'll get Mrs. Hasson." Even before he approached the front door, James dreaded this moment. The boy appeared to be alive, but he looked none too good. Reluctantly, he knocked on the front door. "Mrs. Hasson! Colonel Hunley's back and it appears he has your son! He's wounded, but looks to be alive!" He called through the door.

Almost immediately, Mrs. Hasson opened the door, her face optimistic and hopeful. "Where? Where are they?" She cried, rushing through the doorway and onto the porch.

Hunley and Thompson carried her son up the front walk, and she ran to meet them. "My son, my baby boy!" She cried, tears flowing freely down her cheeks as her fingers brushed his cheeks. "Is he ok? Is it serious?"

Letters

"Don't know, ma'am," Sol responded. "Dr. Hamilton's on his way now, but I'm afraid he's hurt pretty bad."

"Take him inside---the living room---I'll tend to him there until the doctor arrives," she instructed. She stroked her son's head, pushing back the long strands of hair that hung limp over the bandages. "You're home now, James. You're with Mama, now," she consoled quietly.

Sam and Matt looked over at James when she mentioned the young officer's name. Henry's color turned pale and he stepped away from the stretcher. Matt was the only one who noticed Henry's discomfort.

"I'll take that for you, Colonel," Sam said, offering to take his commander's end of the stretcher.

"I've got it, Sam. I brought him this far."

Hunley and Thompson took young Hasson into the house, and the boys stayed on the porch. "He looks bad," Sam observed. "I couldn't even tell if he were breathing or not. I feel sorry for that Mrs. Hasson. She's a fine lady."

"He was," answered Matt, "I saw his chest risin' and fallin'."

After a few minutes, the door opened and Sol came out alone. "Hey boys, nasty bit of business, huh?"

"How'd you end up with the boy, Sol?" James asked.

"Actually---I was looking for you boys, and I saw the Colonel checking Reb bodies back down by the breastworks. Didn't know what he's doing, so I asked him. He told me what he's doing so I asked him---"

"Dammit, Sol!" Matt interrupted in exasperation. "We just wanna know how you found the boy! Not the history of the damn war!"

Sol looked over at James and winked. "Well now---I was just getting to that part when you interrupted me, Rupert. Anyways, Colonel and me found him not fifty yards from here. Don't think he's got much chance though. Nasty head wound he's got."

Later on, Colonel Hunley came through the door, hat in hand. "You boys're staying here tonight," he ordered. "Long as we're in Franklin, your job is to stay with Mrs. Hasson. I've other duties to attend to now. And, James---she wants to see you---inside."

James looked up, surprised. "W-why? What does she want

with *me*?"

"Don't know. But, whatever that lady wants, you do it."

"How's the boy?"

Hunley's lips tightened and he shook his head. "We don't need Doc Hamilton anymore. He passed on thirty minutes ago."

There was a collective moan among the men.

The Colonel nodded his head at the door. "Go James, she's upstairs, first room on the right as you go down the hallway. I'll make sure the rest of you get some food and supplies sent your way. Don't want you bothering Mrs. Hasson for such."

In spite of the turmoil and occupation by the Union forces, the house was clean, nothing was out of place. For the life of him, James couldn't help but wonder why she wanted to see him, of all people.

The ceilings throughout the home were tall and cavernous; the air was cool; the rooms were dark; he felt like he was walking in a surreal dream. As he entered the death room, he saw Mrs. Hasson and her son. The scene struck him like something from a painting, another part of the dream. She sat straight, rigid, and proper in a stiff-backed wooden chair beside the bed where her son laid; her hands were folded in her lap as she smiled at her son's still and lifeless body. He almost didn't recognize the young officer as he laid peacefully by his mother's side. The grime and blood had been bathed away, hair neat and combed straight back from his face now, and the bulky, bloody bandage had been removed and replaced with a small clean cloth that covered the fatal wound at the hairline. James noticed an empty chair placed next to Mrs. Hasson.

"You wanted to see me, ma'am?" James asked hesitantly, nervously griping his hat in hand.

"He's a handsome man, isn't he, James?"

"Yes ma'am, he is."

"Did you know him?"

"I saw him from time to time, ma'am. I know he was well liked---and that speaks highly for an officer---if you know what I mean, ma'am."

She smiled, "I do young man, indeed I do. I think you and my James probably had a lot in common. I've been watching you---you've got some of the same mannerisms, you've certainly had a good upbringing. You're well-spoken and don't sound like someone fresh off the farm---not that there's anything wrong being a farmer."

"I understand, ma'am."

Mrs. Hasson patted the seat of the empty chair next to her. "James, will you allow me to hold your hand for just a moment? Then, I'd like to be alone with my son."

"It'd be my honor, ma'am. You know, you remind me some of my own mother."

She moved her head slightly and smiled lightly at James. "Times like these---I'm soldiers' mama, I guess. You're all my sons, now."

James stepped over to sit in the empty chair next to Mrs. Hasson and reached over and clasped the trembling hand in her lap.

/

Chapter Twenty-Six

"THE COLORED BRIGADE"

DECEMBER 15, 1864
NASHVILLE, TENNESSEE

The stay in Franklin was short and James was glad of it. The Eighteenth got orders the next morning to prepare for their march to Nashville. He'd spent about an hour with Mrs. Hasson, listening to her reminisce about her lost son and husband. She finally released James's hand, gave him a light kiss on the cheek, and returned to her silent vigil over her son's body. None of the boys pried or asked questions upon his return, and he offered no explanations.

The Army of Tennessee and the Eighteenth, surprisingly, encountered no resistance from the Yanks as they made the fifteen-mile northern trek to Nashville. Evidently, the retreating forces from Franklin were more interested in taking refuge in Nashville than laying in wait to ambush any advancing Rebel troops.

For two weeks, the Rebel army camped and prepared defenses on the southern outskirts of Nashville all the while watching Yankee re-enforcements pour in from the northern positions. The Eighteenth was once again in a reserve status, covering the left flank. They were positioned behind a stone fence that covered the breadth of an open pasture; it was some fifty yards from the edge of a forest, located outside city.

The night was brisk and foggy, limiting visibility. The mood around the Eighteenth's encampment was edgy; tempers were short, and nerves raw. What was left of E Company was waiting for their orders to man the wall while different groups gathered around camp fires, or got much needed sleep in order to forget about empty and growling stomachs.

James and the boys gathered around their own fire, finishing a meager meal of hardtack and weak coffee. Not much had been said after they mustered out of Franklin weeks earlier. Even the passage of time hadn't erased the images of their arrival on the city, and the death scenes were still fresh and disturbing.

The silence around the fire was beginning to grind on Matt's nerves so he decided it was time to express an opinion about the army's strategy of the past couple of weeks and the defects of their commander. In other words, he was ready to start complaining again.

"What the hell is General Hood doing, you reckon? Sittin' on his duff---eating well and waitin' for the whole dang Yankee army to arrive in Nashville? We been simmerin' here two weeks now, watching them damn bluebellies roll into town, in all their glory."

"Well---that brilliant strategy don't seem to be working so far, now does it?" Added Henry bitterly, ready to get into the fray. "We haven't done nothing but sit. Them Tennessee boys throw in a few shots now and then from their side of town just to stir 'em up, then the Yanks pound the hell outta us with them big guns they got aimed down our throats. Hell of a way to run a war."

"Yeah, well---how come we've been building breastworks and digging in?" Matt added. "Ain't we supposed to do the advancing into town, instead of waitin' to be run over again? That's what I want to know." He turned to James. "What does the professor think about it?" Matt challenged.

James had been silent most of the evening, mostly thinking about his time with Mrs. Hasson and had just picked up bits and pieces of the conversation, not really paying full attention. He shrugged. "We just do what we're told, I guess. I don't see that it's gonna make much difference much longer anyways."

Matt jumped up and threw his hands in the air, and then started circling around the fire. "Well, ain't you the cherry one today," he snapped. "You know---you boys used to be fun to be around, but here lately, ever'body's moping 'round, getting like it's the end of the world or something. Damn, boys, we survived three years of crazy generals and bad food---that is, when we even got it. Mud, freezin' rain, idiots, an' no shoes! Hell---the soles of my feet are tougher than any shoe leather made. Henry acts like his best friend's gonna drop dead any minute now. Sam thinks he's gotta protect ever'body from the boogieman, an' James gives speeches about ever damn thing he sees. I'm the only normal person 'round here anymore---and that scares the hell outta even me!" He went back to his spot by the fire and sat down.

"There," he stated with a firm nod, "I finally got that off my chest. You boys are drivin' me crazy." He crossed his arms over his chest, crossed his legs, and waited for the barrage of insults from his friends.

James, Henry, and Sam stared at Matt, dumbfounded by their friend's outburst. James finally broke the silence. "You're right, Matt. We have changed."

Matt guffed, "You ain't gonna give us a speech about why we've changed, are you?" He squinted his eyes at James as though daring him to put more than two words together.

"No he ain't," Sam interrupted, "cause I got something here in my knapsack I've been saving for a special time---and I think the time is right for it."

"Ol' Sam's always got something workin'," Henry joked. "Can't be very big if you're keeping it in a bag, though."

"You don't worry none---it's big enough." Sam threw back the flap of his rucksack and pulled out something wrapped in a dirty white cloth. He balanced it in the palm of his left and pinched the top of the rag between his fingers, "Wah- la!," and snatched off the rag as if it was magic. He held a quart jar of thick and clear liquid in his hand.

"Your surprise is a jar of water?" Matt wisecracked.

James and Henry snickered, trying to maintain their composure. Sam was the only one able to keep a straight face. "You know, Matt---I hope I die before you---cause I'm gonna have to do some powerful explaining to St. Peter about you before he considers letting you in the Pearly Gates. No, Matt---this is the real thing---what you see here boys is the o-ri-gi-nal Tennessee moonshine! Traded for it with one of those backwoods Tennessee boys."

"What'd you trade him?" Henry asked.

"A pair of socks."

Henry's eyes narrowed, suspiciously. "Where'd you get the socks from?"

Sam started laughing and back-crawled on his butt away from the fire and Henry. "I believe it was your knapsack, Henry."

"Damn it all, Sam! My sister Caroline sent me those socks! And what're you doing going through my stuff, anyway?"

"You got two pair---I seen 'em!" Sam argued.

"Now wait a minute, boys!" James chuckled. He decided to play the role of peacemaker, even though it wasn't necessary. "Let's think this out together."

His three best friends in the world turned on him like a pack of dogs and yelled, "Shud-dup!"

"Then, perhaps we should have a drink, my fellow soldiers-at-arms," James shot back.

Sam held the liquid treasure with both hands and said, "Circle in boys, an' let's pass the jar! One good sip and a toast each, gentleman---we gotta stretch out the life of this magic elixir an' save it for the last day we're in this stinkin' war." He hoisted the jar above his head. "A toast---to good friends!" He took a swig, crossed his eyes, coughed, and passed it to Henry.

Henry raised the jar to salute his friends. "The last time we did this I ended up joinin' the army for another three years! Ah, to hell with it! To a three pound steak cooked til it's burnt to a crisp on the outside and a cold glass of milk!" He took his drink, feeling the raw alcohol burn his throat on the way down. He coughed up most of what he swallowed, and passed the jar off to James, still hacking from the effects.

James took the jar of hooch and raised it in a salute. "I don't

know if I want any of this rot-gut or not, but here goes. To Matt---
who makes us realize---," he hesitated, knowing they expected
something profound, "how really smart the rest of us are!" He took a
big gulp, forced it down, and felt his insides fry from the tip of his
tongue to the bottom of his toes. He passed it off to Matt.

He grabbed it with both hands and seemed to relish the clear
liquid. "I guess I gotta show you boys how to handle a little
moonshine. To a new pair of boots!" He threw his head back, passed
a sizable amount down his throat, and smacked his lips. "We gotta do
this again sometime!" He passed the jar back to Sam, who replaced
the lid then stashed it away in his knapsack.

The boys kept the fire stoked the entire night and talked until
dawn. Tom. Darryl Giles. Gambler's Paradise. Luther Megs. The
Yank. Mrs. Hasson. And, on and on. All of it. It took all night and
morning.

"Amazing what a little moonshine can do for a man," Sam
thought, as he watched the sun crest over the next Tennessee hill.

Orders to man their posts came soon after a scant breakfast of
the same thin coffee from the night before and some hard biscuits Sam

had traded for when he got the moonshine from the Tennessee boy. Not even the lack of sleep and empty stomachs failed to dull their senses when they heard the rattle of distant equipment as the Yanks made an approach through the woods towards the Eighteenth's position behind the stone fence. The two hundred remaining soldiers of the original Tuscaloosa regiment that the boys had joined three years earlier braced themselves for the upcoming assault; they were spread thin, attempting to defend the entire length of the stonewall.

Colonel Hunley paced his stallion at an easy gait---back and forth from one end of the line to the other. "There's nobody here but us, boys! They break through us an' they'll flank General Hood's army! And, by God, I've never seen a day that a soul from Tennessee could point a finger at an Alabama boy and say he didn't do his job!"

Cheers rose up from the thin gray line, inspired by their commander's flattery. "We're spread thin, so we'll adjust as we need. Every third man to cover the flanks when I give the order!" His fast paced patter continued as he strode the line. Calling his men by their first names, a light remark to lighten the moment, letting his men know he was with them all the way.

"'Bout time we get to shoot at somebody. I was beginning to think my Springfield was gonna rust up," Sam said as he laid extra ammunition on a cloth by his knee.

"Me too," answered James. "If this army goes down---it's gonna be fighting---not throwing up our arms to be shipped somewhere like a herd of cattle."

"Atta' boy," smiled Sam.

"Damn, they ain't even tryin' to hide their arrival, are they?" Matt observed.

Only fifty yards separated the edge of the woods from the stone wall, a too short distance for a killing ground. The sound of five hundred men grew louder; fingers tensed on triggers; bodies tensed; throats dry; senses acute to every sound and movement. Battle cries, curses, saber rattling, and nervous, snorting stallions crushed through the forest.

"Here they come, boys!" Hunley shouted. "Make your shots true!"

The first line of a hundred men charged from the trees into the killing ground, yelling and hollering to beat the devil. Four more lines of the same amount bunched up behind them, ready to follow their tracks. The sight of the screaming colored regiment brought a split second of hesitation from the gray line---shocked by the black faces outline by the blue uniforms they wore.

"Fire!" Yelled Colonel Hunley at the top of his lungs. "Kill the black devils!"

The fatal barrage of two hundred guns cut down the first line and badly mutilated the second as they emerged from the edge of the forest. White officers, staying to the rear of the lines, screamed and cursed---threatening the colored infantry within an inch of their lives if they didn't advance to the wall. The blacks were no match for the veteran Confederate sharpshooters, and their ranks broke, fleeing back in a frenzied rampage to the shelter of the woods. Not one shot fired from their muted muskets.

"What the hell was that?" Henry shouted as he reloaded.

James checked his own weapon, reloaded and braced against the wall---ready for another assault. "I heard there were colored units, but I didn't believe it."

"Well, you can believe it now. If those murderin' coloreds get loose down home---there'll be hell to pay. This is bad," Sam cursed.

"They're comin' again!" Hunley shouted. "Take 'em down!"

Once again, the clatter of loose equipment and stomping horses shattered the morning. Charging and screaming of another line of a hundred colored soldiers broke through the trees. This time, there was no hesitation from the Rebel guns. Hate and disgust lined their rifle sights. The first hundred men dropped from the vicious firepower before they'd made ten yards of the opening---more advanced, hurdling over the bodies of their own dead. And then, a sight that repulsed even the Southerners who felt betrayed by the coloreds raising arms against them as a line of white infantry soldiers were literally pushing the blacks into the deadly fray of the open killing field, cursing and threatening, using their sabers and bayonets, forcing the frightened black men forward. But, no amount of brutal coaxing could keep the unit from a second panicked retreat.

"That ain't right," Sam spat. "I hate the coloreds for fightin' against us---but no man should be forced to fight at the end of a bayonet."

"Look at Hunley," James said, pointing at the furious

commander, "he doesn't like it either."

Hunley paced his horse back and forth---not taking his eyes from the wooded edge--- pointing his saber at them in defiance. "Come out here and fight you cowardly white trash! I know you hear me! Yellow-bellied cowards! Murderers! White trash!" The colonel's face was fire-red, spittle spewed from his mouth as his anger took control of his emotions.

Matt took to his feet, shook his fist at the Yanks and shouted, "Come and get some of this, white boy!" Pointing to the seat of his baggy pants. The fury of Company E intensified, infecting the rest of the regiment---every man jumped to his feet---shouting insults, trying to provoke the white Union soldiers.

Hunley knew he had to get his men back in order---this encounter was far from over. "Back to your places, men! Prepare to fight---they aren't done yet!"

The rebel rousing gradually ceased---rifles loaded---eye-balling their sights for the next charge. Once again, what remained of the colored unit that charged the Confederate stronghold. Volleys of death-spitting fire decimated the blue lines---except this time a large number of white infantry fell beside the tormented blacks. The Eighteenth was picking their shots. The final charge was brief, but costly for the Yanks. The white infantrymen in the rear ranks were the first to break and run this time. The noisy retreat faded deep into the dark woods, until the only sounds heard on the killing field was the cheers of the Eighteenth. The only casualties that lay on the bloody earth were in blue uniforms.

The Eighteen's victory was one of the few highlights of the Nashville siege; Confederate forces were outnumbered and constant frontal attacks by massive Union units finally forced the reluctant General Hood to finally pull his forces back to Franklin. Nashville remained in the hands of the Union Army.

Colonel Hunley met with his subordinate officers to give them orders for their next destination. "We're headed south, gentleman--- deep south. To be honest---we're running out of places to go. But I'll tell you this---our final stand will be in our own backyard, and we aren't going down without a fight. There's one place left for us to defend what's left of our pride and honor. Gentlemen---prepare your companies---we're headed to Mobile, Alabama."

Chapter Twenty-Seven

"KILLER HARRY"

MARCH 15, 1865
SPANISH FORT
MOBILE, ALABAMA

Spirits were running high among Union troops as regiments by the thousands arrived on the outskirts of Mobile. Confederate forces were surrendering in large numbers throughout the South; Mobile was the last holdout of the Rebel army and its fall was inevitable. Fifty-five thousand Yankee troops severed any possible escape by land or water by Mobile Bay or the Gulf; gunboats patrolling Mobile Bay eliminated any possibility of rescue from the rear positions. There was nowhere to run for the less than five thousand remaining Confederate troops defending Spanish Fort and Fort Blakely. Artillery batteries pounded the defensive breastworks twenty-four hours a day. Snipers peppered the weakened picket lines from dawn to dusk.

Harry's only complaint was the competition of too many snipers and not enough targets. He had a personal goal of kills to meet before the war was over, and he didn't plan on being denied. Mac and he decided to pair up, with one staying guard at their coveted sniper post at all times; unattended spots had a tendency to get snatched up by other sharpshooters, if left alone.

It would be dusk soon and Harry waited for Mac to relieve him. He couldn't believe their luck. Union forces held the high ground, while the hapless Rebels had to trudge through the soggy bottomland with their backs trapped against the bay. This was supreme target practice. "Ducks in a pond," Harry mumbled.

Mac finally showed up about dark with four canteens filled to the brim with fresh water and enough food to sustain them for the next twenty-four hours. "How's it goin', Harry?" Mac grinned as he set down the fresh supplies.

Letters

"Pretty good. The Rebs are wising up a bit, but pickings are still good."

"You know, this is the end of it, don't cha', Harry?"

"Yeah."

"What're you gonna do when it's all over?"

Harry shrugged. "Don't' know. Hadn't thought about it that much. Probably stick 'round the South. Maybe go to Texas. It's still wide-open territory. Plenty to do for a fella like me. There's always somebody wants somebody else done away with. Besides, the Yanks'll be runnin' this country now---spoils to the victors. I plan to cash-in."

"How're you gonna do that?"

"Like I said, don't know yet. Watch. Listen. Be in the right place at the right time. Ain't worried 'bout it too much right now. Still have things to finish up here."

Mac smiled, "Yeah, know what you mean. Hey, got an idea. Maybe, me and you can partner up when this is all over with, Harry. I ain't got no definite plans, myself and we make a pretty good team 'tween the two of us."

Harry didn't want somebody like Mac tagging along with him, unless he could use him to his advantage. Mac was a ruthless killer and could have his uses, but he could also be a liability. He wasn't making any decisions about that, right now. "Yeah maybe, Mac. We'll see. Maybe." Harry grabbed his rucksack and Sharps. "If you're settled in, I'm going back to camp to get some shut-eye. I'll see you in the morning."

"See ya, Harry." Mac shot back, making himself comfortable for the night. He figured tomorrow would be another high numbers day, and he wanted to be ready for it.

Harry picked his way through the multitude of regiment camps, heading back to the Ninety-Sixth's location. The atmosphere was euphoric. Laughter, card games, war stories, fights, and general tomfoolery progressed from camp to camp. He didn't like crowds and avoided eye contact all around. Soldiers that glanced his way took notice of dead, fearless eyes; strollers stepped aside without comment---giving him a wide berth to walk. Many had heard of "Killer Harry," but few recognized his face. Harry enjoyed his anonymous notoriety and knew his reputation had spread far and wide. There were even stories circulating about him shooting at Yankee infantrymen when he ran out of Rebel targets. Harry smiled to himself and whispered under his breath, "Step aside, losers. Killer Harry's comin' through."

Chapter Twenty-Eight

"THE LAST LETTER HOME"

MARCH 1865
SPANISH FORT
MOBILE, ALABAMA

James knew his foul humor was due to the fact that he'd received no letters from home in over a month. He couldn't understand why. After all, he'd engaged in vicious fighting all over the South and had time to write under such perilous circumstances; so, why couldn't those safe at home at least take the initiative to pick up a pen and paper to write him. Nobody was shooting at them.

For now, he just wanted some time alone to brood and wallow in his own misery for a while. The overall morale of the men had been surprisingly upbeat, but for the world of him he didn't know why. The rumor was that the peace talks had broken down and there was no favorable outlook for peace any time soon. Constant barrages of artillery behind the lines and sniper fire on the picket lines made living to see the next day rather precarious. Only 130 men remained of the Eighteenth since the brutal and hasty retreat from Nashville to Mobile took place. James knew that fate had dealt him two choices for the future---death or capture. The build-up of Union forces had eliminated any real chance of an honorable retreat.

Upon arrival in Mobile, the Eighteenth relieved two of the "boy regiments" from Spanish Fort and weeks of hard work preparing sufficient defenses lay before them. The inexperienced youths made no efforts to refortify their position and left themselves susceptible to Yankee firepower. The name "fort" was misleading. Spanish Fort was simply an ineffective semi-circle of breastworks reaching from the water's edge on the eastern shore to nearly a half mile above the marshlands south of the town Spanish Fort, and back to the main wharf on the bay. This marsh was, perhaps, two hundred yards wide. It was thought to be impossible for the enemy to pass over it; this turned out to be a bad assumption. They worked day and night strengthening the breastworks, securing the line that ran through a forest of immense yellow pine trees. Trees were fallen haphazardly, making enemy advancement more difficult. An additional little surprise for the Yanks was a number of portable racks with sharpened spear-like branches angled out to discourage charges on the picket lines. The work was difficult and exhausting, but it occupied otherwise idle time and hopefully would serve its purpose of hampering the enemy's frontal attack. Once done, it was time to wait for the inevitable advance that was sure to come soon.

After a time of brooding in his own misery and realizing it was doing him no good, James made his way back to camp; he'd had enough of feeling sorry for himself and it was time to get back into the fray of things. Matt sat cross-legged in front of the fire, whittling on a piece of stick; Sam practiced one-handed cuts with a deck of cards; Henry was stretched out taking a nap. "You boys look a little stressed out. You need to try to relax more," James joked as he strolled into the campsite.

"Where you been?" Henry asked, barely opening his eyes to glance at James.

"Oh, just wanted to get away for while. Anything going on?"

"Yeah, Colonel Hunley came by earlier and said he wanted me an' you to come by the command post as soon as possible," Henry answered.

"Really? Wonder why?"

"Probably wants to promote ya'll to generals since nobody else seems to know what they're doing 'round here," Matt quipped. "Couldn't do no harm, that's for sure."

"Don't know," Henry said, "but he said to skedaddle up there as soon as you got done doin' whatever it was you're up to."

"Well---I'm back. So, let's go."

Henry lifted himself from the ground and brushed himself off. "I was just getting into that nap, too."

"Come'on, let's go see what's so important," James urged. He felt like this visit was more than just a 'Howdy boys, how're you doing' thing and was anxious to see the Colonel.

James clipped along down the path at a quick pace. "Slow down, James! What's the rush?" Henry gasped as he tried to keep up with his cousin.

"Just want to see what's so important that Hunley made a personal trip to fetch us, that's all."

The command post area was a bevy of activity. Message runners dashed about relaying messages from one officer to another, makeshift tables scattered around the campsite strewn with maps and being studied by hunched over officers pointing their fingers and shaking their heads. Organized mayhem ranked supreme. Nobody was sitting around the campfire chewing the fat in this part of Spanish Fort. The boys approached Colonel Hunley's tent and were stopped by a corporal on guard.

"We're here to see Colonel Hunley," James reported. "He sent orders for us to come see him."

"Names?" The corporal asked.

"James and Henry Durrett," James answered.

"Send 'em in, Corporal," Hunley's voice called from inside the tent.

The corporal folded back the tent flap and allowed the two to enter. Henry was the first to react. "Albert! I-I mean Colonel Brown! What're you doin here? I thought you're over Mississippi way!"

Henry chirped, surprised to see his sister's husband standing before him.

Colonel Albert Brown's smile was weak, but he tried to put on a happy front for his brother-in-law. "I was---but they told me you were keeping company with some pretty unsavory sorts around camp, and I thought I should come and see for myself,"

Brown was tall and lanky. The most outstanding feature concerning his looks was the long, wavy shoulder-length blonde hair combed back behind his ears. It was obvious that he was not a well man; his once fitted uniform now hung from his thin frame and his coloring was pale, the whites of his eyes were red from lack of sleep, and he had a lung-rattling cough that exhausted him after every spasm attack. But, the air of authority and respect his very presence commanded was not lost on anyone, in spite of his illness.

Hunley smiled. He was glad to see a cheerful reunion of friends and relatives instead of a mourning woman hearing about the death of her father or son. "I'll leave you gentleman some time alone. We'll meet up later Colonel Brown, when you're done."

"Thanks, Peter. We won't be long." As Hunley left the tent,

Brown casually waved to his fellow officer and returned to the Durrett boys. "How're you doing, James? Been a long time since I've seen either of you," he said, reaching out to shake James's hand. "You look fit--- considering things as they are."

"You too," responded James.

Colonel Brown chuckled, "Don't need to lie to me, James. I've been sick this past month and I can't shake this infernal cough. I know I look like hell, but never mind that, now. I've got some news from home you boys might be interested in."

"How's sister Caroline doing?" Henry asked anxiously. "I got the socks she sent me, but I lost a pair somewhere," Henry said sarcastically as he looked over at James.

"Be glad you got anything at all in the mail these days. And, your sister is doing fine, Henry. The family seems to be holding up good. I went by there a couple of months ago for a visit. Everybody's health is good, but times are tough with all the men folk being gone off to war."

"What about Tom?" James asked, anxious to know some news about his brother.

"Actually, Tom's doing good. I don't think he's got any chance of being part of a prisoner exchange both sides were negotiating earlier. I think that's all a mute point for now. It won't be until the war's over before he's released." Brown smiled, "But from what I understand, he's still giving the Yanks a headache."

"Figured he'd do that," James chuckled. "What kind of mischief is he causing now?"

"He and ol' Bob Bateman have been coordinating escapes from that Rock Island prison they're in. They're in cahoots with some woman from Kentucky that lives right there in the city. The Yanks know she's helping the Southern boys escape, but they can't prove anything. Somehow, she gets info to Tom, and he works it out from the inside. Your Mother filled me in on all this when I went back. She's something else, James. Making those treks up north, sees Tom, collects intelligence from those Yankee officers, and then brings it back to Lee. Unbelievable. She's one brave woman."

"I know, she drives me crazy. The Yanks don't take too kindly to spies---they hang 'em---pretty lady or not. I don't hear from her for months at a time, and I don't know what's happening. When she does write, she never really says anything in her letters."

"Well, you don't have to worry about that anymore. She's making her last trip, now. Things are getting too hot up north. She's afraid they're catching on to her visits with Tom, and she knows they're watching her close to see if she corresponds any with that Kentucky woman, but they'll never catch her. She's too damn smart and clever to let a Yankee outsmart her. Your father seems to be healing okay. That Minie ball that grazed his neck doesn't seem to have slowed him down much physically, but his spirit seems to be busted up a bit. But don't fret, now that your mama's going back soon she'll bring him around."

Colonel Brown patted Henry's shoulder. "Henry---your family's doin' fine. The farm's in pretty good shape. Your sister runs roughshod over everybody like she always did, so all the aunts and kids stay busy. Everybody's just ready for the war to end. So, things'll get back to normal again. Just between us, boys---we haven't got a chance in hell of coming out on top on this deal. We're outnumbered ten to one, all our flank and rear positions are cutoff, and the Yanks are out for blood. We've sent communiqués to the commanders, trying to work out an honorable settlement---but they're not interested. Keep your heads down and don't take any unnecessary risks. The whole damn war will be over before this battle will, I'm afraid."

Henry kept his eyes steady on his brother-in-law. "Well--- leastways, thanks for the heads-up on keeping low. We've been doing that for more than three years now. Don't plan to change our strategy at the last minute."

Brown nodded. "To be honest, it's a miracle that you two have gone through this war unscathed. I've seen too many families devastated from all this. Mrs. Boone, that has that farm down south from your place James, has lost all six of her boys." The Colonel shook his head sadly. "She's just a shell of a woman, now. From what I heard, she won't even come out of the cabin anymore."

That little bit of news from home brought a quiet, solemn pall over the three men for a matter of seconds before anyone spoke again. James and Henry knew the Boone boys intimately.

Henry shuffled a foot and said, "Well…we've all seen much the same here too, Albert. Uh, do you mind if we pass the word on to a couple of buddies of ours back at camp…about what you said before.

You know, about how we're in for it. We kinda stick together, our bunch does."

"That's fine, Henry---just don't start spreading a panic."

"These boys aren't going to run on you, Albert," James injected. "We've come too far to run. Everybody here knows the situation and they're willing to deal with it."

Colonel Brown smiled at James's defense of his comrades. "You boys in the Eighteenth got quite a reputation out there, you know. Wish I'd been hooked-up with ya'll myself. That's why you get the tough jobs; says a lot about every one of you." He waved them on. "Okay, you boys go on, now. You need to get back now. New orders will be coming down the pike soon and you need to be ready. God bless you both, and, by the grace of God, we'll all still be alive when this damn war's over." Colonel Brown reached out and shook the hands of both men.

"We'll be seeing you Colonel, don't worry," James said.

"You can't get shot, Albert---sister Caroline would get powerful upset if you did."

Colonel Brown grinned, "Well, upsetting her is the last thing I want to do, right?"

As the boys approached their camp from the HQ site, Matt was the first to spot them. "Well? Did ya'll get promoted? I don't see no new stripes on your sleeves," Matt commented, still whittling on the same stick.

They took their place in the circle. "No, but we saw A. H. --- he's transferred over here from Mississippi, and he's just filling us in on home news. He looks bad though, I'm worried 'bout him," Henry answered.

"What'd he say?"

James grinned, "Well---ol' Tom's raising Cain in prison. Him and Bob have some system going on with a Kentucky woman--- helping prisoners escape out of that hellhole they're living in. Can you believe it?"

Sam looked up, "Only Tom could find a Kentucky woman in the middle of Yankee land an' figure out a way to escape from an island. Why don't he get out himself, you reckon?"

"Tom probably figures he can do more on the inside than out, I guess." James frowned. "Now listen, boys, Colonel Brown says we're in for trouble---says it's about over. Sam, you still have a way to get letters outside the Yankee lines?"

"Yeah, I gotta boy in town that can help. I'll need to trade him something, but I got that covered. Don't worry 'bout it. Just write your letter home."

"I've got some extra coffee if you need it," James offered.

"Nah---got something better," he grinned.

James didn't asked. He knew it'd do no good to carry on. "I think I'll do just that then, start writing before it gets dark."

James got his writing material from his tent and wandered away from camp to find a nice writing spot. He found a big yellow pine, sat down, leaned against the trunk, and scrunched his knees up to write on. He started writing, what he hoped, wouldn't be his last letter home.

March 12, 1865
Spanish Fort, Alabama

Dear Sister,

Sunday evening is here and again I am writing to you. If I get half as many letters as I write I could not grumble, however I will not grumble anyhow. I would like very much to hear from you now to know how you are getting on in this troublesome world of ours. I fear you are almost by yourself since Mamma is gone. Tell me all about it when you write. What did Mamma carry to Tom and when do you expect her to come back? Who is staying with you, for I cannot think Mamma would leave you alone. I must tell you something of our situation here. I find only 130 in my regiment of the 800 brave men who left here three years ago. We are camped on a hill rising from the bay with nothing but pines and sand around us. We have a fine view of the bay, but as is generally the case with everything in this world, there is something unpleasant in the sight, for there are four Yankee gunboats in plain view at all times, except when dark. "Our boys" all seem lively and in good spirits, but personally speaking I have had the blues lately. Spanish Fort is twelve miles from Mobile and just opposite across the bay. Tarrant's battery is stationed at Blakely, six miles above here. Henry is well and sends respects. We get along finely now, do our own cooking, eating, etc.

There are rumors of an anticipated attack on Mobile, but rumors are so plentiful that we pay no attention to them. The topic of greatest interest with us now is the arming of the slaves in the South. We know but little of the policy of such an act, but look upon it with dread as to the consequences, but willingness if it is for the public good, however politics is not my forte so I will leave such things to wiser heads. The consequences will not affect us personally, materially, but Heaven protect our defenseless loved ones at home. The anxiously looked for mail has come at last, but no letters for me. I have not had a letter since I left Tennessee. I am almost ashamed to own it to my family, but it is so and who is to blame, I cannot tell. We have too much time to think here. Though not very industrous, yet I hate to be idle. I feel like the best of my life is passing away and I am not improving myself or anyone else. I must close my letter. Give my respects to the Doctor, Miss Evie and Miss Stella. Remember me kindly to George, tell him I almost envy him the privileges he enjoys and the chances he has of learning and improvement, tell him to make good use of his time and he will never regret it.

I remain your friend.

-J. A. Durrett

James put down his pencil and writing tablet and rested his forehead on his knees. His letter was not full of flattery. Instead, he was venting; he was angry because no one was writing him; he was angry because he wanted to be home with his family; he was angry because there was no point in dying now.

Chapter Twenty-Nine

"THE LAST BLACK BEAN"

APRIL 2, 1865
SPANISH FORT
MOBILE, ALABAMA

There was no peace to be found anywhere. Union artillery from gunboats on the bay and from the western front zeroed in and hammered the Confederate positions from the semi-circular picket line to the waterline, twenty-four hours a day; any slack or let-up by the cannons' deadly barrage was immediately taken up by constant sniper fire that peppered the picket lines, which had lost any value as a defensive position, but functioned more as an alarm against an all-out attack by Yankee infantry. Soldiers, who had the unlucky assignment of being on the front line, were forced to crawl on their bellies along the hastily constructed ditches to keep from getting their heads blown off. Picket duty had become a death warrant assignment. But, one that had to be served.

James and Sam lay exhausted back at their campsite after having returned from a four-hour turn at the front. Their clothes were caked with mud from crawling through the sloppy defensive ditches; their bodies ached from tense, raw nerves, and the physical exertion required maneuvering in the earthen deathtrap.

"This all seems kinda one-sided to me, don't it you, James?" Sam said as he stared at a gray cloudy sky.

"Just a bit. The Yanks seem to be doing all the shooting. Maybe, we should send them a note and tell them we don't think this is a fair fight. Think they'd listen?"

"No, but you could try writing one of your letters, anyway, if you think it'd help." Sam's eye's searched around the camp. "Where you reckon Henry and Matt are? They said they'd meet us back here before dark."

"Don't know, they'll show up soon, I'm sure. It's their turn to fix dinner tonight and I know they don't wanna miss that privilege."

Letters

Neither boy wanted to even entertain the thought of moving from where they laid. "I'm too tired to even think about eating now, though." Laying there exhausted, James's mind drifted back to home again, which seemed to consume most of his thoughts lately. "You think you can still get a letter out in spite of all the turmoil. I think I've got just enough energy and brainpower to write one more before there's nothing left to say, and there's nobody left to deliver it." James rolled onto his side, turning his back to Sam, "I don't know why I even bother---they don't write back anyway," he muttered.

Sam heard the soft murmur. "I'll try, James. If I can catch the next runner that's heading back to Mobile, we might be able to get one out. Don't you think you're being a little hard on the folks back home? I doubt they've forgot about you, James. Times are hard everywhere, an' I doubt any mail could get through to here unless some bird could fly it in for you. That'd be the only way to breach the lines." Sam's eyes brightened the way they did when a new idea popped into his head. He nudged James with his foot. "Now that's a thought, ain't it? Train a bird to carry the mail for you during the heat of battle. Might find a way to make some money from something like that. What do you think, James?"

James just smiled, thankful for the momentary distraction from his blues. "Sam---if anybody can figure a way to do it, you can." Then, he spotted Henry and Matt coming through the trees, shoulder to shoulder. He recognized the looks on their faces and the stride of their walk that something was amiss. "Here they come," he said pointing, "something's up."

"Sol Thompson's dead," Matt blurted out, coughing up the words when the boys were within ear-shot. "Poor soul was sittin' under a tree eating some soup and got clipped by a damn sniper. The guy must have been shootin' cannon. Blew half his shoulder off, an' ol' Ed Jones from Company I told me he could see his heart an' lungs an' all."

"Can't believe it," Henry added. "He actually lived 'bout thirty minutes before he died. Nobody should have to suffer like that. Never knew what hit him."

Matt kicked at ground, creating cloud of dust. "Dammit all! I'm startin' to lose it, boys. I wish'd they'd just do me now, get it over with. I'm tired of seein' good people blown to hell." Even though he wouldn't be seen by the enemy, Matt twisted his body around facing the Yankee lines and shook his fist in their direction, "Com'on ya' bluebelly cowards! Take your best shot at ol' Matthew Rupert! Couldn't hit me if ya tried, ya sorry low-lifes!"

Sam got up and wrapped his arms around Matt from behind, pinning his arms to his side and twisting him. "You damn fool! Them snipers'll take you up on your offer if you don't stop! Just like they did Sol. The four of us is stickin' it out together, you hear me?" Sam shoved Matt roughly off to the side, almost knocking him off his feet. "Next time I see you offering yourself as a target---I'll shoot you myself."

Sol's death had created a depressing pall over the boys; he was from their hometown, well liked, and had quickly become a part of their little close-knit group even if he was an officer. Losing friends and relatives was becoming commonplace for almost everybody in the army, but some deaths hit closer to home than others, and it was beginning to happen too often. In the background, they heard the persistent sounds of gunfire and explosions reminding them that their own number could be up any moment.

James picked up his knapsack. He wanted to be away from his friends right now. "I'm gonna find my place if it hadn't already been blown to hell and write home. I've gotta get away from here for a bit." He threw his knapsack over his shoulder, reached for his canteen, and headed out of camp. James found his writing tree, sat down, and got comfortable. "At least they haven't blown you away yet," he said as he softly touching the large roots of the yellow pine.

Dear Sister,

I have not written before in over two weeks and would not have written now, but there is a probability of a blockade between here and home and I thought I had best write while I could. We have a merry time here preparing for the Yanks. Work day and night, building fortifications, cutting timbers in front of them, mounting guns, etc. I suppose from the signs of the times, there is every reason to expect an attack, perhaps a long, weary, deadly struggle like the siege of Vicksburg, perhaps only a raid to frighten the good people of Mobile, but certain Dame Rumor is very busy spreading the news of a large force, great numbers, etc. landing on both sides of the bay below this place, and if I trust my eyesight, there is a fleet of twenty-one vessels in sight day before yesterday, shelling our batteries and displaying their mischief loving propensities in various ways, but there are only seven in sight, this morning. I don't know what villainous projects the other fourteen may be hatching down the bay, but certain they have no good will for us and there is no love lost between us, so if they persist in troubling us there is a probability of somebody getting hurt.

I will suppose that all are well at home, for that is all I have of coming to any conclusion about the matter that is by supposing a case, but I would like to know if Mamma has got back, however I can't even suppose that I will ever know any more about it than I do unless by accident. Are you all dead or is there no stationery in Tuscaloosa that I don't get a letter? You need not expect to hear from me any more shortly if you get this, for if we are attacked here, I won't have any chance to write. Give my love to Beckie and Johnnie and Mamma if she has got back home.

Your affectionate brother
J. A. Durrett

P. S. Don't mind about answering this, I don't get your letters.

1

April 3, 1865

It was late afternoon. Harry joined Mac at their sniper post. "What time you got, Mac?" asked Harry, settling in beside his partner arranging his ammunition and supplies.

Mac pulled a scratched up gold watch from his vest pocket and held it up to the light. "Damn near two o'clock. There'll be some fresh meat comin' on to the pickets 'bout three if the Rebs stay to their regular schedule on the pickets. Your timing's good."

"I'll have to admit, them Rebs are makin' it tougher on us. You can just barely see the tops of their heads for the shots," Harry complained. "Tough to get a clean bead anymore."

"Well, when you hit 'em, at least you know they are dead for sure," laughed Mac. "Kinda hard to survive a head-shot, wouldn't you say?"

2

2:00 P. M., Spanish Fort

Less than fifty men of the Eighteenth were still fit to fight and fifteen of them were about to 'volunteer' for picket duty. The line was ragged and ill-formed line, formality ignored as they shuffled their feet nervously, each anticipating his turn to reach into the familiar burlap sack for the three o'clock duty. White bean? Black bean?

"It's sort of ironic that the color of a bean can determine a man's fate...you know, living or dying in the next hour." James said, reaching into the sack. "White," he said, holding the bean up for the others to see. "Looks like I'm drawing camp duty today."

Sam drew his bean. "White," he stated with the same lack of enthusiasm, "see you in camp."

While the others continued the drawing, James handed Sam the letter he'd written the day before. "Can't seem to stop writing lately. Still think you can get this out for me?"

Sam shrugged unsure and nudged James with his elbow. "I'll try. Hey, let's see what ol' Matt draws. Bet it's black." They watched Matt close his eyes, reach in the bag, and dramatically withdraw a bean between his forefinger and thumb.

"Damn, black, of course. That figures," he said, turning to Henry and spitting a stream of tobacco at his boot.

Henry drew last from their group. "Black." He glanced down at his boot. "Hope you're a better shooter than spitter," he shot back.

Colonel Hunley retrieved the bag from his aide and addressed his brave, but ragged veterans, "Gentlemen, best we can do is to try to hold those scallywags off and give up as little ground as possible---at least until we can hope for some relief. The word I'm getting is a full pullout by the sixth, in four days, giving us three more days to hold out until we put our full defenses here and at Fort Blakely. But who knows---this war's going hour by hour at this point." He nodded at the fifteen men who drew the black beans. "You picket boys keep your heads down and don't take any risks. Best you can do is to give us warning if there's any kind of movement or indications of an all out attack. I don't want any dead heroes out there today."

James stepped forward and raised his arm, getting the Colonel's attention. "Sir, Henry and Matt drew black beans and I drew a white one. You know how we stick together; luck seems to favor us that way. Do you care if I join them on the front? I'll trade out with someone else, if they want."

"I certainly don't want to stand in the way of Lady Luck for someone. I doubt you'll have any trouble finding anybody to trade out with you, it's fine by me, James. Just keep your head down."

He nodded, affirming the Colonel's instruction. "Will do, thank you, sir." James got back in line, not even considering he might have done something that his friends considered foolish.

Hunley motioned to his sergeant to dismiss the ranks and left.

"Dismissed!" The sergeant called out, and the men began to disperse quietly.

Henry grabbed James by the shoulder and twisted him around forcefully. "Just what the hell do you think you're doin', James? You drew camp duty an' by God that's what you're gonna do!"

James retreated a step, pushing Henry's arm away. "What's your problem? I've had picket duty plenty already. What makes today any different?"

Henry shuffled his feet uncomfortably. "There's no need to voluntarily put yourself in harm's way when it's not necessary. Just want you to stay here, that's all. A feeling...that's all."

"Maybe, you should listen to him, James. Couldn't do no harm, leastways. Hell, your odds of gettin' killed in camp are probably higher than on the picket line anyway," Matt added.

"You boys are getting on my nerves---I'm going," James stated defiantly.

"Then, I'm goin', too," Sam announced. "I ain't gonna get blown up in camp all by my lonesome."

Matt spit at Henry's boots, hit the target, and winked at his friend. "I'm a good shooter, too. Let's quit jawin' and moonin' over who's going an' who ain't. Time's a wastin'."

3

3:00 P. M.

Harry scanned the picket line in his sector with binoculars, surveying potential targets and movement. He spotted about fifteen gray uniforms, hunkered down low, dodging and weaving through the piney grove just short of the earthen ditch. "Company's comin' right on schedule," he said, shaking Mac's arm waking him up. He brought up his Sharps, adjusted the scope, and scanned the tree line for a target. There was a short span of sandy ground the Rebs had to cross before making it to the picket line. He should be able to pick off at least one before they made it to cover, he thought. Patiently, he watched them run in zigzag patterns. "That ain't gonna do you no good, Johnny Reb. You zig---I zig. You zag---I zag," he giggled. His target finally picked, he squeezed the trigger. "Boom!" The Sharps recoiled hard against Harry's shoulder. The target fell. The other runners stopped momentarily to assist the downed soldier, but for fun, Harry let loose a warning shot at their feet to discourage giving aid. The three Rebs immediately heeded the warning and scattered for cover.

"Bingo!" Mac shouted enthusiastically. "You're off to a quick start, Harry!"

"Dammit all! He's still movin'---look!" Harry cursed, pointing at the downed soldier.

"Finish him off, Harry! You can still nail him! Quick!"

"Nah," Harry said, ejecting the spent shell and reloading. "If I can't kill him on the first shot---he deserves to live. There's plenty more where he came from."

4

"Inch your way slow like! Don't let 'em see you're still alive!" Sam shouted as Matt lay wounded on the spit of sand. "Where are you hurt? Do you know?"

Matt pushed himself forward along the ground, one arm in front, pulling for leverage, one bloody arm hanging by his side. "Well hell yeah I know where I'm hurt! What kinda fool question is that?"

Sam switched his eyes to James. "That boy could aggravate the devil, himself."

"Looks like it's his arm or shoulder---maybe it ain't too bad. I wished it'd been anybody but him, we'll never hear the end of it," Henry bemoaned. "Now, we're gonna have to look at more scars. Com'on, Matt! You can make it!"

Matt griped a handful of sand with his right hand, grasping for a hold. "I'm scootin' 'bout as fast as I can, you know. How come they always aim at me?" Within a few feet of the protective ditch, James and Henry grabbed his good arm and pulled him in to safety.

5

3:15 P. M.

"I like them four down on the left end---how 'bout you, Harry? Angle looks right, don't it?"

"I think you're right, Mac." They are messin' with that wounded Reb, and just might get careless. You want the inside or outside two?"

"I'll take the inside," Mac answered.

"Fine---watch for the caps."

6

"Let me take a look at him," James said, crawling over Sam's back to get to Matt.

"Stay low, boys---they are just waitin' on us to pop our heads up for target practice," Sam cautioned.

Henry eased his head up, in spite of the warning, searching the hills for the shooter. "Can't see a damn thing."

Matt wiggled around, his shoulder burning like fire. "Damnation, burns like the devil!"

"Be still, Matt! I can't see how bad it is if you keep squirming around like this," James reprimanded.

Sam reached around James to help hold Matt still.

James looked up, seeing his upper body was exposed to the ridge. "I need to move," he thought.

7

"There's a lot of movin' and shakin' goin' on down there. If they keep messing with their wounded buddy that way, every one of 'em will buy the farm. Harry sighted another target. A head shot. The crosshairs of the scope zeroed in on hat. The seam between the bill and the cap. The shot was clean and on target. "Hell-o-o number one hundred." He squeezed the trigger. The target dropped like a sack of potatoes.

8

"No-o-o-o!" Sam screamed as James's head jerked back in a violent motion. "No! No! No!" He screamed over and over.

Matt instantly moved in, covering James's body with his own.

Henry scrambled by Sam on his stomach to his mortally wounded cousin. "Oh James, James," he cried. "Not you, James." When he reached him, he buried his face in his James's shoulder.

Sam fell back against the wall of the redoubt, pulled his knees up to his chin, wrapped his arms around his legs, and rocked back and forth on his haunches, mumbling, "No, No, No."

9

"Damn, Harry! You messed up my shot!" Mac whined and observed the melee below. "Man---they're all over that boy! He must have been s-u-u-m-bo-d-y!"

"Not anymore," said Harry. "He's just another duck in the pond. Another notch."

10

The three friends gathered closely around their fallen friend.

Each touching him, wanting the feel of his warm skin to come alive again.

One held his head, stroking back the loose hair from his brow, looking into James's blank, open eyes staring into a black void.

One took James's hand in both of his.

One held a bloody cap against his chest.

Chapter Thirty

"HEROES TO THE END"

Matt continued holding James's hand in his, not willing to let go. Then, he felt a small twitch. In a desperate quick motion, he tore the front of James's shirt open, popping the buttons free, pressing his ear against his dying friend's chest. "He's still breathin'! I can feel his heart beatin'! He's alive!" Matt croaked.

Henry still cradled his cousin's head, not saying a word as Sam, clutching the bloody cap, finally scooted over to James's side to see for himself.

"See for yourself, Sam! Tell me I'm not crazy," Matt urged.

Sam gently pressed his ear to James's unmoving chest. "He's right, Henry, it's barely beating, but he's alive! We gotta get him outta here. We gotta get him to the infirmary, now!" Henry stared in a

catatonic trance, not acknowledging anything being said. "Henry!

Dammit snap out of it, boy!" Sam yelled, punching Henry's shoulder

hard. "We gotta get him outta here!"

"He's dead. What's the use?"

"He ain't dead neither, Henry," Matt snapped.

Henry stated in a monotone voice, still not comprehending the

situation.

"How you plannin' on getting him out? We're pinned down by them

snipers. They'll pick us off for sure if we try to carry him out."

Sam ignored him. "Matt, you and Henry stay here with James.

I'm gonna get us some cover whilst we make our run." Leaving his

rifle and knapsack behind, Sam scooted on his belly along the ditch

making sure not to expose himself to the sniper's sights. He'd spotted

small puffs of smoke from the shooters position when they'd initially

wounded Matt. He made his way to the closest soldiers, about fifteen

to twenty yards from their own position.

"What's happenin' down there, Sam?" Asked Simon Hensley,

watching Sam scoot along the dirt like a crab. "Ya'll getting shot up over there?"

"Yeah, Matt's hit in the shoulder, and James took one in the head, but he's still breathing. We gotta move him back to the rear lines and get him to the field hospital. We need some cover from you boys so we can get him back."

Simon frowned, "Can't hardly get a shot off, Sam. They pick us off every time a head pokes up. You know that."

Sam held his temper knowing this wasn't a time to lose it. "Look, I know exactly where those bastards are perched. I spotted their smoke. If you pass the word on their location down the line, then every other man pops up an' shoots at the same time, then the other half fires around a second later---you'll blow them dirty Yanks to hell. That'll give us cover we need--- and you'll have some payback. We'll get James an' Matt to the tree line by the second volley. Okay?"

Simon thought a second and grinned. "Sounds like a plan, Sam. I'd like the satisfaction of knowing I took out at least one of wily characters before this was all over an' done with. Where are they?"

"Up that western ridge there," he said pointing Simon in the right direction. "It's about a hundred yards up that way. There's an outcrop of rocks that sticks out an' they're using it for cover. You square yourself straight on an' it's right above you." Sam assured Simon with a pat on the arm. "You don't even have to hit anything. Just make 'em keep their heads down." Sam nodded at the line of boys to Simon's left. "The boys down the way will have a better angle at 'em. I'm running outta time here, Simon. Pass the word down an' give us five minutes before you cut loose on them. We'll move when you do, on the first volley."

Simon nodded. "Go take care of your boys, Sam. I'll handle it from here. Five minutes." Both soldiers moved in opposite directions through the ditch, each with their own mission.

"Is he still alive?" Sam asked, crawling up to the boys.

"Barely," said Henry, seeming to have snapped from his trance, hope etched his face. "An' Matt ain't lookin' too good neither."

"I'm okay," Matt said, covering up the pain that stabbed his shoulder.

Henry gave Sam a weak smile, "Ol' Matt ain't complained once."

Sam winked at Matt. Then, it was back to business. "Henry,

me an' you gotta cradle James to the trees in about one minute. All hell's fixin' to break loose, boys. Matt, can you keep up, or do you need help getting outta here?"

"Hell no, matter a fact, I'll lead off to the left an' draw their fire. You boys head to the trees straight on. Them Yanks ain't good enough to hit the same target twice in a row," he smirked.

"Since when did you become a hero, Matt?" Questioned Henry.

"Since the only person that cared a hoot about me got shot."

"Oh, I don't know 'bout that," Sam smiled. "Now let's get ready, boys---hell is on its way." Henry stated in a monotone voice, still not comprehending the situation.

Chapter Thirty-One

"NO MORE BAGGAGE"
HARRY

Mac searched down at the picket line while Harry sat with his back against a large boulder, carving his centennial notch into the stock of his Sharps. "They's up to something down there, Harry. Pickings might be steppin' up here in a minute. Come take a look see."

"Nah," Harry said admiring the handiwork on his stock. "Wonder what that feller's name…" Suddenly a thunderous roar of rifle fire echoed from below the ridge. Harry heard the sounds of Minie balls slamming the rock fortress like a hundred sledgehammers. "What the hell?" Harry screamed as he scrunched down lower trying to make himself one with the ground. The Sharps fell to his side and he pulled his knees up to his chin, shutting his eyes tight into their sockets, covering the top of his head with his arms. He felt a warm wetness spread across the front of his pants, but didn't care. Then, he heard a thumping sound beside him. The firing stopped as suddenly as it began. Cautiously, he opened his arms so he could detect the origin of the annoying, repetitions sound, his eyes glancing quickly, not wanting to dwell on the fear that threatened to erupts in his gut.

Mac lay on his back; next to Harry, his eyes and mouth wide open with the top of his head blown completely away. The nerves in his leg twitched, causing his heavy-booted foot to thump sporadically against the boulder Harry sat against. He knocked Mac's foot away as though it was an attacking rattler and slid away from him, afraid. Harry started to make for his knapsack to retreat from the deathtrap when a second volley of fire peppered the rock again. He dove for the ground and rolled himself up into a tight ball---screaming---yelling for the guns to stop. Then, there was silence. He didn't move---he waited for the third volley to begin. It never came. When he finally thought it was safe, he opened his eyes and once again saw Mac with that blank stare on his lifeless face. Crawling over the rocky surface, Harry grabbed his knapsack and ran for the cover of the trees behind him.   "Time to quit when the ducks start firin' back," his voice trembled.

Harry disappeared into the woods, his Sharps still on the ground next to Mac's body.

Chapter Thirty-Two

"BEYOND THE CALL"

At the sound of the first volley, Matt sluggishly bolted from the ditch and angled to the left towards the line of trees. The loss of blood from his wound slowed his gait and coordination, making his run more of a drunken stagger than a sprint.

"Hell---just give him to me, Henry," Sam said, pointing to James. "I can run faster carrying him myself than the two of us stumblin' over each other."

Henry hesitated a second, "Okay, I've got your backside covered then." He helped lift up James's limp body from the ground while Sam cradled him in his arms like a mother carrying her baby.

Right on cue, the second volley of musket fire shattered the moment between the two boys. "Go!" Yelled Henry. "I got your back!"

Sam didn't hesitate. He ran with all his strength, trying not to jostle James too much, holding his head snug against his shoulder with one hand. Henry stayed within a few feet of Sam's back, running backwards and sideways acting as a protective shield, sacrificing himself to make sure Sam made it safely to the tree line.

Matt stumbled, out of breath, into the edge of the woods first and cut back to the right to intercept his comrades.

"Nice job, Matt," Henry said, following Sam into the trees.

"Thanks." Matt's color had grown even paler. The exertion of running had drained what energy he had reserved.

"Henry, I'll take James to the hospital. Why don't you help Matt, and I'll meet ya'll there."

"No---he's my kin, Sam. I'll take him. He's family."

Suddenly Sam felt ashamed. "I'm sorry, Henry. I didn't mean to be bossin' you. I think of him as my own brother too, you know." He moved nearer to Henry, settling James into his arms. "Here, take him an' go quick. I don't know if he's gonna make it." Sam shifted

James's head against Henry's shoulder. "Go---he's running outta time."

Henry labored his way through the yellow pine forest, tears streaking his dirt smudged face as he made his way to camp.

"You okay, Matt?" Sam asked, sitting down beside him.

"No."

"Me neither."

Sam put an arm around Matt's shoulder and they sat in silence together.

Numb.

Chapter Thirty-Three

"LAST RITES"

Henry sat next to James's cot, holding his cousin's hand. An orderly had helped clean James's face and hands and placed a clean bandage on his wound. He silently watched his cousin slowly give in to his Maker. Looking up, Henry saw Colonels Brown and Hunley approaching, threading their way through the aisles of cots containing wounded and dying soldiers. Both men silently sidled up next to Henry and simultaneously removed their Stetsons.

"M-my God, Henry. What happened?" Stammered Colonel Brown in disbelief and gazing as James's peaceful repose.

"Sniper bullet on the picket line brought him down, Albert."

"His mother will never recover from this," Brown mumbled.

"First, Tom gets captured and now her youngest is near dead. How much more can we endure?" Lamented Colonel Brown.

"She'll make it alright, Albert. She's a strong-willed woman with the deepest faith of anyone I've ever known," Henry answered. "His breathin' is shallow. He ain't got much longer to be here." He finally glanced up at Brown. "We can't leave him here in this God forsaken place, Albert. What are we gonna do?" Henry's voice cracked with emotions he couldn't control.

Colonel Hunley stepped up and spoke for the first time. "We can still get him over to Mobile. The army can't hold out here much longer anyway. We'll get him to Doc Hamilton and make sure he gets a proper burial there."

"Where do you think they'll put him? Henry asked, not taking his eyes of his cousin.

"Probably at the Magnolia Cemetery. I heard that's where they're burying some of the boys," Hunley answered.

"No telling what the Yanks will do to our boys that we leave behind. I'm really sorry, Henry. I'll write to Miss Ann and inform her of the tragedy. I don't look forward to writing this one," Brown said.

Henry looked up with forlorn eyes, "Me neither, but I gotta write her, too. I was with him, so it's my duty to tell her."

"Henry, you stay here with James. When he...passes on, get word to me. Peter and I'll make the arrangements to get him to Mobile where he can be taken care of properly and with some respect." Colonel Brown reached down and lightly squeezed James's arm. "God speed, James."

Colonel Hunley straightened his shoulders and snapped off a smart, crisp salute. Both officers turned and left the hospital to take care of unwanted duties.

Sam and Matt had finally made their way back to camp, arriving after Henry. They stopped by one of the medical tents to get Matt looked at and patched up before heading over to see James. The bullet had passed through Matt's shoulder leaving a clean wound through and through. Orderlies swabbed the entry and exit wounds with volumes of disinfectant, patched him with clean bandages, and directed him to a cot to get some rest, but he refused. He mumbled a few obscenities and said he had important business to take care of. The orderlies were indifferent to his stubbornness. They had plenty to deal with on their own with the constant flow of wounded soldiers coming through non-stop. They were as weary as the men on the front lines.

A sense of apprehension and dread filled the boys as they made their way to James's location. Cautiously, they entered the large open tent. The sounds of the pained and dying filled their ears. "Damn, I hate this place, Sam. This ain't no place to die." They saw Henry towards the back of the hospital, forcing them to walk through the rows of cots, looking down into the faces of men on their last vestiges of life. Henry still held on loosely to James's hand and his head was bowed low as if in prayer.

"Henry? You okay?" Matt asked.

"He's gone, boys. He gave up the ghost an' he's probably sittin' on some big fluffy cloud up yonder having a time of it, now. Laughin' at us, wonderin' why we're so sad." Henry stood, brushed his hair back away from his face, and tucked in his shirttail. "Sam, you got your pocketknife? I need to send a lock of his hair back to his mama. I gotta go write her now, whilst I still can."

"Sure, and send this with it too. This was the last letter he wrote, just yesterday, and he wanted me to mail it for him." Sam stifled a sob. "I-I never got the chance to---" He couldn't finish his sentence. He dug into his pocket and gave Henry the knife and letter, not letting his eyes stray from James.

"Thanks." Henry reached down, took a strand of James's hair, cut it, and reshaped the hair back in place. "See you, boys. Colonel Brown and Colonel Hunley are making arrangements to send James to Mobile for a proper burial. That way, it'll be done right. I'll meet ya'll at camp." He handed the knife back to Sam and left to take care of his own unwanted duties.

Matt and Sam were left alone to say their goodbyes. "He looks so peaceful don't he, Sam? Damn, he was a good one. I---..." Matt's words got choked in his throat, unable to finish. "...I-I'll meet you outside. I think I swallowed my spit down the wrong way or something," he said, brushing a hand across his face. "Gotta go." He turned and hobbled his way from the tent, leaving Sam alone with James.

Sam sat down in the empty chair beside the cot and gently took hold of James's cool, lifeless hand. "I know it's not in your nature,

James---but I'm gonna make you a promise right now. Somehow, some way---I'm gonna find the fella that did this to you, if he's still alive." As he sat quietly, focusing on his friend's peaceful repose, gathering his thoughts, an impish grin creased his face. He leaned back in the chair and folded his arms across his chest. "I'm gonna tell all my kids and grandkids how me and you won the war single-handed, James. I'll make 'em think we were the biggest, bravest heroes there ever was. And when I get up there with you…"---Sam had to stop and hold back a sob, "we'll sit on them fluffy clouds and bet on which bird takes flight first." Sam stood abruptly, twisted his Rebel cap around backwards, smiled, and walked away, following the same path he'd entered by.

Henry didn't even remember his walk back to camp. He was just there---standing next to a burned-out campfire, not sure of what to do next. He realized that he had to write the letter. Finally, willing his feet to move, he rummaged through his cousin's knapsack and found a well-used stub of a pencil and a small bundle of paper tied together with a piece of twine; he knew where to go, now. Clutching the supplies in his fist, Henry made his way to the yellow pine tree where James wrote so many of his letters home since they'd arrived at

Spanish Fort. He'd decided to write James's sister, Rebecca, since

Albert was writing to his mother. He found the familiar tree, sat down,

leaned against the trunk, and thought about what to say. He didn't

have James's gift of words, nor was he able to put it down in writing

the same way. A man of few words when it came to paper and pen;

so, he decided to make it short. Just tell Rebecca what happened, he

thought. Be done with it.

April 3, 1865
Spanish Fort, Alabama

Dear Cousin,

   It is with painful regret that I inform you that Jimmy was this evening mortally wounded, bringing the shot directly through the brain. He was wounded about four o'clock this evening, while in the ditches, he imprudently raised his head to look over at the enemy which was firing at our lines. He is over at the field hospital and will be sent to Mobile tonight. As he had written the letter enclosed with this, I also send with you a lock of his hair.

I am Dear Cousin

Yours, with great sympathy

Henry Durrett

Feeling the weight of the world on his shoulders, Colonel Brown slumped sluggishly into the chair before the makeshift desk in his tent. With an aching heart and trembling hand, he dipped the writing pen into a stained inkbottle at his side and began the letter to Ann Durrett. He prayed God would give him the right words of condolences as he put pen to paper.

April 7, 1865
Mobile, Alabama

Dear Madam:

I very much regret to have to inform you that your son, James, is dead. He died about dark on Monday evening, the 3rd of this month, from a gunshot received that evening near Spanish Fort, about fifteen miles below Mobile. The ball penetrated his forehead just below the edge of his hair and came out near the top of his head. The blow seemed to produce insensibility and he never spoke afterward, but continued to sink deeper into death. Henry Durrett, who accompanied him to the field hospital, was present at his death, and I who saw him about half an hour before, agreed that it would be better to have the body carried to Mobile for burial than to leave it there at a place that the enemy could more likely get possession of first and perhaps retain possession of longer. It is probable that Dr. Hamilton took immediate care of his body on arriving at Mobile, as a letter was sent to him upon the subject. I cannot say enough how I sincerely sympathize with you in the sad loss you have sustained in the death of your youngest son. Oh how long shall we continue to make these heart-rending sacrifices to the cruel demands of this relentless war?

Please inform Sister Caroline that Henry was well at the time of your son James's death, and that as I have some promise of getting away from Spanish Fort sooner than he and of having another opportunity of visiting him. He requested me to write concerning his company's arrival in Mobile yesterday, my company also returned here temporarily. Our troops are closely pressed at Spanish Fort, and I do not think the prospect of holding Mobile permanently is as good as desirable.

My health has been quiet bad for a week or two.
Very truly,

Colonel A. H. Brown

Afterward

On April 8, 1865, at 2:30 P. M., at a farmhouse in Appomattox, Virginia, General Robert E. Lee, Commander of the Confederate Army and General Ulysses S. Grant, Commander of the Union Army sat down together and signed a peace treaty bringing an end to the Civil War.

The next day, April 9th, the defending Confederate regiments of Spanish Fort were forced to retreat and take up positions six miles away at Fort Blakeley. The final assault by the overwhelming Union Army began at approximately 5:30 P. M. The battle lasted only thirty minutes before Confederate forces were completely overrun and forced to surrender.

During the siege of Spanish Fort and Fort Blakeley, 2900 Confederate Army soldiers lost their lives. Losses for the Union Army were 629.

These are the post-war fates of the real-life characters in the novel.

Letters

Tom Durrett: Tom was released from the prisoner of war camp in Rock Island, Illinois, in April of 1865. He returned to his family in Alabama, started a family of his own, and later moved to Texas where he bought land and farmed around the rural town of Maypearl. Finally, just a few years before his death in 1926, he returned to his beloved Alabama. He died at the ripe old age of 86 and is buried in Duncanville, Alabama, at the Mount Zion Cemetery.

Henry Durrett: There's not much information about Henry, except that he died in 1868, three years after the end of the war. Cause of death is unknown; he was 28 years old. He was buried in the same cemetery as Tom.

Ann Beauchamp Durrett: James's mother began her spying activity for the South after Tom was captured and sent to the Rock Island prisoner-of-war camp, in Illinois. Upon her numerous visits to Tom, she would return with valuable intelligence for the Confederate Army; her clandestine activities never discovered by the Union Army. She died April 15th, 1880. Ann Durrett also served as the Matron of the Regiment for the 18th Alabama Voluntary Regiment.

Kentucky Woman: The woman, who called out to the

Confederate prisoners as they were marched through the streets, helped 42 men escape. Union officials suspected her of such crimes, but were never able to catch her red-handed. However, being a pretty Southern belle, she was frequently courted by Union officers.

Colonel Peter Hunley: Survived the battles of Spanish Fort and Fort Blakeley and was taken prisoner with the other Confederate soldiers. He was released at the end of April, as were all prisoners.

James Durrett: James was the man of mystery. In all my family genealogy records and family Bibles, there is no record of when he was born, only that he was the youngest of the family and he died in the Civil War on April 3, 1865.

According to the letter written by A. H. Brown to Ann Durrett informing her of James's death, he was buried in Mobile, Alabama. It wasn't until ten years after the initial writing of this book in 2000 that I finally found and visited James's grave at the Magnolia Cemetery in Mobile, Alabama. Once again, a twist of fate in the mystery. The reason I was initially unable to find his grave was due to the fact that his last name was misspelled. On the gravestone, James's last name was spelled as *Durret*, with one *t* instead of two. Furthermore, in other cases, James's name was misspelled on military records as well, as *Durnet*, instead of *Durrett*. Since all records were handwritten, sometimes with calligraphy-like flourishes, it is easy to see how the double- r could be mistaken as *r-n* in the spelling of his last name. I am in possession of many letters written after the Civil War by Tom, his mother, and sisters---James's name was never mentioned in any of them. As a matter of fact, Tom never made any references to the Civil War or his imprisonment.

There were two legacies that James left behind: One is the beautifully written letters on which this novel is based; the other is the cap he wore when he was killed by the sniper. The story goes, according to my grandfather, Louis Countess, (his mother was Rebecca, the sister that James wrote so often) that it troubled the family so much to have it around the house that they had to get rid of it. No one knows where it is. Hopefully, this novel will give him a third legacy to carry on. The Durrett family never owned slaves.

Spanish Fort: Spanish Fort is a city located on Mobile Bay approximately fifteen miles from Mobile; it was not a "fort," per say. The defenses constructed by the Confederates are now large, overgrown mounds covered in grass in the front yards of residential sections of Spanish Fort and within the town itself. The place of death for James and 770 other Confederate soldiers that occurred in the final, yet barely publicized battle in the history books about the Civil War---is a residential development and a parking lot for a shopping center.

To read the actual scans of all of James's letters and see other source materials, go to my website:

www.bsawyers.com

Letters

About the Author

Buz Sawyers resides in Rowlett, Texas and teaches Creative Writing and Composition courses at Argosy University and the Art Institute of Dallas. *John Doe* is his sixth novel and once again he has crossed into a totally different genre from any of his previous writings. Currently, he is working on a sequel to *John Doe*. Also, Buz is working on the memoirs of Major James Capers who served during the Vietnam War and was finally nominated for the Congressional Medal of Honor in 2007. Buz can be contacted at his website & email:

www.bsawyers.com
buzsawyers@tx.rr.com

Letters

www.ingramcontent.com/pod-product-compliance
Lightning Source LLC
Chambersburg PA
CBHW070907260626
47162CB00007B/2591